I0451724

Solve Gorgoni
Science Agents #3

Pierre V. Comtois

Published by Rogue Phoenix Press, LLP
Copyright © 2023

ISBN: 978-1-62420-765-5

Credits
Cover Artist: Designs by Ms G
Editor: Sherry Derr-Wille

Prologue

Gen. Jefferson surveyed the distant hills with his optic amplifier. All seemed calm under the cloudless blue skies of what was once the state of Virginia. Green meadows covered the hills and in the hollows between, thick forest followed brooks and streams that gurgled invisibly to the Potomac somewhere to the north.

"It looks peaceful enough," said Jefferson's adjutant, Col. Ramirez.

"Looks can be deceiving," Jefferson replied, handing the glasses to Ramirez.

"The Humanists have been in full retreat for weeks now," said Ramirez, looking over the countryside for himself. "Do you think they'll make a final stand on the other side of the river?"

"Doubt it, but no sense getting reckless at this late date," replied Jefferson. "Still, I wouldn't want to delay any chance we have of liberating the Arlington camp."

"What can the drones tell us?"

"Not much," Jefferson sighed. "One thing the Humanists have in their favor is the old satellite system. They work intermittently, but when they do, they can interfere with our drones, preventing visuals. Unfortunately, this is one of those times."

"So if we advance, we'll be going in blind."

"That's what we're doing out here," reminded Jefferson. "We're out front so Division won't be the one going in blind."

Jefferson elected to accompany a fast action scouting group that raced ahead of the main column of the Constitutional Army in hot pursuit of the retreating Humanist forces. However, fear that the enemy might take out their frustrations on the captives in the camp convinced the high command that if the camp could be liberated sooner rather than later, then every effort had to be made to do it.

It was something the Army had experience with. As its units advanced from the South and West, they overran the network of reeducation camps, or 'special enclaves,' established by the Humanist government to remove the last resisters to its corrosive ideology. The camps themselves were not pretty sights with some worse than others...a lot worse. Citizens of the Constitutional Order knew about them of course, but when actual video and first hand descriptions and interviews with liberated inmates began to circulate, hatred of the Humanists grew to fever pitch. As a result, there was little love lost by the troops for the enemy, an enemy that took control of the old United States, and most of the rest of the Western world, turning it upside down with the least of its sins being the 'canceling' of the Constitution itself.

Jefferson had seen the reeducation camps before and shared the hatred of the Humanists they inspired. Inmates had not been treated kindly with malnutrition and crowding common. Conditions in the camps became more acute as the fortunes of the Humanists worsened. Prisoners of war were herded into camps that were not designed to host so many people. There were food shortages and disease. Prisoners began to die and mass graves discovered.

The Humanists were an ideologically driven bunch who brooked no dissent from a pernicious creed that promoted racism, perversion, and an inversion of every value held sacred by western civilization for two thousand years. The result of nearly a hundred years of rule that began in the early twenty-first century, ended with a degradation of technology as well as a concurrent plummet in the quality of life both in the former United States and wherever the seductive, secularist Humanist philosophy could reach. As Humanists captured the different branches of society, its government, its courts, its education system, its media, the pressure to conform to its rules grew so great most people could not resist. If they persisted, they became non-citizens who were banned from restaurants and stores, whose bank accounts were frozen, and jobs lost; a total banishment from the public square. Most people simply gave in but the most stubborn were jailed and finally confined to the camps where they were bombarded with endless consciousness raising programs.

At first, many of those who gave up simply went through the motions, deferring to their racial and "gender fluid" betters in public, mouthing the slogans of equity and social justice; but as succeeding generations emerged from the education system, resistance grew more rare until only a determined, prideful few remained unconvinced. At last, Humanist leaders lost their patience and the 'special enclave' system was established where the unreconstructed minority were confined.

In the meantime, governments of the former southern and Midwest states resisted the Humanist wave, driving its followers from their territories and finally declaring themselves independent from the Humanist strongholds on the east and west coasts of the old United States. Infuriated, the Humanists declared ideological war on the independent states, bombarding them with a propagandistic tidal wave meant to wear down their resolve. The former states retaliated by purging themselves of unrepentant Humanists, driving them north and west. However, the Humanists were not content to leave well enough alone, especially when the gap between each side continued to widen in terms of freedom, wealth, and technological progress. Humanists, it proved, were never content. They could not rest with the knowledge that someone, somewhere had not been indoctrinated. It seemed that as prosperity and contentment grew in the former states, the Humanists were driven to ever greater fury telling their people that those outside the pale were racist, misogynist, homophobic recidivists. Finally, with their citizenry whipped into a righteous frenzy, they declared a jihad against the Constitutionalists. The war came as a surprise to the unprepared former states, who found themselves under assault by Humanist Rainbow Brigades whose mixed gender storm troopers followed a scorched earth policy. Fortunately, the Humanists had little more than their own fanaticism to propel their assault so it was relatively easy to throw them back and turn the tables.

Quickly, the tide turned as the Constitutional Armies drove north from Florida through the old South while divisions from Texas and the southwest invaded California. Because of its policy of equity, the Humanist forces were both inept and hindered by aging equipment that no one seemed qualified to keep in repair. By contrast, the Constitutional

Armies had been raised by a society that valued ability, experience, and common sense above quotas and set asides. As a result, its officers were far more flexible than their counterparts and their more advanced weaponry kept casualties low.

Now, with the Constitutional Army almost to the banks of the Potomac and on Washington's doorstep, the Humanist forces were in full retreat, the detritus of a defeated foe littering much of the landscape and roadways leading north. Which presented the next question: what to do with a conquered population that had been taught for a hundred years that up was down and wrong was right? Jefferson didn't have the answer for that one, but was content to leave it to the politicians.

Suddenly, his thoughts were interrupted by the sound of gun fire.

"Those were pulse discharges," said Jefferson.

"It came from over those hills," indicated Ramirez. "In the direction of the camp!"

It was their worst nightmare: panicky camp guards or maddened Rainbow Brigadiers shooting prisoners at will.

"That settles it," said Jefferson, heading to his armored rover. "We can't wait for the rest of the battalion to catch up. Let's go!"

"Doctorow, comm Division that we're going in," ordered Ramirez. "The rest of you, mount up!"

There was a scramble as men jumped into their vehicles and engines began to rev up. A minute later, a dozen rovers, their pulse cannons charged up, crested the hill top and charged down to the road below that led around the hills to the camp beyond where gun fire could still be heard.

Chapter One

An Unexpected Visit

Jules Santros stretched and took a few seconds to luxuriate on the iso-mattress that dominated the bedroom.

The east wall of the room was sheer plas-glass with the polarizing function not in operation at the moment. As a result, he could look over and see the early morning sun just as it peeked above the eastern horizon lighting up the desert scenery outside. Long shadows began to extend from rocky outcrops lining the smartway leading back to town and the occasional Joshua tree and stovepipe cactus dotting the landscape.

As he did every morning since he and Mooney moved in here, he admired the view and confirmed his opinion they made the right decision in picking the location for their permanent home. After years of living on Mars for him and Proxima for Mooney, it was a pleasure to finally set down roots somewhere and when Jules visited Joshua Tree, Nevada on business a few years before, he knew it would be the place for him.

Whispering, so as not to wake Mooney, Jules commanded the smart home to take up the polarizing of the east wall a few degrees. Not enough to spoil the look of the early morning sunlight as it filled the room, but enough to cut down bothersome glare. Carefully, he slid off the bed and tip toed to the washroom for a quick shower.

Dressed, he crossed the bedroom into the hall and along the fieldstone interior walls to the kitchen as quietly as he could. Even though he liked to get up at the crack of dawn, Mooney was a different animal. Between active assignments for Military Intelligence and in recognition for services rendered, his boss, MI director Henri Leclerc, arranged it so they could work remotely. He as an advisor to MI's science division and Mooney taking part in official indoctrination as an MI operative; something she'd lacked as a former agent for the Exterior

Ministry.

Jules thought the convenience was a fair exchange for having saved the universe not once but twice over the last few years!

As a matter of fact, it was while investigating that first crisis that he'd come to Joshua Tree and a most unexpected run in with Mooney. He'd met her before on a diplomatic mission to the Zhapoologani. That time, she'd been working as a translator; but in Joshua Tree, he'd discovered she was actually an agent for the Exterior Ministry assigned to keep tabs on him. Once her cover had been blown, they decided to work together and made a good team. Good enough, in fact, to end up getting married when it was all over. They'd been on their honeymoon when they were given their next assignment with no less than the fate of mankind in the balance. It was the fallout from that mission that saw Jules more or less back at his old job for MI, that of scientific researcher.

To wit: trying to solve the temperature problem that prevented the use of a substance called nitinol in the construction of the Consortium's warships. In fact, nitinol's civilian applications could be even more revolutionary in that it could make interstellar travel safer than ever. That was due to nitinol's memory shape properties: no matter what was done to parts made with the material, they could regain their original shape in minutes if not faster allowing a damaged ship to repair itself automatically and preserving the lives of its passengers. What always prevented its use in the past however, was its susceptibility to changes in temperature. The problem was that the slightest variance from the temperature in which a part was manufactured when it was assigned its memory shape, would cause the part to lose its assigned shape.

However, one thing his research for MI had going for it was the fact that the problem had already been solved by Prof. Fernando Santanti and a self-replicating computer called the SR1. The SR1 was built by Anton Tamaka using forbidden technology that resulted in a crisis that Jules and Mooney were only narrowly able to stop in the course of their last assignment for MI. The details were irrelevant but the main fact was that the SR1 built itself a spacecraft housing made entirely of nitinol with which it was able to travel through space without the danger of temperature variation.

As a result, Jules knew there was a solution to the problem.

All he had to do was find it.

For that, he'd been directed by Leclerc to return to MI's science research section and track down the solution.

Luckily, that didn't mean he had to work on site at MI's headquarters on Mars but could work from home communicating with the lab directly using the hyper-bandwave function on the special issue telcomm reserved for intelligence purposes.

After fixing his first cup of coffee of the morning, Jules stepped into the plas-glass enclosed solarium that flanked the rear of the house. Its flagstone flooring was crowded with Mooney's dry weather plants: her towering, spindly fouquieria splendens, members of the broad leaved agave havardian family stuffed into the interstices, golden barrel cactus, brittle bush with their little yellow flowers, and who knew what else. Together with the workbench and pottery storage, there wasn't much room for the patio furniture but Jules managed to get himself settled at the table where he was overshadowed by a thick clump of splendens.

Outside, beyond the plas-glass barrier, 'Manda's gardening mania created a jungle of dry weather plants surrounding the house and on cooler days allowed them to hold old fashioned bar-be-cues out back (if you didn't count the laser grill) Just from where he sat sipping his coffee, Jules could see a thick stand of prickly pear cactus (with fruit plainly visible), some Tasmanian tree ferns (were they native to the southwest, he wondered?), forests of yucca of different types, Joshua trees, and even some organ pipe cactus.

Looking around the solarium then taking in the immediate outdoors with the sun now fully risen beyond, Jules felt content. Yeah, I could get used to this.

But now, back to work before Mooney arrives to interrupt me.

Jules keyed his telcomm and accessed the hyper-bandwave function that took him into MI's private cloud network. From there, he had to input a series of codes to make his way past several firewalls until finally arriving at the science research division's sub routines. From there, it was only a matter of identifying himself by using the telcomm's scanning programs for a retina scan. The last step was to press his finger tips onto the screen for a print scan and he was in. Immediately, the nitinol file sprung up in the air before him and he was able to get to work. *Now where did I leave off yesterday?*

He was deep into quantum supra-mechanics versus temperature variants that he never noticed when Mooney made her appearance in the solarium. She knew better than to interrupt him in such a transcendent state however, so let him alone, waiting for an opening. It came.

"Hey, Mr. Mind, ready for breakfast?" she asked when she noticed him taking a deep breath, which usually indicated a mental pause between operations.

"Hun? Oh, Mooney, didn't hear you come in. Yeah. I'm starved."

Making sure to close everything before leaving the solarium, Jules rose to follow Mooney into the kitchen. It was a pain in the neck having to go through the security access routine every time he wanted to get back to work, but better that than taking the chance, a long one though it might be, for someone to hack the open channel and ride the data stream right into the heart of the science division.

"How's it coming?" asked Mooney, throwing the question over her shoulder as she led the way to the back of the house.

"I think I'm making some progress," replied Jules as they rounded the corner of an interior passageway into the kitchen where a table in the breakfast nook was already set. "Santanti's notes seem to point to a temperature sensitivity at the grain structure level. He found a way to avoid long term creep resistance at both high and low temperatures. I suspect that's the key problem we need to solve. If we can do that, we'll have the breakthrough we're looking for, finding that elusive balance between fluidity and brittleness."

"Sorry I asked," laughed Mooney.

Thinking on it, Jules had to laugh too. The jargon did get ridiculous at times. Just as the situation forced on he and Mooney by the circumstances both of being science agents for MI and for the peculiar result of their first mission together that ended with there being two of him! Due to a localized temporal time distortion caused by the collapse of a man made black hole, Jules found himself duplicated and forced to allow 'Jules-prime', who was in every way himself except that he didn't know anything about there being another Jules, go back to his normal life including rejoining his wife, Joan, waiting for him on Mars. The Jules left behind with the knowledge of the duplication, was left to wrestle with his conscience and find a way to make a new life with fellow agent 'Manda Mooney.

Yes, the two had been wed soon after that experience, but Jules continued to struggle both with a sense of having betrayed Joan and about his own identity. At last, though, he'd learned to accept his situation after a long talk with his older brother Andrew, a Catholic priest who explained the philosophical and theological underpinnings to his new reality, settling the question of his being a separate, individual being from that of the other Jules with a right to proceed with his own life path.

Nevertheless, because he'd determined never to let the other Jules know about his existence, he allowed MI to create a new identity for himself to go with his new life. Outside of he and his wife, he was no longer Jules Santros but Victor Conroi. It was as the Conrois that he and Mooney (it was how he addressed her during that first mission; since then, it became a term of endearment, one 'Manda didn't seem to mind) purchased their home and now lived the quiet suburban life.

Jules took his place at the table, the plas-glass outer walls giving a panoramic view of the approaches to one side of the house: the empty driveway, the white ribbon of smart road that passed in front and wound downhill toward the town of Joshua Tree a few miles out of sight. On the opposite side, beyond large sliding sheets of plas-glass, lay the pool area with its retractable clear-lite canopy and snuggled in its own screen of desert plantings. Away from the house, well camouflaged by desert plants, rocks, hills, and opacity controlled plas-glass, were a few other dwellings belonging to their neighbors, one or two of which they had become friends with. Somewhere farther out in the desert, Jules understood there was a Trappist monastery but he had never seen it. *Have to take a drive out there one of these days.*

"Daydreaming already?" asked Mooney, setting down platters of scrambled eggs and bacon on the table.

"Just thinking," said Jules, helping himself to the eggs. "We're a long way from Thebatislivikovo."

9

"A long way," agreed Mooney, setting down the coffee dispenser. "What brought that up?"

Jules shrugged, again gazing out over the desert.

"Just how nice it is to have our own home in such a wonderful setting," he said. "It's a far cry from most of the other worlds we've found ourselves on."

"Mars, Proxima, Callisto; yeah, I agree. But Thebatislivikovo took the cake."

"Well, it wasn't as if we planned to go there," said Jules.

"Certainly not for a honeymoon!"

It was a little joke Mooney liked to bring up now and then because the ironic thing was, Thebatislivikovo, the home world of the Zhapoologani, with whom the Consortium had been at war, did technically end up being part of their honeymoon itinerary. They'd begun their honeymoon on Callisto when it was interrupted by Leclerc who assigned them to a new mission. One that concluded on Thebatislivikovo.

Mooney was heading back to the stove she liked to use for preparing real meals when she hesitated, supporting herself on the island in the center of the kitchen space.

"What's the matter?" asked Jules. "Still hung over from that party last night?"

The two had attended a social gathering back in town, one intended to acquaint locals with one another and Mooney indulged in a couple mixed drinks, Proxima gin and Deneb beer to be exact, never a good combination.

"I'm okay," said Mooney, straightening. "Felt a little light headed there for a second. Must have been those drinks."

"Anyway, we were lucky to get off Thebatislivikovo alive and in one piece," said Jules.

"No luck to it," corrected Mooney, returning with the hash browns. "I spoke Zhapoologani. Had no trouble explaining what we were doing on their Moon and how we'd just saved their whole civilization."

"You make it sound easy. There was the little matter of having caught us red handed having reconfigured their cloud set up in order to defeat the SR1."

"That did take some fast talking," admitted Mooney.

To defeat the SR1 and prevent it from completing its intention to end all life in both the Consortium and the Outer Arm Coalition (leaving itself as the sole sentient organism in the galaxy) Jules was forced to co-opt the Zhapoologani's cloudspace, whose nexus was located on Thebatislivikovo's moon, and use it to transform the SR1 into non-equilibrium matter, forcing it into permanent residence in non-space. It worked. But he and Mooney had little time to catch their collective breaths when a Zhapoologani security team found them in the midst of what looked to them like sabotage.

"It was touch and go there for a while after they rounded us up with Prof. Tamaka."

"I thought they were going to shoot us right there and then," admitted Jules.

"That's when I started talking...fast! And weren't you glad you'd teamed up with a former translator for the Exterior Ministry."

"And how!" Jules recalled again how narrow that escape from death had been. He often wondered if Mooney knew it herself. When she talked of the incident, as she was doing now, it was with such flippancy Jules began to doubt if she did. "What exactly did you tell them to keep them from shooting us on the spot?"

Mooney shrugged. "You know, I don't exactly remember. All I could do was concentrate on those tough Zhapoologani consonants and how in the world I was going to explain what we'd just done when I wasn't even sure myself. It was just a good thing the Zhapoologani commander was good at math because he seemed to put two and two together and came up with four. He got the gist of what I was trying to say about the cloudspace generator we'd altered to use against the SR1 and the unknown vessel that had just wiped out the entire Zhapoologani home fleet."

"That's when he concluded the business was too big for him to handle and decided to hand us over to his superiors on Thebatislivikovo."

"Right. That's how we made history by becoming the first humans ever to visit the Zhapoologani home world."

"An honor I'd rather have forgone," said Jules, sipping from his second cup of coffee of the morning.

"Oh, I don't know," mused Mooney. "It was kind of fun having all those Zhapoologani males ogling me as we were taken through the capitol."

"That wasn't ogling, dear, that was hunger."

Mooney waved off the remark. "Stories about Zhapoologani eating human prisoners are just fairy tales intended to scare kids at bedtime."

"We did make quite a sensation there, I'll admit."

"Never saw such strange architecture with buildings bigger at the top than at the bottom, like upside down pyramids."

"I thought it fascinating too," said Jules. "How, for instance, did they manage to stay up? Must have been influenced in some psychological way by the Zhapoologani physiology. They're upper torso's are so much bigger than the lower."

"No chance of inter-species romance happening there, I can tell you," joked Mooney. "Or am I allowed to say that in mixed company?"

"It's a free country as the saying goes," replied Jules. "Anyway, I did find the way their science developed fascinating. Even though the laws of physics are the same throughout the universe, there's no telling how different people will apply it and the Zhapoologani sure applied it in strange ways."

"You got all that from the Zhapoologani scientist you spoke to?"

"Some. He spoke our chief language well and believe me, I was relieved to be able to explain what we'd done to someone who could understand. After he'd explained it all to the Grand Shamushinashishi, our death sentences were commuted."

"Nice of them," said Mooney, nibbling on a piece of toast.

Again, Jules wondered if she appreciated the near run thing it had all been. Or was she just covering up her own anxiety with humor? With Mooney, sometimes it was hard to tell.

"We were treated pretty well after that, even though they still didn't fully trust us."

"We did spend most of our time in the quarters they'd assigned us," recalled Mooney. "I still shudder when I think of looking out those windows and thinking the whole building was going to fall over and crush us to death."

Jules laughed. "It did have that vertiginous feeling. Too bad I never had the opportunity to watch one being built. Would have loved to see how they did it."

"You, maybe, not me. I wanted out of there. I never had the feeling we were particularly wanted."

"Well, remember, the Consortium and the Coalition had been at war for years. We weren't going to overcome hard feelings overnight even if we'd saved their civilization from complete destruction."

"Still, it was such a relief when I heard we'd be leaving and a Consortium battle wagon was waiting for us in neutral space."

"Have to admit I was anxious to get back home too," said Jules. "Still, our stay on Thebatislivikovo must have had some positive effect because I've heard the Consortium and the Coalition have re-opened negotiations between themselves, might even exchange ambassadors."

"I don't envy whoever the Consortium sent to Thebatislivikovo," said Mooney.

"That may be, but it all ended up for the good. The war has been suspended and we now have detente between the Consortium and the Coalition...all started because of us, really."

"A dividend from our mission no one expected."

"Right. Doesn't that make you feel all warm inside?"

Mooney laughed, almost choking on her breakfast. "I think you'd better get back to your creep resistance and grain structures before I throw something at you!"

"So you were listening," observed Jules, rising from the table. "I think what's really bothering you is that with all this peace and love breaking out, there's less chance of Leclerc sending us on any more missions. Which is fine by me."

Jules refilled his cup with coffee and began making his way back to the solarium.

But he'd spoken too soon.

A chime echoed through the house warning them that a visitor was approaching the front entrance.

"Wonder who that could be?" asked Mooney. "You expecting anyone?"

Jules shook his head. They weren't so settled in the neighborhood that they could expect anyone dropping by to borrow a cup of sugar.

"Can you see who it is?"

Mooney sauntered into the den and up the little landing that divided the front portion of the house from the rear. Glancing outside as she did so, she stopped short.

"What is it?" Jules wanted to know.

"You're not going to believe this."

"Try me."

"It's Leclerc!"

Chapter Two

A New Threat

"I don't believe it!"

Which he didn't. Mooney had to be mistaken.

"Well, it is," she insisted.

Peeking outside, Jules saw an air car parked in front of the house and Leclerc himself studiously following the curving walk to the front door.

"You're right," whispered Jules.

"Do we answer the door or hide and hope he goes away?" asked Mooney, a smile in her voice.

Jules was silent a moment, contemplating the desert scenery that stretched out beyond the air car, and for a moment actually considered the suggestion.

"Well?" prompted Mooney, suddenly serious.

Jules sighed and went to the door.

"Guess we'll just have to face the music," he said.

"Do you think this is a social call or business?"

Jules could tell by the tone in her voice, that Mooney was hoping for the latter.

"Leclerc wouldn't come all the way from Mars just to pay us a social call," said Jules, resigned. "Even if he were called in to New Washington he wouldn't go this far out of his way. No, I think we're in for bad news."

"For you maybe," said Mooney, giving her long red hair a shake. "I hate to think I've been going through all those MI indoctrination papers for nothing."

There was no more time for conversation after that as a tonal change in the door chime indicated that Leclerc had reached the entry foyer.

Jules stepped to the door and opened it himself instead of telling the smart home to do it for him.

"Henri!" he exclaimed, taking the MI director's hand in a firm shake. "I couldn't believe it when Mooney told me it was you."

"Don't blame you, Jules," said Leclerc, stepping inside. "Haven't been to Earth in three years. Keep forgetting how wearisome the gravity can be."

"Then you've been stationed on Mars too long. Time to come home."

"Maybe, but at least under the domes, there's climate control," harrumphed Leclerc. "How can you stand the heat out there?"

"It's not that bad when you get used to it," said Jules. "Mooney spends half her time out there working in her rock gardens."

"Nice in here though."

"Let me get you something cool to drink," offered Mooney after giving Leclerc an unprofessional hug. "A big tall Callistan Cooler?"

Leclerc held up his hand using his fingers in a pinching gesture.

"With a pinch of rum, I know."

As Mooney disappeared in the direction of the kitchen, Leclerc took the opportunity to look around the sun splashed, climate controlled interior of the house.

"Very nice place you have here," he observed. "But how can you stand the weather?"

"Well, it may be hot outdoors, but it's not humid," replied Jules. "You learn to live with it; that, and knowing when are the best times of day to go outside. For instance, the air moves at different times of the day. The evenings are wonderful. Nights it actually gets cold."

"Not used to all this open space," said Leclerc. "And this house. With all that plas-glass, it feels as though you're living outdoors."

"We like it...and the environment. The house was designed by Janson Lionelwell, the architect?"

No reaction. "He's very well known for his ability to combine modern features such as plas-glass and smart living with native building materials and late modern housing styles." Jules took in their surroundings with a wave of his hand. "That's where all the field stone interior walls and the oak beam rafters come in. The plas-glass outer walls all around can either be made clear or opaque depending on the level of privacy we want. They can even look completely clear from the inside while on the outside appear opaque or even different kinds of textures from stonework to old fashioned shingles. Pretty amazing really."

"And paid for by my department," Leclerc pointed out.

"Worth the price for saving the universe...twice!" said Mooney, handing Leclerc his drink.

"I don't disagree," objected Leclerc. "Just making an observation."

"If it helps soothe your conscience, you're invited to stay with us whenever you want."

"I appreciate that," said Leclerc, eyeing the tastefully appointed mix of proto-modern and traditional wood based furnishings scattered about the big, open rooms, "but I think I'm more Martian now than I am Terran."

"Speaking of saving the universe," said Jules, indicating a comfortable looking iso-couch where it faced a stone fireplace. "How are things going with the Zhapoologani?"

Leclerc accepted the chair but stared hard at the fireplace. *Did they actually burn wood in it?* Deciding not to ask, he replied:

"Not bad," he said, taking a sip from his drink. "This is very good, 'Manda! After learning what you two were doing on their moon and how close they'd come to being wiped out, the Zhapoologani, have been eager to sit back down at the negotiating table and talk with us."

"It also helped having their home fleet wiped out by the SR1," added Mooney. "Nothing like finding yourself helpless in deciding to make peace instead of war."

"Be that as it may, and keep this under your hat, the government isn't ready to make the official announcement for a few weeks yet, the Consortium and the Coalition have agreed to a detente between the two empires."

"A thaw?" asked Jules, giving Mooney a significant glance.

No point in letting Leclerc know that the news had already been traveling along the grapevine.

"It really means peace, but the word detente includes that element of uncertainty that will exist for a bit longer as both sides learn to trust the other. To help shore up trust, we'll be exchanging ambassadors."

"No kidding? That is a big step."

"Even so, after spending some time on Thebatislivikovo, I don't envy whoever the Consortium sends to represent them," said Mooney, reiterating what she'd said to Jules earlier that morning.

"No argument there. Whoever the ambassador will be, he'll have his job cut out for him what with being the first Terran to interface directly with an alien species."

"Three, if you count the Drool and the Sangi, the Zhapoologanis' junior partners during the war," noted Jules.

"True. There's still uncertainty in New Washington on exactly how our relations will be conducted among the three. Will the Zhapoologani continue to speak for the Drool and the Sangi? Will those races finally break away and take charge of their own affairs? At this stage, the last thing we want to do is upset the Zhapooloani by treating with what they might still think as their subordinates."

"Wonder if some kind of civil war could break out among them?"

"That's one of the things we have to be careful about," acknowledged Leclerc. "We don't want to get involved in the Coalition's internal politics."

"We've got bigger fish to fry?"

"Exactly. Right now, negotiators are working on an informal alliance with the Zhapoologani," revealed Leclerc. "If the two empires are not going to be at war any more, then what will be the basis of our future relationship?"

"Trade isn't enough?"

Leclerc shook his head. "Unlikely the Coalition will have anything the Consortium really needs. We're pretty much self-sufficient as are the Zhapoologani. That leaves security. Even though the Consortium has yet to run into any alien races within its own space, the existence of the Coalition proves that it's only a matter of time before we do. When that time comes, it won't hurt to meet it with as strong a front as possible. Turns out the Zhapoologani feel the same way, especially while they still need to rebuild their fleet. So, the main object in our new relationship will be mutual security."

"Whew! Who would have thought such a day would come?" mused Jules, not without the same relief that the billions of other Terrans would feel once they also heard the good news. "So, I guess with all this peace breaking out, MI will be winding down its operations?"

"Not likely," said Leclerc, continuing to enjoy his drink. "We're going to have new concerns now; such as transitioning from a Zhapoologani centered intelligence gathering program to other concerns that the Consortium has let slide during the war."

"Such as?" Mooney wanted to know.

"Corporate corruption, forbidden experimentation on human genes, cloning, etc. The whole gamut of interstellar law. We also need to keep an eye on signs of rebellious behavior on Consortium worlds."

"I wasn't aware we had such problems," said Jules.

"Oh, nothing in the offing...so far as we can tell. As you know, the Consortium allows quite a bit of freedom under the restored Constitution of 1789 so dissent is indulged. It's when dissent threatens the common sense order and societal upheaval that the intelligence services must step in."

"Still, the lines don't seem as clear cut as they were during the war," said Mooney.

"That's true. It means MI must take on new kinds of agents, those steeped in political theory and our rights under the Constitution to help discern between healthy dissent and dangerous movements."

It seemed to Jules the conversation sobered Leclerc greatly since he walked into the house. Something was bothering him. Something he wasn't ready to talk about.

"Well, you might be happy to know that my nitinol project is proceeding well," said Jules, changing the subject.

"You've licked the temperature problem?" asked Leclerc eagerly.

Jules was cautious. "Maybe. The team has narrowed down the possibilities and I feel certain the solution lay in the nickel titanium mix.

As you know if you've been reading our summaries, nitinol is composed of almost equal parts nickel and titanium. If the solution lies there, the difference will be one of mili-fractions of a difference between the two."

"So, you're ready for actual experimentation; trying different amounts of the mix?"

Jules nodded. "If we're on the right track, it'll only be a matter of running checks on different mixes until we hit the right one."

"That's encouraging, and will be good news to our engineers," enthused Leclerc. "Even now, the Navy is gearing up for a new generation of warships that will withstand any of those potentially hostile first contacts I mentioned."

"I make no promises, you understand," cautioned Jules. "Just good chances."

"Understood."

There was a pause in the conversation then as Leclerc finished his drink. To fill the empty space while waiting for the MI director to get around to his reasons for dropping by, Jules asked about another touchy subject.

"Um, director, I was wondering about the other Jules."

He sensed Mooney stiffen on the settee beside him. She knew the subject of his other self was one that plagued his conscience for a long time and was always fearful of a relapse.

"How is he doing? He and Joan?"

"He's not with MI, I can assure you," replied Leclerc carefully.

"Back in the field?"

"That's right. I hear that he and Joan are on assignment. A new dig somewhere on the frontier. I don't know any more than that. Want me to find out?"

Jules shook his head. "No need. Just curious is all. Really, I'm over that now."

"Good to hear." Now Leclerc cleared his throat, coming at last to the reason for his visit. "Because I have an assignment for you. Something that's very, very sensitive and must stay within the tightest need to know circle that MI can arrange."

"The tightest I know, is between you and the agents involved," said Jules grimly.

Leclerc nodded. "Anyone else who needs to be brought into this will only be told what they need to know and not the big picture nor the overall context."

"And here we were talking about MI winding down," said Mooney. "I guess you're not here to give me my final exam in person then?"

Leclerc allowed himself a tired smile before going on.

"Have the two of you ever heard of secular humanism?"

Jules and Mooney looked at each other before Mooney replied.

"Ancient history, isn't it? It ended up causing the last great war on Earth before the movement's followers were defeated and their ideology suppressed."

"That was all back in the twenty-first century, early twenty-second," added Jules. "The Constitutionalists finally won the war then helped to defeat the movement in Europe. Ended up breaking the European Union and eventually most nations agreed to adopt the 1789 Constitution and forming the Consortium of Nations."

"Every school child knows about the secular humanists," continued Mooney with vague alarm. "How monstrous they were. Godless maniacs who claimed to worship science and ignoring it completely when it contradicted their nonsensical beliefs. Didn't they outlaw meat and were eating insects near the end?"

"And when they couldn't break those who refused to accept such propositions as the supremacy of the state, a genderless society, the inferiority and basic racism of people of European descent, same sex marriage, polygamy, legalized pedophilia, euthanasia, infanticide, socialism, radicalized feminism...the sordid list goes on...they placed them into re-education camps."

With a growing sense of uneasiness, Mooney scooted closer to Jules who placed a comforting arm around her shoulders.

"Of course, no society could function under such beliefs," concluded Leclerc. "Denial of logic and God could only lead to breakdown, chaos, and repression. It was an evil that preyed on man's greed and self-interest until setting one person against another.

Balkanization, they used to call it. They used their belief in manmade climate change and the rise of strange, new diseases to demand that the state take more and more control over citizens' daily lives until people became virtual prisoners in their own homes. But the most seductive aspect of secular humanism was it made life so easy. It's surface concern for human welfare was Christianity without the need for God. Instead, the state took the place of God, granting and withdrawing rights as it saw fit. Mostly, it took them away. The right to self-defense, the right of free speech, the right of conscience, freedom of movement, freedom of religion, even the right to life itself.

"Eventually, set asides, preferred treatment, reverse racism all set one group against another and the law of the jungle took over. Law and order broke down. It was every man for himself."

"It was a horrible world," said Mooney. "I don't think I like this subject."

"No one does," agreed Leclerc. "Luckily for us, there were portions of the old United States that had not succumbed to the secular humanist argument. They resisted and eventually overthrew the old Humanists and condemned their pernicious philosophy for good, wiping every trace of it from human history."

"Thank God for that," exclaimed Mooney. "The real God, that is."

"It was a horrible time, one that humanity has not had any desire to revisit in the centuries since. The Consortium has done a thorough job of suppressing any serious reconsideration of the Humanists' deranged values."

"So, what has all of that to do with this new assignment you have for us?" asked Jules.

Leclerc heaved a heavy sigh.

"Well, what it comes down to, is a book."

"A book?" asked Mooney. "Do they even still exist?"

It was a rhetorical question. Certainly, many millions of physical books still existed but mostly in the world's libraries or in private collections. Most print was available in digital formats accessible to anyone with a telcomm...which was virtually everyone in the

Consortium.

"They do," said Leclerc, playing along. "Perhaps the rarest of all is a book called *Elements of Humanism*. There's only a single copy in existence and until two days ago, it resided under lock and key and much more at the National Archives in New Washington."

"'Until recently?'"

Leclerc nodded. "Despite the greatest security precautions the Archives could devise, as great as that used to protect the original copy of the Constitution of 1789, the book was stolen."

The others remained silent, the enormity of what the director was telling them, growing slowly in their minds.

"As you know, all literature dealing with the secular humanist philosophy was destroyed over one hundred years ago except a single copy of the book *Elements of Humanism* written by one of the heavy theorists of the movement, name of Samuel Pimdale. This one source, though every word in it is poisonous and can lead the weak minded down darker paths of social error, was the only one to be preserved solely for reasons of historical research and understanding. Over the years, only scholars with special permission from the leadership of the Consortium could consult it. Its contents continue to be regarded as so dangerous that it needs to be kept out of the public eye. When their research is finished, those who are given permission to consult the volume, must undergo stringent psychological examination in order to verify that their minds weren't contaminated by its twisted values. It's that dangerous."

"And you say someone stole it?" asked Mooney.

Leclerc nodded. "I can't emphasize strongly enough how dangerous the book is. When its theft was discovered, the entire resources of the Consortium were mobilized to find it, but because the whole investigation had to be kept top secret, it necessarily hampered the ability of investigators from doing as thorough a job as they could."

"So, the book is still missing," summed up Jules.

Leclerc nodded again. "When the government failed to get anywhere quickly, I was able to convince the authorities to let Military Intelligence handle the case on its own. I told them it was my belief that MI would be able to conduct a more focused investigation. And, of course, I had you people in mind from the start."

"How long has it been since the book was stolen?" asked Jules, anticipating what Leclerc was leading up to.

"Almost a week ago now," said a gloomy Leclerc.

"A week." Unable to sit still, Jules stood and began to pace the room. "If its contents were an actual disease, that would be long enough for it to start spreading into the general population."

"That analogy has already occurred to us," admitted Leclerc. "Whoever stole this book is playing with fire. Which makes it imperative that we find the thieves as quickly as possible. When I think of how ruthless the Humanists were, how nothing and no one was allowed to contradict their beliefs, how they spent untold wealth, sacrificed millions of lives, perverted science, ended individual freedoms all in order to achieve their impossible, unnatural goals...well, it sends a shiver down my spine."

"So, is that why you're here?" asked Jules. "To give me and Mooney the assignment in person?"

"Again, this case is highly sensitive," said Leclerc. "I wanted to brief you in person rather than trusting even to MI's dedicated hyper-bandwidth. The government gave the job to MI because it agreed with me that we could offer a more focused effort, one that would yield results. To do that, the conduct of our investigation will be as tight as I can make it: I'm giving the assignment to the two of you whom I believe can be trusted with absolute confidentiality. Under no circumstances can word of this be made public. Although the general public can be trusted to reject Humanist positions, there are far too many weaker minds, with little or no critical faculties, that might be influenced to accept them. This mission will be conducted under extreme compartmentalization. Which means for the most part, you'll be on your own.

"Finally, a second reason I've decided to give you the assignment, besides your obvious abilities as demonstrated in past cases, is that you're conveniently located on Earth where the theft took place. Being members of the science division, I know this assignment isn't exactly in your line. It's more of a political situation than a scientific one, but I feel I can trust you with this very sensitive matter.

"Oh, and one other thing," concluded Leclerc. "Try to avoid any contact with the regular police and security units that had a role in investigating the case. Their knowledge of the wider ramifications of the case is limited anyway, and we prefer that they remain out of the loop if at all possible, for security reasons."

"Nothing like making a difficult situation even harder," grumped Mooney.

She and Jules exchanged looks.

"We'll start right away," said Jules.

Chapter Three

New Washington

Jules looked down through thinning clouds at the exurbs surrounding the city of New Washington, capitol of the reconstituted United States of America. Whole sections had been rescued after the war by historical preservationists so that, on the ground, visitors could walk for many blocks at a time and never see a dome or a modern style smart home. He read that when the Constitutional armies entered the city after defeating the Humanist forces, they'd found everything run down, buildings in disrepair, the old subway long closed with its old fashioned rail cars rusting on underground sidings, even slums. The Humanists' socialistic policies that emphasized something called equity over ability, discouraged innovation, and suppressed competition. Anyone whose ideas threatened to give them an advantage over others in any way was quickly discouraged. As a result, nothing much was ever accomplished. Improvements in technology lagged, repair and upkeep of existing infrastructure fell behind, entrepreneurship became impossible. People quickly discovered that under such a system, it was just pointless to exert themselves beyond what was necessary. It was a wonder that the Humanist nation lasted as long as it did...and not surprising that it collapsed so easily once the war began.

As bad off as the Humanists were, conditions had been even worse in Old Europe, Canada, and Australia. Luckily, by the time those countries had been subsumed by the Humanist disease, there had been a revolution in China and Russia suffered an economic implosion. Of all the countries in the Western world, only Israel was able to maintain its societal integrity, keeping the Middle East from exploding until the West could get back on its collective feet again. That process began with the civil war between the Constitutionalists and the Humanists, a war that spread to neighboring Canada which was even worse off than the United States. Eventually though, the illiberal forces there were defeated with the result that the former provinces of Canada allied with the states of America in defining a new political entity to be known as the Consortium.

"What are you thinking about?" asked Mooney from the adjoining seat on the supersonic stratoliner they caught back at the rocket field outside Joshua Tree.

"You know very well what I'm thinking about," grinned Jules, turning away from the window.

Mooney leaned forward to look herself. "About the war and the Humanists."

"Yeah," said Jules but with no humor in his voice.

By then, the plane was in the last stages of its descent to the renamed Ronald Reagan Aerodrome and Rocket Field. They had been warned to reattach their harness straps in preparation for the landing.

The plane was close to the ground now and off in the distance, Jules identified the White House, Capitol Building, and other familiar monuments...those that survived the Humanist regime. It was a miracle, now that he thought about it, that the Jefferson Memorial hadn't been torn down. The Humanists, he understood, had chosen to use it as a learning tool for the masses, draping it with signage and slogans denouncing Jefferson as a racist and the Constitution for which he had an unofficial advisory role, as an outdated instrument of white male suppression. With that rationale, the Bill of Rights was canceled and the last remaining copy of the original Constitution scheduled for ritual immolation. Luckily, an underground cadre of Constitutionalists managed to rescue the document and kept it safe until the Humanist regime was finally overthrown.

Jules shuddered.

The slogans that defaced the Jefferson Memorial had long since been cleaned up and the memorial restored to its former pride of place.

Others had not been so lucky.

As the stratoliner banked for its final approach to the Aerodrome, it came within sight of the Washington Monument Memorial. Located at the east end of the long reflecting pool, it was all there was to mark the spot where the once famous obelisk had stood before it was demolished by the Humanist regime. Even now, it was hard to believe it was torn down simply because some believed it had been built with slave labor or that Washington himself owned slaves. Instead, Humanists promoted their own brand of heroes: perverts, fornicators, abortionists, and atheists.

When the Humanists were overthrown, the Consortium decided to mark both the former Washington Monument and the madness that destroyed it with the placement of a simple pylon engraved with the reminder of what had once stood on the site.

"What a nightmare world it must have been," mused Jules aloud.

"Must have felt like a mass lunatic asylum," agreed Mooney, sensing her husband's thoughts.

Having been reminded of the lethal derangements of the Humanist regime, Jules became more than ever determined to find whoever stole the *Elements of Humanism* and to prevent the horrors it gave rise to from ever again reestablishing themselves.

Suddenly, the whine of the 'liner's engines shifted in tone, signaling reverse thrust just before the landing gear touched the ground. There was a brief screech and then they were taxiing along the runway, headed for the terminal.

"I'll never get over how smooth these 'liners come down," Mooney was saying. "I hardly felt it when the wheels hit the runway."

"I didn't feel it at all," replied Jules. "If I hadn't been looking out the window, I never would've guessed we landed."

In minutes, the forward half of the 'liner inserted itself into a bay at the terminal and passengers all around them rose to gather their things. They exited from the forward hatch directly into the waiting area where travelers were already waiting to board after them.

They were traveling light, so instead of diverting to baggage claim, they made their way immediately to the glassite covered concourse where lines of robo-cabs stood waiting to whisk passengers to the city. Through the open ends of the concourse, other stratoliners were taking off to parts unknown, the pulse of their supersonic engines being felt more than heard.

"So, we're hitting the case cold," said Mooney as the 'cab pulled away and accelerated immediately to high speed before bursting out of the concourse into the bright Virginia sunlight. "No briefing with the Consortium Security Service."

Jules nodded. "According to Leclerc, they were never able to get very far in the investigation. It's probably better for us to start from scratch. It's less likely we'll miss anything and not be influenced by false leads they may have come up with."

"Do we let them know we're on the case?"

"Not unless we need to. If we get in trouble with local law enforcement, we can always refer them to MI for clearance. But I hope it doesn't come to that."

"They'll probably resent it if they find out we've been called in to go over the same ground they did. It'll seem to be calling their competence into question."

Jules shrugged, watching the multi-colored glassite business and government towers grow in height as the smart road negotiated the robo-cab through traffic. "It's only human. But I trust that they'll be professional about it."

"You trust more in human nature than I do," smiled Mooney.

As they spoke, the 'cab emerged from the city proper into the heart of New Washington by taking the Arlington Bridge across the Potomac River. Now the architecture shifted to a more classical style in keeping with local ordinances. All the older buildings of the former United States government had been preserved including the White House, Capital, Supreme Court, Library of Congress, and the National Archives.

"I understand a lot of these buildings had to be completely remodeled after the Humanists were driven out," observed Jules.

"Fumigated you mean," said Mooney, as the 'cab pulled into an underground garage beneath the Archives Building.

"They say there are still some Humanist remnants on the walls of the sub-basements," said Jules, helping Mooney from the 'cab.

"Left there for archival purposes," added Mooney. "Only

accredited scholars who've passed anti-susceptibility psyche testing are allowed to see them."

"The same exams required to study *Elements of Humanism*," noted Jules.

While having no special interest herself in seeing any of the old, faded graffiti, Mooney couldn't help trying to spy any on the garage walls out of the corners of her eyes. But had the garage been added only after the war?

She was still trying to remember, when they entered an up-capsule. "Second floor," said Jules and immediately the cabin began to rise.

"Are they expecting us?"

Jules nodded. "I called before we left. I was told archives director Alfo Bikari wouldn't be available but there'll be someone there to answer our questions. I decided not to wait around for the director to show. Wanted to get to work as soon as we arrived. We can worry about a hotel room later, if we need it."

"You expecting things to move quickly then?"

Jules shrugged. "You never know. Better to expect the unexpected and be ready to move when it happens. The trail is cold enough as it is."

As it was in the second floor corridor where the up-capsule deposited them.

"Chilly in here," noted Mooney, hugging herself.

"Climate is kept on the cool side, the better to help preserve ancient documents," explained Jules.

"But does that have to include the hallways and offices too? I thought environmentally sensitive material was kept under glassite."

"Maybe personnel need to be preserved too," joked Jules. "Here we are."

An inscription on the clear plas-glass double doors read 'Office of the Director, National Archives, Alfo Bikari'. Jules pushed one of the leaves open for Mooney who preceded him into the room. There, a male secretary rose from his desk to inquire as to their identities.

Jules told him.

"The director isn't here right now, but I'll get you guard captain Ponto," said the secretary.

A few minutes after the secretary placed the call, a uniformed officer made his appearance.

"Mr. Conroi?" he asked.

"Yes," replied Jules, shaking hands. "And this is Mrs. Conroi."

The man raised his eyebrows.

"We were contacted by Military Intelligence two days ago telling us to expect a special investigator," said Ponto. "But I didn't think there would be two of you..."

"Mrs. Conroi is my partner in this case. We work as a team." explained Jules, using his telcomm to identify himself.

Mooney did the same.

Reassured, Ponto nodded.

"Why don't we use the director's office. We can talk privately there," he said, motioning for Jules and Mooney to precede him.

Inside, they took a pair of pneuma-chairs that were arranged before the director's work station.

"Now then," began Ponto before Jules stopped him with a raised hand.

"Just a precaution," cautioned Jules. "The matter we're investigating is of the utmost priority with top level compartmentalization. That means, in case you haven't been informed, the matter we're here to discuss must remain strictly among the three people in this room. Are all recording devices and monitors in the room shut off?"

Ponto, clearly intimidated, spoke to the room. "Now they are."

"Including the secretarial channel?" asked Mooney. "No notes will be taken of our conversation by you or the secretary outside."

"That channel is off as well," assured Ponto.

"Tell us what you know about the theft of the book," said Jules, getting right to the point. "We know it was stolen over a week ago now."

"All the more reason to move quickly with our investigation," added Mooney.

Ponto cleared his throat. Loosened the collar of his uniform coat.

"That's right. It took place over a weekend. Most of our employees were off at the time. Only a few administrators, including director Bikari, were in the building in addition to the security staff."

"How tight is security?" asked Jules.

"Well considering the fact that the archives were not believed to be high risk, not very," admitted Ponto. "We have four guards on the ground floor who watch the entrances and another three on this floor watching monitors mostly."

"What are they monitoring?" asked Mooney.

"Images from cameras set up in rooms and entrances," said Ponto. "And that's done mostly from the guard shack. In addition to cameras, you see, we also have a web of motion and sonic detectors covering areas where more sensitive material is kept."

"Such as?"

"What original Founding documents that the Humanists never got around to destroying mostly. But there are also rare books and correspondence collected over the years from political figures from the old United States. We even have some physical artifacts of too great historical importance to leave with the Smithsonian."

"Are there any security measures taken other than those for visual monitoring, motion, and sound?"

"Well, there's the vault we use to protect the Constitution. As I'm sure you're aware, every effort is made to keep it on display for the public, but when it's not, it's lowered into a vault in the sub-basement of the building that's designed to keep it safe even in the event of a pulse cannon or ion boring beam strike."

"Impressive," admitted Jules. "Were the same precautions made for *Elements of Humanism*?"

"Precautions there were almost as stringent," insisted Ponto. "Although it isn't...wasn't...kept in a sub-basement vault, it was kept in a walk-in safe of its own here on this floor. The safe is constructed of pure tintinnabulum. The same kind of metal used in our naval battlewagons. Together with the other security measures, the book should have been as secure as anyone could make it."

"Except that it wasn't," noted Mooney.

"Let's have a look at the guard shack," suggested Jules.

Ponto led the way from the director's office, down a series of corridors into a central suite where a large plas-glass booth dominated the area. Inside, a pair of uniformed guards sat watching a score of monitor screens tracking movement of personnel as they went about their jobs.

"As you can see, the equipment here leaves no area unobserved," Ponto was saying.

"These gauges indicate sounds and movements within restricted areas," offered one of the guards on duty, obviously enamored of Mooney's figure and long red tresses. "If there were any unauthorized activity in off limits areas, alarms would sound, automatically closing and locking intervening doorways and of course, alerting us here in the shack."

"And nothing of the sort was reported on the day of the theft?" asked Jules, rubbing his chin.

Ponto shook his head. "Nothing. Guards had been posted and rotated out as usual as their shifts ended or began. The equipment registered nothing out of the ordinary."

"Have you run any testing programs on the equipment?"

The duty officer looked annoyed. "We have. Right after the theft was discovered, we ran a system wide check. Everything was okay. There was nothing wrong with the equipment or monitoring devices."

"So, how would you explain the theft then?" asked Mooney.

The officer shrugged. "We can't. Isn't that why you people have been called in?"

"Let's look at the safe," suggested Jules.

After Ponto ordered the monitoring equipment in the area of the safe to be shut down, he, Jules, and Mooney went for a closer look.

Inside the room there was a table with some chairs used by the few accredited scholars cleared for study of the *Elements of Humanism*. There was nothing else except the door to the safe itself, set into one wall. There was no handle or timing device of any sort visible on its plain surface.

"How do you get in?" asked Mooney, running her hands against the door's cool tintinnabulum surface. "I don't see any signs of tampering."

"The safe can only be opened from the guard shack," replied Ponto. "When a visitor enters this room, the door to the outside is closed and locked behind them. Only then, when the signal that the door is secure is received by the guard, is the safe opened remotely."

Ponto spoke the command that closed the outer door. A few seconds after it slid into place, hidden servos were engaged, the safe door impressed itself inward, then rolled aside behind the tintinnabulum walls.

"When unoccupied, sensors placed around the room are active," said Ponto. "Although unobservable, they include devices for motion and sound as well as a video feed. The monitors for sound can even detect the pulse of a person's heartbeat."

By then, the safe door had fully opened, revealing inside a lone pedestal protected by a bubble of clear glassite.

"This glassite, is shatter proof," said Ponto. "Of the kind used to create the protective domes on Mars."

"The book was kept under the glassite?" asked Mooney.

"It was. The glassite bubble was in turn secured in place by an electro-magnetic field making it unmovable except when the field is canceled from the guard shack."

"And yet, even with all these precautions, the book was stolen," said Jules.

"An inside job?" asked Mooney.

Jules looked at Ponto.

"Of course, the possibility was considered but we were able to account for the whereabouts of all our employees," said Ponto.

"Are you sure?" asked Mooney. "Overlapping schedules? No one was left alone for any amount of time? Especially among the guards?"

Ponto hesitated. "We keep records of such things. The building's computer system tracks all comings and goings. If there were any such irregularities, I'm sure we would have caught them."

"Humans have been known to outsmart computers, Mr. Ponto," noted Jules.

"What about your own movements, Mr. Ponto," queried Mooney,

playing the bad cop. "Were they checked as well?"

Ponto struggled to control his indignation. "I wasn't in the building that day. I was out of town with my family."

"That can be double checked. Are you sure...?"

"Absolutely!"

"Nothing personal, Mr. Ponto," soothed Jules. "We have to cover all the angles."

"How about absenteeism? Has anyone taken any time off lately? Called in sick?" pressed Mooney.

Ponto thought a moment. "Well, people come and go. They come in late now and then. Or leave early. They miss lunch."

"But has anyone taken leave and not come back?" pressed Mooney.

"Well, Lou Sigman has been out for a few days..."

"How many exactly? When did he first take leave?"

"Since Monday. He worked that weekend and then called in for some personal time off."

"What was he employed as?"

"He's one of our security team. He manned the guard shack..." Ponto's voice trailed off as he realized an angle he had not considered.

"What's Sigman's address?" demanded Jules.

Ten minutes later, he and Mooney were once again in a robo-cab headed out of town toward Stone Ridge, a suburban area of New Washington popular among government employees.

"Do you think Sigman has potential?" asked Mooney, watching as the glassite towers of outer New Washington give way to older architecture in the style of the early twenty-first century.

"Maybe," said a thoughtful Jules. "It was an inside job to be sure, but the more I think about it, the more I'm convinced it couldn't have been done by only a single person."

This piqued Mooney's interest. "A two man job?"

Jules nodded. "A single person couldn't be in two places at once. Someone had to man the guard shack in order to manipulate the safeguards while another man retrieved the book. Remember, the outer door to the vault room couldn't be open at the same time as the safe door.

Someone had to be inside to let the guard shack know when he was ready to leave."

Mooney was quiet for a moment. "Supposing Sigman was in the guard shack, do you have a candidate for the second man?"

Jules hesitated before replying. "Maybe."

The robo-cab glided along leafy, tree lined streets until pulling up before an old fashioned red brick apartment building.

"Fancy," noted Mooney, stepping to the sidewalk. "I heard these historical jobs were on the pricey side rent-wise."

"Our man doesn't do badly," observed Jules.

"Government pay or something else?"

"Maybe both."

They mounted a short flight of steps and noted the names above a row of antique, but no longer used mail shutes.

"Here it is," said Mooney, pointing.

Sigman's unit was located on the third floor.

Not wishing to alert Sigman of their arrival, Jules used his telcomm to access the MI band which quickly provided him with the entrance code.

Mooney tested the door and it gave.

Together, they entered a foyer on the other side and Jules led the way to the emergency stairs.

Their footsteps rang hollowly in the fire tower as they made their way upstairs. At the third floor, Jules poked his head out of the old style swinging door and saw that the hallway outside was deserted. He led the way to Sigman's living unit and they took their positions on either side of the door. They produced their MI issue ion pistols.

"Why don't you make yourself known," suggested Jules. "He's less likely to be alarmed at sight of an attractive female."

Mooney made a face but made sure her pistol was out of range of the unit annunciator which here was equipped with a video component. Taking a position before the annunciator alerted the tenant that someone was at the door and presently, Sigman's face appeared in the annunciator's screen.

"Yes?" he said, his expression indicating pleasure at sight of

Mooney.

"Mr. Louis Sigman?" asked Mooney, putting on her most friendly smile, the one with the dimples.

"I am."

"I'm with the Archives benefits program and going over your paperwork, found that there was some information missing from your employee file. We need that information in order to make sure you receive the full range of benefits when you retire in a few years."

Holding out the possibility of extra cash, no matter if it was needed or not, always resulted in a positive reaction and so it proved this time as Sigman wasted little time in unlocking his unit door and pulling it open by its quaint doorknob.

Instantly, Jules crowded in behind Mooney who had been just a little faster. Both had their pistols in plain sight and at the ready.

Sigman, taken by surprise, backed off quickly, nearly tripping on the unit's thick soma-rug.

"Hold it, hold it!" he cried, raising his hands by way of demonstrating he was harmless.

After a hasty look around the room, Jules swung the door shut and put some distance between himself and Mooney, the better to keep other doorways and each other covered.

"Take what you want," Sigman was saying. "Nothing here is worth my life."

"Sit down, Mr. Sigman," soothed Mooney, indicating a nearby pneuma-couch with her pistol.

As Sigman took the advice, Mooney moved over to another doorway and quickly inspected the bedroom. It was empty.

"Are you alone?" she asked, after she returned to the living room.

Sigman nodded, still frightened, his hands still lifted.

Jules returned after looking over the other rooms.

"He's alone," he told Mooney. "You can lower your arms, Mr. Sigman."

"What's this about?" Sigman demanded, regaining his composure.

Mooney returned her pistol to the hidden pocket in her bizsuit which was specially designed to make sure weapons didn't show.

Jules retained his own, but left it dangling in his hand, assuming a casual demeanor.

"We're agents of Military Intelligence," announced Mooney, projecting their credentials from her telcomm. "And you are part of an investigation into the theft of a book from your place of employment, the National Archives."

Bingo! Thought Mooney, looking at the screen of her telcomm that was indicating an immediate rise in Sigman's pulse rate.

"We won't waste your time or ours, Mr. Sigman," continued Mooney. "We have evidence that you were part of a two man operation that stole the *Elements of Humanism*. You know about its sensitivity and the level of precaution the Consortium has placed on it. You're also likely aware of the penalties that go along with being involved with any compromise in its security."

Having little definite evidence that Sigman was involved in the theft, he and Mooney decided that the best approach was to try and bluff him.

It worked.

Sigman visibly collapsed, as though the confrontation and accusation released pent up anxieties from which he longed to be free.

"I knew it," he was saying behind hands that hid his face. "I knew it. He said that it would be easy, that no one would ever find out."

"Who told you that?" pressed Jules. "Bikari?"

Mooney looked up from where Sigman was sitting to Jules. Though she'd suspected Bikari had been on Jules' mind as the second man, hearing him say the name aloud still took her by surprise.

Sigman nodded. "Yeah. Bikari. He offered to pay me ten thousand credits if I helped him to steal the book. What was a book anyway? It was nothing to me. And who'd ever find out? With the director himself covering for us, I thought the whole thing would be a cinch. But when he didn't show up for work the following Monday and then the whole rest of the week, I started to worry. I checked my account and found I still only had the first two thousand credits he'd transferred as a down payment. He was going to transfer the rest when the job was done. But here it is almost a week later and nothing...and no sign of Bikari! Things went south fast. I figured...I knew, security would catch on to me sooner or later. Just didn't think it would be this soon."

"Do you know where Bikari is now?" asked Jules. "What about the book?"

Sigman shrugged. Obviously a defeated man.

"He told you nothing about his plans following the theft?"

Sigman shook his head. "Nothing. Told you he was supposed to cover for us. I expected him to come back to work the next day as usual and pretend someone else had broken in and stolen the book."

Jules looked at Mooney and pulled her aside.

"This guy's telling the truth," said Mooney before Jules could speak.

"I think you're right. Doesn't sound as if he's been contaminated either. I don't think he ever even saw the book let alone read anything inside."

"That's good. Do we call in a team to pick him up?"

Jules nodded. "We're not going to get anything more useful out of him. What we need to do now is get over to Bikari's residence as quickly as we can."

"Not likely he'll still be there at this late date. He's had almost a week to make himself scarce."

"Agreed. But what else do we have?"

They stayed with Sigman only until a detail from MI showed up to place him in custody. As per Leclerc's instructions, extreme compartmentalization was in effect so local law enforcement was left out of the loop. In the meantime, Jules searched the unit but came up blank.

In a robo-cab again, he and Mooney traveled at best speed to the Georgetown section of New Washington where the address given them by Ponto was located.

"Nice neighborhood," observed Mooney as the 'cab rolled along O Street Northwest, past Georgetown University. Still operated by the Society of Jesus, it managed to survive the Humanist pogroms of the twenty-first century, reformed after the war, and reestablished itself as the Consortium's source for top diplomats.

Away from the university's sprawling campus, architecture gave way to a bewildering variety of contemporary and neo-modernesque buildings with a sprinkling of ugly specimens left over from the Humanist years tucked away here and there. Then the 'cab turned down Prospect Street which was dominated by ranks of old style brownstones with plenty of curbside landscaping.

"Archives directing must pay pretty good," said Mooney, impressed, despite her bias for the wide open spaces of their own desert home.

"Unfortunately, we're not here to admire the scenery," reminded Jules as the 'cab pulled up in front of a narrow, three story building tucked among a row of similar units.

Outside, the street was busy with pedestrians enjoying the warm Virginia sunshine. A baby was wailing from somewhere and the shade was cool beneath a row of dogwood trees that punctuated the bricked sidewalk. It was all very peaceful. Not the setting for a sinister plot to let loose one of the most dangerous ideologies ever to have plagued mankind.

"This is it," said Jules of the building unit before them.

His judgment was confirmed by the bronze name plate fastened to the center of the door: "Bikari."

Repeating the procedure they'd used at Sigman's, Jules stood aside, his ion pistol held discreetly away from view of any passerby on the sidewalk.

Mooney positioned herself before the annunciator and activated it. She waited a moment. No reply. She tried again. Still nothing.

"What now?" she asked.

From a pocket in his suit jacket, Jules removed a small device and aimed it at the lock mechanism embedded in hidden circuitry within the false wood door. Mooney recognized it as an MI issue universal laser key.

"I didn't know you had one of those," she remarked.

"Have to have some secrets of my own," replied Jules, smiling.

There was no outward sign that anything changed regarding the status of the door, but it was a measure of Jules' confidence in his key that he simply pushed against the barrier with the full expectation that it would yield.

It did.

Together, their weapons drawn but held at a disarming angle, they entered a small foyer. Beyond, a glassite wall and door prevented immediate entry into the unit proper. Once again, Jules moved to push the inner door open.

Cautiously, he slipped into the hall beyond where a staircase led to the upper reaches of the unit and an arched entranceway opened into a dining room. There, a polished table of shiny teak surrounded by high backed chairs sat silently. A chandelier hung from the ceiling. Back in the hall, a lone table with a vase of flowers was the only item in evidence.

"Hello," called out Jules. "Anyone home?"

No reply.

"Alfo Bikari," he tried again. "Are you home?"

Still nothing.

"Think he was warned we were coming?" asked Mooney, bringing her pistol up guardedly.

"Not from Sigman."

"Might there have been someone else at the Archives who was in on the theft?"

"Possible. Bikari could have had more than one insider helping him out but kept both or all, unaware of the others."

"Sounds too elaborate to me," said Mooney, watching the top of the stairs. "The simpler the better would have been best for a job like that."

"I'm inclined to agree with you."

"Then what?"

"Don't know what to think at the moment. Let's try over there."

They broke up, each taking one side of the archway leading to the dining room. After a quick survey, Jules made as if to enter...but bumped into a wall.

How did he make a mistake like that?

"Hey, clumsy," teased Mooney as she stepped into the dining room. "Watch your step!"

Then the same thing happened to her.

She bumped her nose against the molding framing the entrance.

"Ow!"

"Now who's being clumsy?" returned Jules, making his way around the wall to the dining room.

Again, he was met with resistance as he ran into the wall again.

"What...?"

"I'll check upstairs," said Mooney, giving up on the dining room.

But when she tried mounting the first step, she ran into the banister stanchion instead.

Reaching out to steady herself, she missed the banister by several feet and, losing her balance, stumbled to the floor.

"Darn it! Why am I so clumsy all of a sudden?"

By then, Jules had gone to her side to help her to her feet but ended up a few yards away, too far to do her any good.

He found himself facing the table with the vase and with suspicion rising, reached out to it experimentally.

He ended up grasping at empty air a few feet away.

"What's wrong with us?" asked Mooney again. "We suddenly can't do anything right."

She was still trying to find that first step up the stairs but missing it every time.

With rising suspicions, Jules turned, saw Mooney by the stairs and stepped carefully in her direction...but failed.

Instead, he'd tripped over the bottom step of the stairs!

Chapter Four

Death in New Washington

"Don't move," warned Jules. "If either of us stays in motion, we'll get farther and farther apart and maybe never find each other again."

Mooney froze.

"It's some kind of gas," guessed Mooney. "An odorless gas. It's dulling our senses."

"I don't think so," said Jules. "We can still see everything clearly. Nothing wrong with our perceptions."

"Then what?"

"I think we're caught in a quantum uncertainty loop."

"A what?"

"Try to reach out for my hand," he said, holding his own in her direction.

She reached to take it but missed. Tried again but missed again.

Mooney shook her head as if to clear it. Regaining her composure, she brushed some stray locks from before her eyes and reached out more slowly, concentrating.

She still missed Jules' hand, finding herself grasping empty air a few feet away.

"This is weird!"

Jules dropped his hand.

"It's just what I thought," he said. "If you kept trying for a million years, you'd never find my hand."

"I don't understand," said Mooney, concern in her voice for the first time.

She was becoming frightened, something that didn't come easy to her.

"I think we're stuck in some kind of quantum uncertainty loop," repeated Jules. "We might be able to find a door eventually but more likely we'd starve to death first."

"Oh, now that's reassuring!"

"I don't suppose you've ever heard of the quantum particle observer effect?"

"Sounds vaguely familiar," admitted Mooney cautiously. "You're not going to begin a lecture now, are you? Not when we're going to starve to death."

"No lecture. Just some background," said Jules. "The quantum particle observer effect is based on the principle that particles are in a state of potential until they're observed. The observer effect was proven back in the twentieth century when experimentation revealed that sub-atomic particles are in a constant state of potential until they're observed. In other words, on the quantum level, particles such as protons travel in only a single direction along a wave length, but if measuring devices are used to track them, they shift orbits and begin traveling along different routes depending on the observer. But the real revolutionary bit about the discovery was that the outcome of being observed would be only one of an infinite number of possibilities. Thus, the outcome changes every time it's observed."

"So, what does all that have to do with our situation?" asked Mooney. "We're not operating on the sub-atomic level."

"Doesn't matter. On a sub-atomic level, matter doesn't exist with certainty in definite places, but only has potentiality. Continuing research, and mind you, most of quantum research has long since drifted into the philosophical due to a failure in the language of science to account for the theoretical possibilities inherent in the observer effect, has since proven that all of reality, if we can call it that, is made up of a web of integrated energy patterns. Patterns, some believe, that humans could potentially learn to manipulate on a personal level."

"You're kidding!"

Jules shook his head. "No. Logically, it makes sense, but is that the way reality really works? If humans use quantum physics on a subconscious level to shape their individual destinies, then how can reality be any kind of orderly place with billions of individual minds working to fashion each their own destinies? Now that doesn't make any sense."

"I take it scientists...or rather, theologians...are working right now to make sense of it all?"

"They haven't stopped since the observer effect was first discovered," reassured Jules. "But if it's any comfort, Jesus Himself might have hinted at it when He taught us to do unto others. If it's true that we all subconsciously create our own realities, then it would behoove us to treat each other kindly to ensure our own well-being."

"Makes sense."

"It does."

"But does it help us right now?"

"Good question and I think I have an idea."

"Was wondering why you seemed so cool about all this," observed Mooney. "At least we know we're on the right track. Nobody would set up a trap like this in any ordinary home."

"Right. Therefore, there must be a device around here some place. Let's call it a quantum scrambler for lack of a better term."

"Okay. Now, what does it look like?" asked Mooney, glancing around the hall and what could be seen of the dining room for anything out of the ordinary.

"Have no idea," admitted Jules. "But we'll have to find it and disable it if we're going get out of this trap."

"But even if we knew where it was, how could we reach it, let alone disable it, if it shifts position every time we reach for it?"

"Which brings me to the solution to our problem," concluded Jules. "At least I hope it does."

"Me too. What is it?"

"One of us will need to be hypnotized. Without self-consciousness, the hypnotized person should be able to move about normally without disturbing reality. All they'll need is some direction from the control to find the scrambler and turn it off."

"That's it?"

"Makes sense, doesn't it?"

"I think so...depending on whether I fully understand what you've said about the observer effect."

"It better because it's the only thing I can think of."

"Hypnosis then, is what you have in mind?"

Jules nodded, careful to make eye contact with Mooney. Fortunately, the quantum scrambler didn't prevent them from seeing what they wanted to see, only from acting on it. As soon as they did, the conditions surrounding the object of their interest changed, preventing them from finding it. But eye contact didn't seem to affect the local quantum field.

With Jules looking at her, Mooney herself couldn't help returning the gaze as he explained what he had in mind.

"Hypnosis," he was saying, "is a human condition involving focused attention, reduced peripheral awareness, and finally, an induced capacity for the subject to respond to suggestion.

"Are you listening?" he asked, his eyes still holding Mooney's.

Mooney nodded; her eyes fixed on his.

"There are two sides to the human brain," Jules continued. "The right side controls creative functions on a conscious level while the left side is the practical one operating on a sub-conscious basis. That's the side we're going to try and access through hypnosis. What I'm hoping is that the person who's in a trance can operate within the scrambler's field without effecting the reality around them because they won't be consciously trying to do so. It'll be the person giving instructions to the entranced who will be making the conscious decisions."

Jules gazed into Mooney's eyes, studying her reactions. She was standing still, unblinking now. Looking neither to the right or the left. He'd taken a chance on using hypnotic eye induction to put his unsuspecting spouse into a trance. The simple method, he guessed, would work better if she hadn't been aware she was being hypnotized.

Jules continued speaking, softly, steadily, without obvious inflections, for a few minutes more. It didn't matter what he said, just so long as the soothing drone of his voice lulled Mooney into a sleepless calm. He hadn't known if she were susceptible to hypnosis but using the eye induction technique was so uncomplicated, so unobtrusive, it was a simple matter to begin the process and see where it led.

And it worked. Mooney was now in a trance and, he hoped, open to suggestion.

"Mooney," he began. "I want you to go into the dining room and then through the rest of the first floor of the house. You're to look for a small device. It need not be large. It'll likely be out in the open since there'd be no need to keep it hidden. When you find it, look for a switch and turn it off. If there's no switch, smash it."

Nonchalantly, as if she were strolling through their own home back in Nevada, Mooney turned and walked through the entranceway into the dining room.

Jules smiled. It was going to work. There was no way she could have found the entrance with her conscious mind.

He saw her looking around the dining room, stooping to look under the table, then disappearing out of his sight, presumably headed for the kitchen. He heard her footsteps on the cortextured floor beyond before they faded in distance and among the unit's walls. If she returned without any change in the conditions, he intended to send her upstairs, but that proved unnecessary.

A minute later she returned with a small, pyramidal shaped object in her hand and stopped before him. The object was damaged.

Jules reached out for the vase of flowers on the hall table. His hand found it easily.

Satisfied, he turned to Mooney and pinched her cheek.

"It's all right dear, come on out of it," he soothed. "Wake up now."

Suddenly, the light of consciousness that had been absent in Mooney's eyes returned. She blinked.

"So, you think hypnosis will let one of us navigate the quantum field and find the scrambler?" she asked.

"I'm positive."

"How can you be so sure? Maybe neither of us is susceptible to hypnosis."

"Well as it turns out, you are."

"Huh?"

"Look in your hand."

Mooney looked and saw that she was still holding the scrambler. "Is this it? How...?"

"You proved easy to hypnotize. Sorry, but I thought it'd be easier to try it on you without warning so you'd offer the least conscious resistance."

"It was that easy to hypnotize me, huh?"

Jules nodded.

"Doesn't say much for my strength of character, does it?"

Jules allowed himself a laugh out of relief that the trap had been so easy to overcome. "Has nothing to do with strength of character. Only on conditions and, like I said, the subject offering no conscious resistance."

"The funny thing is, I still remember everything you were saying about hypnosis and eye induction," said Mooney. "What happened after that?"

"I asked you to search the first floor and you did. I think you found the scrambler on the kitchen counter or something. In any case, I doubt it was hidden. It's turned on and off by a simple telcomm signal, the reason why you had to disable it physically."

"Hard to believe a little thing like that could give us so much trouble."

"I don't think it's meant to be a permanent solution to anything but only a temporary one," said Jules, turning the damaged scrambler over to reveal a label on the bottom. "Quantum Security Systems" he read, followed by a serial number.

"Sounds like those things are commercially available."

"It does, doesn't it? I think what we have here is a clue."

"Besides the fact that someone here didn't want any snoopers stopping by?"

"Speaking of snooping, let's do some."

Quickly, they made the circuit of the downstairs. They found nothing as Jules expected. No one would remain behind with the scrambler in operation.

Upstairs, they'd find a different story.

They mounted the main staircase cautiously, ion pistols at the ready even though Jules believed no one remained in the house.

The first room they checked, looked as if a whirlwind had been through it. Items were spilled over the floor, drawers ripped from bureaus, bedding scattered. It was the same story in the second room.

But in the third room, there was something different. All around was the same evidence of a hasty search as in the first two rooms, but this time a new element had been added: there was also a body.

"I think we've seen this cinevid before," deadpanned Mooney.

Jules admired his wife's sang froid but knew it was a bluff. Murder continued to disturb her as much as it did him.

In the room, the body sprawled grotesquely on the synth-carpeted floor. It lay face down, arms beneath the body, apparently held where it had been shot. There was a tiny hole about midway up the torso, nearly between the shoulder blades.

"Bikari?" Suggested Mooney.

"Most likely," replied Jules, slipping his pistol back into his suit jacket and crouching next to the body.

Mooney, her own pistol still at the ready, made a quick search of the bedroom including adjoining bath but found nothing amiss.

Meanwhile, Jules had rolled the body onto its back.

It was Bikari all right. He'd been shot in the chest by an ion pistol set at maximum. Leaving little blood to stain the carpeting, the weapon left a needle thin hole in its target, obviously the heart, which went on to pass completely through the body and out the back.

"Here's where it hit after coming out his back," said Mooney, fingering a small hole in the wall beside the bedroom door.

"An amateur," said Jules.

No one properly trained in the use of an ion pistol would be so sloppy as to use it at maximum which allowed the beam to pass through multiple objects after hitting its primary target.

Jules rummaged through the man's pockets. Nothing.

"No telcomm in the room?"

Mooney shook her head.

"Well, whoever killed him was at least professional enough not to leave his telcomm behind," said Jules. "Which doesn't help us of course."

"But why was he killed in the first place?" asked Mooney. "Doesn't make any sense. He must have been one of them."

"Maybe. Maybe not. The fact that he was killed suggests not. Remember, in its later stages, Humanism devalued life. The unborn, the elderly, were done away with in the name of unburdening the planet. Suicide was encouraged as a means of ridding society of the mentally and emotionally disturbed. Overpopulation was considered a burden on Gaia that needed to be relieved. It's only a sign of how important it is that we catch up to these people because obviously, they've already absorbed the Humanist mantra that the ends justifies the means."

"And what were the ends being met here?"

"Covering their trail," said Jules. "But if there's one thing I've learned in this business, it's that no one ever does as good a job of covering as they think they do. For instance..." he reached into a pocket and pulled out the remnants of the scrambler.

Mooney smiled. "Then what are we waiting for? Let's get to work!"

"I'll take the bathroom," said Jules, heading in that direction.

"Suit yourself."

With experience behind them, it didn't take long to conduct a very thorough search including HVAC venting, carpet edges, lighting fixtures, and window sashes. They conducted electronics and digital sweeps using a special function of their telcomms. Finally, they checked out the work station using a highly secret MI 'cloud chaser'.

After all that, only the more obvious places were left and when those had been eliminated as well, Jules couldn't help feeling disappointed.

"Nothing," he said.

"Been saving the best for last," said Mooney, walking over to a bird of paradise, one of several small indoor trees resting in large planters in different places around the bedroom.

Removing a wooden support stick from one of the planters, she used it to probe the soil.

"Where'd you learn that trick?" asked Jules.

"A girl has to have some secrets."

Finished with the first planter, Mooney repeated the operation with the second, a miniature bamboo palm and struck something.

"Bingo!"

"Got something?" asked Jules, joining her by the plant.

In answer, Mooney dug her fingers into the moist potting soil, and when she pulled them out again, was holding a small object in the palm of her hand.

"I do believe I've found a clue," she declared, before heading to the bathroom sink to wash the object clean.

"What is it?" asked Jules, looking over her shoulder.

"A vanity compact," replied Mooney. "It's usually keyed to the owner's voice so it can't be used by anyone else, but often owners don't bother and leave it at the neutral setting. Since this one was likely hidden by our Mr. Bikari, it follows that he could open it."

"Making it likely that the feminine owner never keyed it to her voice alone?"

"Right. Open," Mooney said, holding the pearl tinted compact to her lips.

There was a standard musical sound and a holographic image of a vanity space appeared in the air over the compact and, with some adjusting of her hand, Mooney was looking into an area that reflected her face. Holo slides and rules beneath the mirror image allowed adjustments with a sweep of the hand.

"Not bad," said Mooney, admiring her own image in the holo-mirror.

"I could have told you that," flirted Jules.

"Why thank you, kind sir," replied Mooney, ordering the compact to end program. "Can we assume that this compact did not belong to Bikari?"

"You assume right," said Jules. "But he must have had a reason for hiding it in the planter."

"Insurance?"

"I'd say so."

"Which leaves the question: whose compact is it?"

"Girlfriend? Mistress?"

"Or seductress."

Jules looked at his wife. "You're bad."

"Just putting myself in Bikari's place. There'd be no need to hide a compact belonging to a girlfriend or mistress. But if he were conspiring with a woman to steal a certain book..."

"No honor among thieves, huh? Well, it wouldn't be the first time partners in crime didn't trust each other. But the picture begins to get clearer. Bikari meets a woman who becomes his lover. Somehow, she convinces him to use his position at the Archives to steal the book. She might have suggested they could sell such a rare item and run away with the proceeds to live happily ever after..."

"Everyone knows how dangerous that book is," said Mooney. "It would take some convincing to get him to steal it."

"She was probably real convincing, if you catch my drift."

"Now who's being bad?"

Jules shrugged.

"Anyway, turns out Bikari is no fool, or at least not a complete fool. He doesn't fully trust his partner and holds onto the compact as insurance. But how did he intend on using it if he was forced too? Was he going to use it as proof of some kind that it wasn't his fault, that he was tricked somehow?"

"Probably."

"But why was he killed? Why would this woman kill her willing partner?"

"Seems right now that he was merely a means to an end."

"Unless, the woman noticed her compact was missing and suspected Bikari."

"If she were part of a Humanist underground, that's all it would take for her to eliminate a possible threat," suggested Jules.

"An underground?" repeated Mooney, startled.

Jules nodded. "This wasn't simply a theft by Bikari acting alone with the potential threat of ideas in the book infecting him, spreading to acquaintances. and so on. If this woman, as we suspect, seduced him into stealing the book, I'm sure she wasn't acting alone. Eliminating Bikari suggests the covering of tracks. Look at the way these rooms were turned inside out. She was desperate not to leave anything behind that could be traced. For sure, she didn't get ahold of something as sophisticated as the scrambler on her own."

"Makes sense."

"That quantum trap was meant to delay an investigation of the theft," guessed Jules. "It was never intended to stop anyone permanently. Hopefully, whoever set it, won't have expected us to escape as quickly as we did. That means time is of the essence. We need to catch up to this woman as soon as we can before she has a chance to disappear completely."

"Are you suggesting I do the catching up?" asked Mooney, still holding the compact in her hand.

Jules nodded. "While I follow up with Quantum Security Systems."

"Well, I can already tell this item is pretty high end," said Mooney. "I think I'll go do some shopping..."

Chapter Five

A Flaw in the System

For the second time in several days, Jules found himself looking out the window of a stratoliner. This time however, the view wasn't of a formerly American city but that of Toronto, at one time a part of old Canada. Already, the near silent whine of the 'liner's engines signaled its final descent as the city's gleaming, multi-colored towers rose higher and higher in his vision. Located on the shores of Lake Ontario, the city had once been a major North American metropolis but after a hundred years under the domination of Humanist culture even more severe than that experienced by the United States, it had fallen on hard times. Its vast population of nearly ten million had been reduced by half due to socialist policies that left the city devoid of jobs and opportunity. Those who could, fled. The rest festered and died in poverty, starvation, and freezing winters. However, once normalcy and common sense had been restored by the Constitutionalist armies and Ontario entered the Consortium, Toronto's resurgence was remarkably swift until it had once again assumed its place as an entrepreneurial entrepot with a rising population.

Which was why Jules was not surprised to find the company he was coming to investigate, Quantum Security Systems, was headquartered here.

It had been simple enough to find it. There had not even been any need to have MI do any checking for him. A simple search of publicly available business listings via his telcomm yielded an address and contact information. A few jumps away, and Jules was able to learn all he needed about QSS from its own cloud site. From there, posing as an interested client, he had made an appointment with the company's sales representative for a personal meeting and demonstration of its chief product, 'quantumguard', what Jules continued to refer to himself as a quantum scrambler.

The irony, of course, was that Jules would need no demonstration of the device's effectiveness. He'd had, after all, firsthand experience with how well the damn thing worked.

Recollection of his experience with the scrambler reminded Jules of the absent Mooney. Though he knew perfectly well that she could handle herself, she was still his wife after all and that gave him the right, if not the duty as a husband, to worry about her. As it was, being left on Earth and on the trail of the mystery woman in Alfo Bikari's life, seemed, on the face of it, a low risk task. There was nothing to worry about.

Or was there?

Staring out at the rapidly approaching ground, Jules recalled past assignments that he'd shared with Mooney and how seemingly safe avenues of pursuit quickly turned into potentially deadly situations. No, there was nothing about this business that he or Mooney could afford to be complacent about.

Suddenly, there was an increase in the tempo of the engines as the 'liner eased to a stop over its assigned landing apron. Horizontal thrust was exchanged for the vertical and the big aircraft slowly settled to a stop. Jules braced himself for the inevitable rush of his fellow passengers to get off the 'liner and on with their lives and just as inevitably, a human traffic jam resulted.

It was some minutes before he was given the space to leave his seat, gather his carry-on bag and exit the 'liner through the extension corridor. Wasting little time, he made his way through the terminal and found himself a robo-cab, giving it the QSS address.

The drive was uneventful with the cityscape around him little different from many of those elsewhere in the world. Pity. For real departure from architectural monotony, one had to visit the cities of Europe which had been largely successful in preserving their cultural heritage despite ravaging by their own versions of humanism. Cities in the rest of world, particularly in Asia, had mostly rebuilt themselves in early twenty-first century glass and neon which now seemed quaint and old fashioned in comparison with the new glassite towers of the West.

It was still before noon when the robo-cab deposited him at an older office building on the outskirts of Toronto's downtown. From information derived from his telcomm, Jules knew the way to the offices of QSS on the building's nineteenth floor. An up capsule took him there in seconds and a pair of genuine glass doors emblazoned with 'Quantum Security Systems' on one leaf.

Inside, a pretty secretary smiled and asked his business.

"I'm here to see Mr. Jarel," said Jules, trying his best to look like an eager customer. "I have an appointment."

The secretary made a show of checking her records before confirming the appointment.

"Won't you have a seat, Mr. Conroi?"

Jules did as she advised, considering his decision to pose as a client rather than as himself. He didn't want to take the chance of spooking Mr. Jarel, or worse, if he was involved in the theft of *Elements of Humanism*, to allow him a chance to disappear or warn others who might be implicated in the plot.

"Mr. Jarel will see you now," the secretary was saying.

Jules rose and headed for the old fashioned door with Jarel's name on it.

Pushing it open, he was met by a man wearing the latest cut of synthsuit, presumably Mr. Jarel.

He was right.

"Mr. Conroi, is it? Pleased to meet you. I'm Donka Jarel," said the man, extending his hand in welcome.

Jules took it and then the pneumachair indicated by Jarel. The manager himself resumed his place behind the big work station that Jules suspected was more ornamental oak than actual holo-console and touchscreen.

"Now then, Mr. Conroi," began Jarel, smiling. "I see by your inquiry, that you've expressed interest in our quantumguard home and business security unit. Let me assure you that it's the best, most reliable product on the market, recommended and endorsed by police departments throughout the consortium. Here, let me show you some of its more salient features."

So saying, Jarel motioned over the holo-console embedded in his work station surface and one of the stereopticals on the office wall shifted from an abstract image to the company's latest sales pitch.

"As you'll soon see..." began Jarel before Jules interrupted.

"If you don't mind, I'll just stop you there," said Jules.

"Freeze program. Am I going too fast for you?"

"Not at all, it's just that buying your product isn't the reason I'm here."

"Not the reason? I don't understand," said Jarel, turning to face Jules more fully.

Behind him, the auto-curtains had been pulled back to allow a generous view of Toronto's downtown area. The blue skies with the occasional fleecy white cloud reflected soothingly in its forest of glassite towers. It all made for a warm, peaceful atmosphere in the QSS offices.

In reply, Jules pulled out his telcomm, accessed his secure MI file and called up a holo image confirming his identification as a special agent.

"You're with Military Intelligence?" asked Jarel faintly.

"That's right. And I'm here investigating a case dealing with Consortium security."

"And you think QSS is involved?" asked an astonished Jarel.

Jarel, thought Jules, was either a good actor or expressing genuine surprise at his visit.

"Why didn't you simply identify yourself from the start? Why this subterfuge about being a client?"

"Because I had no idea whether or not QSS was involved with the case," explained Jules. "If you were, I didn't want to alert you to the fact ahead of time giving you the opportunity to warn any possible confederates of the investigation."

"That's preposterous," protested Jarel, rising from his chair and beginning to pace. "Our company has nothing to do with anti-Consortium activity."

"I'm prepared to believe you," soothed Jules. "Nevertheless, I've ordered..."

"Mr. Jarel!" Exclaimed the secretary, bursting suddenly into the room.

"Miss Peddera. What's the meaning of this? You know I'm in conference..."

"It's our comm lines," said the secretary. "They're all down! I can't even use the inter-office annunciator!"

"That's impossible," declared Jarel, clearly becoming flustered with a morning filled with surprises.

Speaking to his work station, he ordered it to place a call to manufacturing. Not only did the call not go through, but the entire holo-console had gone dark.

"That's my fault, I'm afraid," said Jules at last.

"What do you mean?"

"Military Intelligence has overridden your company's comm codes rendering QSS dark."

"What? What gives you the right to do that? Don't you know we have a multi-million credit company to run? Going dark will wreak havoc on our supply chain to say nothing of customer relations."

"I'm aware of that, and I'm sorry to have ordered it done," said Jules. "But as I said, it's not clear what role QSS has in our investigation and until it's cleared, all communications by the company must be suppressed." Jules held up a hand to forestall more protest. "That decision is final."

Angry and frustrated, Jarel waved Miss Peddera from the room and retook his chair behind the now useless work station.

"So now what?" he asked. "What can I do to convince you that QSS isn't a security risk nor involved with any investigation you might be working on?"

"First," began Jules, pulling out the scrambler he retrieved from Bikari's living unit, "I need to know to whom you sold this quantumguard product?"

"That particular one?" queried Jarel, taking it from Jules.

Turning it over in his hands, he took note of the serial number engraved beneath the company's name on the base of the unit.

"It's damaged," Jarel noted, examining the device more closely.

"I know. It was the only way to disable it in order to escape its effects."

"You were caught in the unit's quantum field?" asked Jarel, surprised.

Jules nodded.

"And escaped?"

Again, Jules nodded.

"How did you do it?" demanded Jarel. "Our Quantumguard units are guaranteed to hold intruders until police activate a pre-registered code that disengages the device allowing capture and arrest. QSS guarantees it!"

Jules shrugged. "Obviously, it's not escape proof."

"But how?"

"That information will be kept confidential for the time being."

Knowing how to escape the device would be useful information for MI to have in the event any of its agents ever found themselves caught by it again. In fact, Jules also considered how useful the scrambler could be for MI itself and made a mental note of suggesting the department put in an order to QSS in the future. Then again, it had taken two victims being caught in the scrambler's field at the same time to enable he and Mooney to escape it. How likely would such a circumstance happen if agents encountered the trap in the future? Already, he was thinking of possible alternatives: self-hypnosis?

"By what right can you withhold the information?" demanded Jarel. "The Quantumguard patent belongs to Quantum Security Systems."

Jules shrugged. "It's apparent from first-hand experience, that your device is very effective and could be used against the interests of the Consortium. Military Intelligence needs a safeguard against such a contingency."

Jarel thought for a moment before making a suggestion. "Perhaps QSS can work with Military Intelligence to share information. You reveal how the Quantumguard can be bypassed and we will share any improvements we make to circumvent the flaw."

"That might work, providing there's still a way for authorized agents of the Consortium to escape the Quantumguard's field," said Jules.

Jarel fell silent after that, wondering no doubt, if there could be any escape once the flaw discovered by Jules was corrected.

Taking advantage of Jarel's silence, Jules reiterated his earlier question.

"You can help convince me that QSS can work with Military Intelligence by answering my question, namely to whom did you sell that unit to?"

"I can find out by looking up the serial number here, but right now, that's impossible with all our data streaming shut down."

Jules had to admit he was right. Taking up his telcomm again, he used the touch screen function to silently reactivate Jarel's holo-console.

Jarel was momentarily startled when he saw the instrumentation on his console come to life again but recovered quickly.

"Jarel 235-Q," he said. "Display information for scrial 57994066."

Instantly, the stereoptical on the wall changed again, displaying purchase information for the Quantumguard unit in question.

"It was ordered by a private security firm called Lookout Safe," read Jarel. "Delivery address, eThekwini, Zululand."

"Was this the only unit of Quantumguard ordered?"

"Yes."

"What name was on the purchase order?"

"Scroll down," said Jarel, as the image on the stereoptical began to move. "Stop. Someone called A. Buti."

Jules made a note of the name, doubting it was authentic, and rose to leave.

"Wait," said Jarel. "What about our systems?"

For answer, Jules once again used his telcomm, shutting down Jarel's work station.

"I'm sorry," Jules told the crestfallen manager. "You'll be notified as soon as the situation has been cleared up. In the meantime, your offices and employees will be kept under surveillance to make sure none of what we've discussed goes any farther."

"But I'm not even sure what we discussed," protested Jarel. "A purchase order? A flaw in the Quantumguard? None of that strikes me as remotely deserving of such overreach."

"We'll let you know when the business environment has improved," said Jules, walking out the door.

Chapter Six

Compact With Danger

It was called a vanity compact for a reason.

As Mooney rode along in a robo-cab headed for New Washington's high end shopping district, she took the opportunity to study the compact she'd found in Bikari's living unit more closely.

Of course, the manufacturer's logo was embossed on the reverse as was to be expected. But Mooney dismissed that as a possible lead. Bikari's unknown girlfriend hadn't likely bought it direct from the manufacturer. No. She purchased it from a retailer. A high end retailer. Of course, she could have bought it in another city but Mooney hoped such a small item, possibly given to her as a gift from Bikari himself, was purchased right here, in the Consortium's capitol.

It was coming on evening now but it was like daylight here, deep among the city's towers whose interiors glowed in different colors depending on the settings of their glassite tonalities. On the smart streets, an army of robo-cabs zoomed along in traffic free coordination with numberless private vehicles, some even being lifted up the sides of buildings to overhead stalls. Despite the seriousness of her mission, Mooney couldn't help feeling a bit of a thrill to be visiting many of the city's designer boutiques where the compact she held would have been purchased. She might even find something for herself among them.

Just then, however, it was back to business.

Consulting a list of likely businesses where the compact might have been purchased, Mooney gave the 'cab the first address and presently, it shifted lanes and pulled easily to a stop before the Ladies' Handmaid, located along H St Northwest.

Stepping from the 'cab, Mooney was immediately struck by the sounds of the city all around her, the soft, sifting drone of the passing traffic, the talk and laughter of the crowded sidewalks, the echoes of larger robo-trucks among the canyons formed by the towers that lined the street into the distance. The hustle and bustle, the aliveness that contrasted with the peace and quiet of her own home back in the Nevada desert country, filled her with excitement and anticipation. She found herself disappointed to have only a limited number of possibilities where the compact might have been bought. She wouldn't mind taking more time to move about the milling streets.

Stepping across the sidewalk, she found herself entering the Ladies' Handmaid, and plunging into a world of clear plas and plas-glass display cases and gleaming white tile all lit from hidden sources that chased every last shadow out of the store. A handful of customers browsed among the displays, all of which were fabulously expensive. Maybe too expensive even for the vanity compact Mooney held in her hand.

She had hardly stepped into the store when a clerk approached her.

"Can I help you," she asked.

"As a matter of fact, you can," said Mooney, conscious that her casual daywear consisting of a dark, one piece jumpsuit and flats, suitable for any contingency that might come up during a mission for MI, was wildly out of sync with the crinosynth skirt and ensemble worn by the clerk. The contrast, however, didn't seem to bother the young woman. "Can you tell me if this compact was purchased here?"

Mooney handed the compact to the clerk for examination.

The clerk turned it over in her hands and frowned.

"We don't deal in data based product," she sniffed. "We specialize in retrowear for the discriminating client. Strictly twentieth century. But there might be a way. Can you open it?"

"It's not keyed," said Mooney, leaning in and saying "open."

There was that musical tone again and the compact sprung open.

"There's usually a statement of quality and guarantee information somewhere among the data," the clerk was saying as she wiped her fingers over the holo's control panel. It took some digging, but she finally reached the copyright information that included the name and address of the store where it was purchased. "The Feminine Touch. That's in Crystal City, near the old Pentagon ruins."

"Oh! Thank you!" said Mooney, taking back the compact and trying to put as much sincerity in her voice as possible. "I received this as a gift and really wanted to get another one for a friend. I really appreciate this!"

The clerk had no time to say anything as Mooney was already half way out the door.

On the sidewalk, she signaled for one of the numerous robo-cabs that always circulated through the downtown area and hopped in as soon as the door lifted to accept her.

"The Feminine Touch, Crystal City," she ordered, as the unmanned vehicle scooted into a traffic lane. It found its way across the Arlington Bridge and soon, the dilapidated remnants of the historic Pentagon building bulked in the nighttime darkness. Merely a shell now, it served mainly as a tourist destination for those curious about pre-Humanist days when the United States boasted a strong military establishment.

The 'cab breezed along a six lane smartway before taking the Crystal City exit and after a few twists and turns, deposited Mooney at the front entrance to the Feminine Touch.

In contrast with the Ladies' Handmaid, the boutique was located in the heart of a modernesque plaza whose buildings were all outlined in colored light. Light blazed from a jumble of plas-glass cubicles piled atop each other that looked nothing so much as children's building blocks equipped with interior lighting. The overall effect was dazzling and seductive to any inveterate shopper. Not immune to the effect, Mooney had to struggle not to slip into that frame of mind.

The inside of the boutique proved as different from the Ladies' Handmaid as it was possible to be. The set-up and displays seemed more suitable to a tech store than a ladies' accoutrements seller. Feminized work stations were scattered about the synth-carpeted floor space, with individualized modules and WIFI accessible personal spaces interspersed. Plas-glass cabinets and counters showed off required articles the modern woman could not live without including digitized handbags, figure enhancing netting that used broadcast power, anti-grav pumps, programmable makeup masks, and independent power units disguised as hats from pill boxes to sun bonnets.

Looking around, Mooney was impressed. Her own tastes ran to crino-synth formal and retro basic, but there were some toys here she wouldn't have minded fooling around with.

In keeping with the tone of the shop, the female clerks were adorned in spotless white coveralls that accentuated their figures and Mooney even noticed a male or two in white suit jackets who seemed to be tech advisors rather than anyone expected to wait on female clientele.

As a result, the first person that caught Mooney's eye was a tall brunette who wore her coverall in a way sure to catch any man's eye.

"You look a little lost," said the clerk with a laugh in her voice.

"Maybe I am," admitted Mooney. "Who do I speak to about identifying the purchaser of this compact?"

The clerk looked at the compact in Mooney's open palm. "I can help you with that."

"I found it and knowing a high end product when I see it, thought I could give it back to the person who lost it."

"That should be easy enough to check," said the clerk, taking the compact.

"It's not been keyed," Mooney pointed out.

"Is that right?" the clerk asked the compact to open; again there was the musical tone and the holo display.

Unlike the clerk at the Ladies' Handmaid, this one jumped straight to the chase and found the personal file with purchaser information.

"Here it is," she said, holding the holo image at an angle that Mooney could read.

"Constance Shores," read Mooney. "Lives at 400 Potomac."

"Huh!" grunted the clerk.

"Something wrong?"

"The Potomac hundreds are reserved for those rebuilt paddle wheelers that cruise up and down the river," said the clerk. "Shores must be pretty well set up."

"She bought this compact from you, didn't she?" noted Mooney.

The clerk gave her a sharp look, not sure whether to be insulted by the sarcasm.

"Thanks for your help," said Mooney giving a little wave over her shoulder. "I'll be sure to get this to Constance as soon as I can."

Outside the boutique, Mooney checked her telcomm for 400 Potomac and confirmed what the clerk had said. The hundred address numbers; 100, 200, and so on, were reserved for a half dozen solar powered boats that were exact replicas of the old steam paddle wheelers that used to ply the rivers of the old United States. Aboard, the interiors were designed as multiple living units, very high toned, very expensive.

So what was Shores doing there? Was it all a front to impress Bikari? Make it easier to first seduce him, then get him to steal *Elements of Humanism*? Or did Bikari himself supply the funds?

Shores became even more of a question mark when Mooney received a reply to her request from MI for a background check on the woman. That raised an eyebrow or two. As she was driven in a 'cab for the wharf where the 400 boat was currently moored, Mooney contacted Jules to give him an update.

"Mooney," said Jules using MI's closed bandwidth. "How's everything going?"

"Moving right along. I've traced the owner of the compact and you're not going to believe what I found."

"Try me."

"Traced her to an address. Am heading there now for a look see. With luck, I'll get the drop on her and have her in custody in a short while."

"Be careful," warned Jules. "If she feels she's cornered..."

"Right. But here's the big news. Checked with MI and it seems that Constance Shores is a mental case."

"Well, yeah. She's a Humanist, right?"

"There's more. Seems she was part of a group who escaped from an institution on the Moon," reported Mooney.

"What kind of institution?"

"A rehabilitation asylum for hard core non-conformists. Top

secret."

"Interesting. Being mentally unstable, it would make sense that she'd be an easy target for any Humanist propaganda that might be getting out. All the more reason to be extremely cautious when you approach her."

"Don't worry. I have no intention of letting my guard down. But it's nice to hear that you worry about me."

"Good luck."

Mooney cut the connection, noticing she was getting close to the river. Its presence was betrayed by the lights of the city that reflected off the gently flowing waters. The 'cab left the busier thoroughfares for the relative quiet of quayside. It slid to a stop before a manned entrance area sealing off tenant parking, the wharf, and the big boat that rested at 400. Just barely, over the entranceway, Mooney could make out steam rising from the ship's twin funnels. Was it the real thing or just a touch to add realism to the historic recreation? The rest of the double decker was gayly lit with blazons of lights along its passageways and just then, a private party was going on above decks.

Mooney took herself over to the entranceway where a watchman operated a gate that allowed only authorized tenants, visitors, and crew members access.

"Can I help you, Miss?" asked the watchman.

"I'm here to visit one of the tenants, Constance Shores," said Mooney, not bothering to correct the watchman's salutation.

"Is she expecting you?"

"No," admitted Mooney, truthfully.

"Then I'm not authorized to allow you entry. I'm sorry."

"I want my visit to be a surprise. I have a gift for her." Mooney flashed the compact that she still possessed.

The man was unfazed. "Sorry."

"Please?" Mooney placed as much femininity into her voice as she could along with a smile that never failed.

Well, almost.

The man shook his head in regret.

Mooney would have preferred not making her actual business

known, the lower profile she could keep, the better. But clearly, she wasn't going to get past the watchman as plain 'Manda Conroi. Sighing, she produced her telcomm and accessed her MI identification pattern.

Holding the holo image up so the man could see it clearly, she said, "Happy to see you so steadfast in your duty...Begonal..." reading his badge, "But as you can see, I'm here on official business."

Begonal studied the identification closely and gulped. If he had surrendered to Mooney's earlier provocation, he might have lost his job!

"I've never seen anything like this before," he said. "How can I be sure it's for real?"

"Listen," warned Mooney. "I'm in pursuit of a suspect in a sensitive investigation and I don't want to call any more attention to myself that I can avoid. If you force me to call in back up in order to prove that this is legit, it might spoil everything. Do you want to be responsible for that?"

The man gulped again. Something in Mooney's voice told him she wasn't joking.

"All right, but you'll have to sign the register."

Mooney laughed, not in derision, but in delight at the naivete of the question.

"Not likely!"

Begonal caught her drift and laughed himself.

"Tell you what," said Mooney. "I'll fill you in later, on my way out, okay?"

"Thanks. I have a feeling I'll need something to explain this to my supervisor."

With that, he let Mooney pass the gate and into the parking area.

Quickly, she made her way to the gangplank that connected the siding with the steamboat which bulked larger and larger as she approached, surprising her with its size. In the background, beyond the black water of the river, the lights of New Washington shone with the Lincoln Memorial and Capitol Building beyond prominent amid Charles L'Enfant's still recognizable street plan.

On the lower deck, crew members hurried to and fro and Mooney guessed they were about to cast off. In which case, she'd arrived just in time. Glancing to the rear of the boat, she noticed the paddle wheel, which towered over the second deck, was slowly revolving in place, as if warming up for full power.

"Sure you want to come aboard, Miss?" called the mate. "We're casting off and moving down river to Alexandria."

"That's okay," replied Mooney, clearing the gangplank, and stepping aboard.

The mate shrugged and signaled the shore party to raise the 'plank.

As Mooney made her way along the deck, the big wheel picked up speed and the boat drifted away from the siding, heading for mid-river. But by then, she'd ducked into a side corridor looking for a way upstairs.

She found it in the main lobby where she double checked the tenant listings to make sure the unit number she acquired at The Feminine Touch was correct.

It was.

She proceeded up the staircase to the second deck, passed a few cross corridors, and on a door facing the water, found the unit she was looking for.

Pausing, Mooney withdrew her ion pistol and held it at the ready, but being sure to keep it out of sight of the living unit's annunciator with its standard video feed. She'd considered briefly calling in back-up, but dismissed the idea based on the highly sensitive nature of the mission. Besides, she was confident she could handle the situation on her own. Once she had her suspect in custody, she could contact Leclerc directly for pick up. Composing her features to give away as little as possible, she waved her hand over the annunciator and waited.

No reply.

Mooney tried again.

Still nothing.

She thought of the party she could still hear overhead and wondered if Shores was in attendance, celebrating her victory over the hapless Bikari.

On the other hand, she might not even be aboard. But was that likely if she knew the ship was scheduled to depart for Alexandria? Not unless she had no intention of coming back. Its usefulness being over.

What to do?

With a mental shrug, Mooney replaced her ion pistol and removed her MI laser key. But not just any kind of laser key. This one could quickly decrypt any door lock no matter how sophisticated. And how sophisticated could the lock be in a standard living unit? As it turned out, not very.

Putting away her laser key, Mooney once more armed herself with the ion pistol and slowly pushed open the door.

"Anyone home?" she ventured.

No answer.

Coming more fully into the room, Mooney looked around.

She stood in a small but comfortable living room with synth-carpeting and plush furniture. Shores had good taste in décor at any rate.

Beyond the living room, a small galley served as kitchen with a couple portholes giving a view of the outside. Nothing there. The bathroom was empty too. Wet towels had been thrown on the floor. Mooney tsked.

She was about to check the bedroom when she was stopped by a voice from the door.

"Who are you?"

Mooney whirled, gun in hand. A woman stood there, hands on hips, and judging by how much space she took up in the doorway, was not of the petite kind. Her dark hair was bobbed in the latest style and she wore her things just the way a man would like. Altogether, she cut a formidable figure.

"Constance Shores, I presume?"

"You have me at a disadvantage, dear," was the reply. "And why the gun?"

In response, Mooney lowered her pistol just a hair.

"Very simple," she explained. "You're under arrest."

"Arrest? For what?"

"For murder to start."

"Murder? Just who are you? Why have you broken into my unit?"

"I'm with the police," Mooney said vaguely. "We have reason to believe you killed Alfo Bikari."

"Never heard of him."

In response, Mooney used her free hand to retrieve the compact and show it to Shores.

"Recognize this?"

Shores sighed heavily and threw herself into a chair, as if unaware of the gun that tracked her across the room.

"So what's next?" she asked.

Mooney pocketed the compact. "For starters, how about telling me where the book is?"

"It's where it can do the most good," replied Shores, making no attempt at protesting her innocence.

That came as a refreshing change to Mooney.

"And where is that?" she pressed.

Shores answered her with a question of her own.

"Ever think about the way things are?" she asked. "It could be different you know. Once it was. We used to have freedom."

Aware that her prisoner was trying to change the subject, Mooney decided to play along, hoping she'd let slip something of significance.

"Don't believe everything you've been told about Humanist times," Shores was saying. "They were times of great freedoms for humankind. The greatest ever. People were freed from racism, sexism, and all the other isms. The patriarchy had been trodden underfoot. The rule of the European descended was leveled. The wealth of the elites had been transferred to the people. There was no more political strife. The people were in charge and they broke all the chains that had been holding them back since the beginning of recorded time. Genetics were mastered freeing people from the tyranny of gender..."

"Political strife was ended because any other opinion but the correct one was suppressed, crushed," replied Mooney. "Anyone who dared to think differently, was made into a non-person. Ultimately, for those who refused to conform, there was the jackboot of the reeducation camp. In the end, it took war to restore sanity."

"After that, it was the Constitutionalists' turn to put people in the camps," returned Shores.

"They couldn't very well allow the poison that ruined millions of lives the chance to reinfect society. Freedom was restored and with a proper, enlightened education system based on the old United States Constitution, a healthier, more sane society could be built."

Shores shook her head as if in pity for her captor. "You need to break loose from that moral and religious straightjacket they've put you in."

"You're not the one to be talking about straightjackets," Mooney pointed out.

Realizing she wasn't getting anywhere with her basic argument, Shores switched tactics going from a broad Humanist argument, to the more personal.

"Putting all that aside," she said, "what about your position as a woman?"

"What about it?"

"Your own personal freedom is curtailed in ways you perhaps don't even suspect," argued Shores. "Woman are still trapped as the major component in the domestic arena. The state has withdrawn support for child care programs that would release women for greater participation in the work force or public life. The patriarchy..."

"And who do you think would be working in these child care programs?" retorted Mooney. "Other women of course. Don't they get to be free? Why should they be cheated out of the satisfaction of a career? No, the concept of more freedom for women is a trap. True freedom comes in having a choice between career and family, not being made to feel guilty or unfulfilled by choosing to have children and taking the responsibility of raising them yourself instead of foisting them on strangers.

"I'll decide for myself whether to pursue a career or a family," concluded Mooney. "As for the opportunity of a career, seeing as how I'm here, with the gun, it's obvious that opportunity is open to me. It could just as easily have been a man standing here, but it isn't. It's me. There's no patriarchy holding this woman back."

"But what if you found yourself pregnant?" persisted Shores.

"Wouldn't that interfere with your career? What if you were and you didn't want it to interfere?"

"Not going to happen," said Mooney. "I'll get pregnant when I want to. I'm in control of my body. I have the freedom to choose."

"But what if it was unplanned?"

"In this day and age?" said Mooney incredulously. "There are a half dozen ways to prevent pregnancy for anyone with forethought. Even for men. Any woman who gets pregnant by accident today is just a fool."

For a brief moment, Mooney thought she'd struck home. There was a brief flash in Shores' eyes that just as quickly vanished.

"Just for argument's sake," continued Shores, "what if someone did find themselves with an unwanted pregnancy, in our society, they wouldn't have any choice but to bring the child to term."

"What other choice is there? It wouldn't be the child's fault for being conceived. Why should it suffer death for something it had no role in?"

"But don't you see? It's the woman's body, she has the right to control what happens to it!"

"That would be fine if the unborn child wasn't a person but when does personhood begin?"

Shores was silent then.

Mooney persisted with her argument. "If you or anyone can identify exactly the moment when a fetus becomes a person, you might have an argument as to the value of the unborn child, but you can't. Science proves that personhood begins at conception. There's no identifiable break between a simple fetus and personhood. Because of that, no one has the right to end an unborn life. That life has its own natural rights that can't be sacrificed to one woman's moment of carelessness."

At that point, it dawned on Mooney that she was being somewhat careless herself, but that moment of hesitation was all it took.

Having apparently lost her patience, there was only one thing left for her captive to do and before Mooney knew it, she was grappling with Shores for possession of the pistol.

As the old saying went, the best laid plans never survive contact with the enemy and what Mooney soon realized was that it went for personal combat as well. Trained initially as an agent of the Exterior Ministry before joining Military Intelligence, she was certified in different forms of hand to hand combat but all that did little good in the face of an opponent who didn't follow the same rules of engagement.

Shores flew after her in a mad, undisciplined rush, throwing Mooney back on her heels. In that first unexpected assault, her wrists had been seized, she'd been forced back toward the door leading to the corridor outside, and her gun hand slammed against the door frame. Pain numbed her hand, forcing her to loosen the grip on her pistol.

It dropped to the floor, but Shores made no attempt to retrieve it. Instead, she continued to force Mooney outside and the next thing she knew, she was being forced over the railing that ran along the sides of the steamboat. Below her, she could hear the dark waters of the Potomac rushing along the hull and around her, the sounds of partying overhead and the revolving paddle wheel at the stern mingled to add to her momentary confusion.

Slowly, however, she recovered herself and remembered the lessons in the use of leverage she'd learned to throw off Shores and free her wrists.

"Don't be a fool, Shores," she warned. "There's no place you can run to aboard this ship. Even if you get away from me, you'll be found."

"You think so?" Laughed Shores. "What if you weren't around to call for help?"

With that, she charged again. Mooney stepped aside to avoid a bodily collision, but Shores was prepared for that, clipping her side with a knee.

Mooney doubled over, holding her side, cursing her carelessness.

But Shores wasn't waiting for her to recover from the blow. Grabbing Mooney's arm, she whipped her around, slamming her against the ship's railing.

Now the vast swishing sound of the big paddle wheel filled her ears and Mooney took a moment to look over her shoulder at the wheel as it plunged into the water a few feet away. It had only been a second or two that she stood catching her breath from the strike against the metal railing, registering the position of the paddle wheel, but it was enough for Shores who charged in, grasped Mooney's middle in a bear hug, and lifted her clear of the deck.

In a single motion, with Mooney's hands still clinging to the railing, Shores tipped her bodily over the railing and threw her overboard.

Mooney's grip on the railing was too weak, her wrists failed her and, in another moment, she was falling headlong into the narrow space between the plunging paddle wheel and the boat's stern. Dark water closed over her head and she was gone...

Chapter Seven

More Insanity

Posing as a client worked well enough in getting in to see Jarel at QSS that Jules decided to try the same ploy with Lookout Safe.

This time, though, expecting to hit closer to home, he decided not to take any chances.

Before climbing aboard an Africa bound 'liner, he called Leclerc at MI for some back up. The director agreed to dispatch a small but tight tactical unit that could then be kept incommunicado until the case had been wound up. The tac team would meet Jules at his eThekwini hotel after he arrived.

He'd also been somewhat reassured about Mooney when Leclerc relayed the information that she'd picked up a lead on Bikari's girlfriend and was in pursuit. But the kicker was the information that this Constance Shores had escaped from a high security asylum on the Moon. *What was that all about?* Jules wondered as the 'liner swept across the Atlantic toward what used to be known as South Africa.

It had been a long time since that country had been a single nation. Having been broken up in the Humanist years, the remnants of its White population hounded from the sub-continent, South Africa became several statelets, all of them currently failed. One of them, Zululand, was deemed the most chaotic. Little wonder that those behind the theft of the *Elements of Humanism* chose to hole up there. Complicating things for Jules, was the fact that none of the failed statelets belonged to the Consortium. For sure, individuals seeking movement out the area were not prohibited from doing so by the Consortium, but there was no clear identification of authority in the statelets themselves to negotiate membership.

All of which spelled out uncertainty and danger as Jules landed at Zululand's ramshackle excuse for an airport.

He'd reserved a room at eThekwini's finest hotel but he had little idea what that meant. Lacking smartways, he found himself conducted to the hotel by a rickety internal combustion vehicle that was actually driven by a human being.

"Get you there in a jiffy, Mon," called the driver from over his shoulder. "No traffic today."

The man laughed at what was obviously intended as a joke. The lack of traffic on the road seemed to indicate the man was being sarcastic. Likely, this was the normal condition of the city's roads.

What vehicles Jules did see were technicals; civilian machines converted for paramilitary use with the addition of mounted pulse rifles or old fashioned smart rockets. They seemed to be stationed at every corner but from his background reading on the 'liner over, he knew they guarded territories claimed by different political factions that ruled the city. Luckily, they cared little about foreign visitors deeming them no threat to their power.

Presently, the taxi halted in front of the hotel, clearly a building of pre-Consortium design, and Jules paid off the driver. Inside, he was relieved to find his reservation had gone through. Soon, he found himself in a room that had all the appearance of the latest domestic updates having been past-adapted to the average living unit, and that clumsily. Luckily however, he had no plans to use the room for very long.

Using his telcomm, he sent a prearranged signal via MI's secure bandwidth and a moment later, there was a discreet knock on the door. For a second, Jules wished the room came with an annunciator so that he could check who was at the door, but in eThekwini, it was for sure you couldn't have everything.

"Who is it?" he asked instead.

"Daly," was the one word reply.

Satisfied, Jules opened the door and 'Daly' stepped in.

"Any problem getting in country?" asked Daly, who was Black as would be the rest of the tac team working mostly undercover in an African country.

Jules shook his head. "You?"

"None. We're here as a missionary group," said Daly, smiling.

"I should have thought of that," complimented Jules. "I'm just a potential client for Lookout Safe."

Jules had checked up on Lookout Safe and found a suspicious lack of trade for the company. What clients were listed had either gone out of business or were non-existent. With his guard up, he called the company before leaving the Consortium to make an appointment as Victor Conroi, a business executive looking to update his security systems. He hadn't been surprised when he sensed some hesitation on the part of Mr. Buti, but he eventually allowed the appointment.

That hesitation put him on alert. As a result, he thought it prudent to call in a special ops unit as back up. He'd be going into the offices of Lookout Safe with his eyes wide open.

"What do you know of the situation?" asked Jules of Daly.

"The director himself briefed us on background but no real details of what exactly you're working on," said Daly. "Leclerc said that was irrelevant. Our part was simply to make sure you weren't killed."

Jules nodded. "Thoughtful of him. But that's essentially it. I intend on going in under cover as a client. You can accompany me as my assistant. The rest of your team can secure a perimeter on the outside of the building, discreetly of course."

It was Daly's turn to nod. "Doable. When do we start?"

"My appointment with Buti is in one hour."

An hour later, Jules, with Daly a half step behind him and holding a businessman's briefcase for appearances sake, presented themselves at Buti's office.

When Jules left the hotel with Daly, the balance of the tac team was nowhere to be found. And when they arrived at the building on the outskirts of eThekwini where Lookout Safe was headquartered, it still appeared to be absent. Jules was too professional to ask about it and Daly didn't volunteer any information, but presumably, the team had already taken its positions around the building. If so, Jules had to admire their skill. Even he, knowing they were there, couldn't spot them.

Inside the building's foyer, Jules checked a tenant board to verify which floor had Lookout Safe's offices. An old fashioned cable operated elevator took them up the seven flights to suite eleven where the lack of an annunciator system compelled them to let themselves inside.

There, a secretary's work station was unoccupied but apparently their presence had been detected because a voice from an inner office invited them to enter.

"In here, Mr. Conroi," called the voice.

Inside was an expansive office space with a work station at the far end. There, a white man sat at his ease, a smile playing about his lips. The room was somewhat gloomy, lit mostly by two bars of vertical lights set on either side of the man behind the work station.

"I understand your...company, is interested in our security services?" asked the man.

"That's right," replied Jules cautiously. He didn't like the tone in the man's voice. "But I was told that a Mr. Buti would represent..."

"I am Buti," said the man.

"You? Isn't Buti a Zulu name? I was led to believe..."

The man shrugged. "A necessary deception. Just in case someone such as yourself managed to escape the numerous...discouragements...I placed in your way."

"The quantum scrambler trap."

"Among others that you seem to have avoided falling into."

"You know who I am?"

"I know who you represent."

"And just who is that?"

"Maybe you'd like to say what..." Here, the man chuckled. "...Lookout Safe might do for you?"

"Just who are you?" asked Jules, realizing his cover had been blown, if it had ever been believed in the first place.

"I can tell you because you'll never leave this place alive," said the man. "In fact, I have found fertile ground here as you can hear outside."

Just then, the dull sound of pulse weapons could be heard from somewhere down in the street.

Instantly, Daly dropped the briefcase prop and retrieved an ion pistol from inside his suit jacket.

"Who are you?" demanded Jules again.

"Prof. Morgul Romak. A name that won't do you any good, I'm afraid. Freedom from the moral straightjacket of the Consortium has at last reached the ears of those most in need of hearing it. There has always been an inchoate resentment in Africa for the colonialists. All it needed was for someone to articulate the reasons for it."

"You'd open that pandora's box again?" demanded an angry Jules. "All the race hatred, mistrust, and jealousies that led the old Humanists to divide people, to set them at each other's throats? That ultimately cost the lives of millions of people?"

"That's the way it has always been taught to you," laughed Romak. "In truth you don't even see the chains that bind your mind and your soul. That crushes your freedom and keeps you in thrall to the forces of the so-called free market. You're just a plaything for unaccountable politicians, for advertising men, technocrats, for oligarchs who control the unseen forces that dictate every facet of your life."

"It's you that's laboring under a delusion," countered Jules. "The values of a prevalent Christianity have enlightened men giving them the ability to see through pretense, to evaluate moral choices through a clear prism of eternal values suited for every person in whatever culture, of whatever background. Just as are the values enshrined in the old Constitution, itself a profoundly Christian document."

"Enough!" declared Romak, clearly impatient. "I have no time to debate the niceties of moral philosophy with you. Not when my followers below are prepared to settle the question in a more direct manner."

With that, lights around the edges of the room began to flicker, drawing their attention away from Romak. At the same time, the vertical lights that flanked the work station began to move inward and even as Jules and Daly watched, blinking, Romak disappeared.

"Where'd he go?" asked Daly, stepping in front of Jules.

Suddenly, there was the sizzling sound made by the invisible beam of a focus heater as it burned into the wall behind them.

"Out!" shouted Daly, shoving Jules toward the door.

Daly was right behind him as they immediately crouched to

either side of the doorway, trying to find Romak in the gloomy office.

"Can you see him?" asked Daly, looking for a target. "Did you see him leave the work station?"

"No," said Jules, squinting into the room, trying cut down on the glare of the moving lights.

And yet, it wasn't so dark in the room that he couldn't miss Romak if he'd still been there. Which he was, proven by yet another shot from the focus heater that burned a neat gouge into the door frame over their heads.

Daly fired into the room, hoping to hit Romak. But he didn't have a target.

"I don't get it," he said. "Where is he? There's no place to run in there. No place to hide."

Jules said nothing, still squinting against the lights, shading his eyes with his hand, trying to see.

Those damn lights! If only...

Could it be? Asked Jules of himself. Could it be something so simple?

"It's an illusion," said Jules.

"A what?"

"It's an illusion called a standing wave," repeated Jules. "Professional magicians use it all the time to distract their audience's attention from where a switch is being made."

"A magician's trick?"

"Yeah. It's a phenomenon noticed by neurologists a couple centuries ago. Neurons in the brain that deal with the vision respond to moving lights like those, automatically cut out extraneous information like whatever lies between the two lights. It's called lateral inhibition. A magician taking advantage of the phenomenon can in effect make himself invisible to a spectator. The kicker though, is that the retina in the eyes are still registering the hidden object. It's just that the neurons fixed on the lights are preventing the conscious mind from seeing anything."

"So how do we beat it?"

"By taking out those moving lights," said Jules.

"That's all?"

With that, Daly took aim and blew out one of the lights with his pistol.

Jules did the same with the other; but when the fumes of the shattered lights dispersed and they looked again, Romak was gone.

"He must be in the room someplace," guessed Daly, making ready for a dash inside.

But Jules doubted it. The misdirection had a purpose beyond simply giving Romak the advantage in an exchange of fire. Nevertheless, he followed Daly into the office, moving quickly, using items of furniture for cover.

There was no defensive fire. Romak was gone.

"There must be a hidden exit in here somewhere," said Daly, pounding the walls with his fist.

"No doubt," agreed Jules. "But I don't think we'll have time to look for it. I hear your men coming up the emergency tower."

It was true.

The sounds of pulse rifles crunching into walls and ion pistols returning fire filled the halls and passages of the building as members of the tac team retreated upward.

"Time to call in our back up," suggested Jules.

With that, he took out his telcomm and accessed the bandwidth that had been reserved by MI specifically for this mission.

"Ground force to sea force," he began. "Calling for Emergency Extraction Vehicle at current signal origin. Do you read?"

"Sea force reads," came the immediate reply. "EST for EEV six minutes."

"Acknowledged,"

With the sounds of battle getting louder, Jules moved quickly to the room's work station. As he'd expected, it was inoperable. Romak made sure of that. All that remained were fused components, melted together in a congealing heap. Crude but effective. If it had simply been wiped, he might have salvaged something but now there was no chance of retrieving any information using MI's cloud chaser.

Frustrated, Jules resorted again to his telcomm. Switching

bandwidths for direct communication with Leclerc. The director replied immediately.

"I see you've called for emergency evacuation," he said without preamble. "Is the situation under control?"

By which he meant was Jules safe.

"No problem," said Jules. "Will have to ask EEV for an emergency measure however. Am I cleared?"

"You have final say while in the field," confirmed Leclerc.

Jules nodded grimly. "One final request at the moment. Find out all you can about a Prof. Morgul Romak. Will check in again once aboard the EEV."

"Acknowledged, but what about the book?"

"I've been looking the office over and there's no sign of it," said Jules. "I'm convinced Romak either didn't have it here, or he took it with him."

"That's disappointing," was all Leclerc said, but it was enough.

Jules recognized the reproof but was also comforted by the fact he'd come closer to recovering it than any other investigator who'd been on the case previously. He also knew Leclerc recognized that fact as well.

"Carry on," said the director. "Out."

Replacing his telcomm in his suit jacket and taking his pistol in hand, Jules turned to Daly who'd been using his own unit to scan the walls of the office for Romak's secret exit.

"Never mind that," said Jules. "Have your men continue to retreat up the stairs to the roof. But make sure they don't discourage pursuit. When we're picked up, I want Romak's men to come up behind us."

"Right," said Daly, contacting his team deputy via telcomm. "We better move ourselves. They haven't far to go."

Together, the two men retreated from the office suite to the hallway, seeking the fire tower. With Daly in the lead, Jules' ears were assaulted by the din of battle as the half dozen men of the tac team fell back upward. They were only a floor below now with bits of formacrete scattering over the stairwell as pulse weapons shot up the walls over their heads.

"Up here," called down Daly. "Only a few flights to the roof."

"Careful not to discourage those gangsters from coming up after us," added Jules.

"They don't need any encouragement," called back one of the team members. "It's all we can do to keep 'em at bay!"

Slowly, methodically, the team retreated up the stairs. One floor, then another, and another.

Finally, Jules burst through the door giving access to the roof. Beyond were blue skies and hot sunshine as he looked for some evidence of the EEV he expected.

Suddenly, there was a disturbance in the air and a door sized opening appeared out of nowhere as a set of stairs were lowered toward the roof. A uniformed man stood in the opening surrounded by blue sky. A light breeze ruffled the sleeves of his blouse and his hand was raised, motioning for them to come aboard.

When not opened to admit passengers, the Emergency Evacuation Vehicle was totally invisible to outside observers. Its fuselage composed of a reflective material operable in moisture laden oxygen atmospheres, it was able to defract its surroundings, projecting whatever was behind it toward the front. If blue sky was behind it, then that was all an observer in front of it would be able to see. Couple that with its dead silent engines and aerodynamic shape that prevented even wind currents from making a sound, it was the perfect transport for espionage activity.

"All aboard!" shouted Daly to his men as they boiled out, one after another, from the interior of the building.

With a man holding their attackers at bay, everyone else dashed to the lowered hatch and ran into the waiting EEV. Daly gave the order for the last man to abandon his position by the doorway and together, they were virtually scooped up by the rising stairs.

Inside, Jules watched through an observation port as the Zululand militants emerged onto the roof, looking about in confusion, their pulse rifles at the ready. With the absolute stealthiness of the EEV, they had no idea what happened to their prey even as they hovered a few feet over their heads.

Leaving his position at the rear of the EEV, Jules made his way quickly to the pilot's cabin where the operator was making ready to depart the area.

"Hold it a minute, lieutenant," said Jules. "What are your orders?"

The pilot looked at him saying "Victor Conroi is the agent in charge of the mission. His orders are to be followed to the letter."

"I'm Conroi," said Jules, displaying his identification from his telcomm.

"Acknowledged," said the pilot. "What do you want me to do?"

"I want you to circle back and drop a nul grenade onto the roof of that building."

Jules knew it was an unusual request but the pilot showed no surprise. Instead, he brought the EEV around and when the vehicle was directly over the roof where the local gunmen were still milling about in consternation, threw a switch.

A slight shudder shook the EEV but otherwise there was nothing to indicate anything had happened.

But the scene on the rooftop was another story.

There, a score of gunmen were sprawled on the formacrete roof, dead.

"Did we just drop a nul grenade on that group?" demanded Daly, joining Jules in the narrow passage to the pilot's cabin.

"Had to be done," said Jules.

"Damn," said Daly, shaking his head. "I don't care about those bastards down there. I just never saw the effects of a nul grenade in an actual combat setting before. Trained with 'em of course, but never seen 'em used on an enemy. Works just as advertised. Sucks the air right outta their lungs. Dead in seconds. No mess, no nothin'."

Jules didn't say anything.

Yes, those men had been trying to kill them all only a few minutes before, but it still seemed unsporting to take them out with a nul grenade dropped from an empty sky.

It had to be done however because Romak had been right about one thing, it had been easy, too easy, to spread the Humanist contagion in a place like Zululand. It had to be stopped in its tracks. Before it could spread any farther. He only prayed that most if not all, those infected, had been gathered on that roof.

That, however, didn't make up for the fact that the mission's main target escaped. Romak was still on the loose and he had nothing more to go on. With a growing sense of frustration, Jules made his way to the rear compartment and found a bench to sit on that was far enough away from the others not to be overheard speaking into his telcomm.

With luck, Leclerc found something in his background search of Romak that could be used to find him.

"Leclerc," Jules said, when contact had been established. "Have you found anything on Romak?"

"Are you ready for the long arm of coincidence?" Leclerc asked.

"What do you mean?"

"Prof. Morgul Romak was an inmate of Special Research Unit 6 on the Moon, the same asylum from which Constance Shores escaped!"

Chapter Eight

Following the Trail

In the dark waters of the surging Potomac, Mooney managed to hold her breath before plunging beneath the surface, but that was all. She felt the water moving about her from the motion of the big paddle wheel as it scooped deep, propelling the big steamboat forward at a deceptive rate of five miles an hour.

Thankful that she chose to wear her jumpsuit rather than a more cumbersome female cut bizsuit, Mooney struggled blindly in the dark, groping upward, hoping to reach air. Instead, her outstretched arm struck one of the blades of the paddle wheel as it passed in the opposite direction. Instantly deciding that going with the wheel would be easier than fighting the suction of the water as it strove to follow the wheel downward, she reached out to take hold of the blade first with one hand, then the other.

Have to hold on, no matter what, she thought, her lungs already near to bursting.

She felt herself being drawn deeper into the water as the wheel dragged her along. She squeezed her eyes shut against the cold, gritted her teeth to keep her mouth shut against the instinct to breathe. She was being keelhauled by the big wheel, her arms feeling as though they were about to be pulled from their sockets as, after a seeming eternity, she felt herself rising, rising...

"Bwaah!" she gasped when she finally broke the surface and was able to breathe again.

Still gulping air, with water streaming from her body, her arms so weak, she was unable to do anything to help herself, she could only continue to ride the upward motion of the wheel to its apogee. There, her lungs filled with air again, she mustered the strength to bunch her legs under her, intending to jump, making a grab for the ship's railing before the wheel could fall away beneath her.

Hoping for a soft landing, she was surprised to see that Shores was still on deck, having just turned away from the railing after assuring herself that Mooney had drowned, dragged beneath the water in the wake of the wheel's motion.

Making sure of her footing, Mooney waited until the wheel reached its apex then freed her hands and leapt, using the wheel's downward momentum to bridge the gap between it and the railing that she'd been shoved over less than two minutes before.

Such was the force of her leap, that she not only cleared the railing but landed squarely on Shores' back, knocking the wind out of her and throwing them both to the deck with such jarring force, it left Shores stunned.

Thanks to Shores having provided the soft landing she'd hoped for, Mooney recovered first and, reaching into one of the pockets in her jumpsuit, produced a pair of DNA nodules, quickly affixing them to Shores' wrists. Clicking them together triggered the DNA read in the devices, locking them in place until a signal could be given canceling the read and releasing the prisoner.

By then, partyers on the upper deck noticed the fight and its aftermath and were crowding the railing above, looking down. Suddenly, Mooney became conscious of her appearance.

My hair! he thought, running her hands through her red locks, brushing unruly strands away from her face. She breathed a sigh of relief over her practice of avoiding the use of facial makeup while on business otherwise she'd really look a fright.

She was standing over Shores' supine form, securing her wet hair in a pony tail when the boat's security officer in company with the manager arrived to find out what the commotion was about.

"What's going on here?" the director demanded.

"I'm making an arrest," said Mooney, impatient after her ordeal.

"An arrest?" repeated the disbelieving manager. "Who are you? Don't you realize that Miss Shores is one of our residents?"

"She's also wanted by the authorities."

"What authorities? I haven't heard anything about her being wanted."

Mooney would have held her temper and continued to explain, but suddenly was reminded of the audience both at the railing above and beginning to gather behind the manager.

"This is not the place to be having this conversation," she said. "I suggest we take the prisoner back to her unit and talk there."

The officer looked to his manager for guidance.

The manager, on closer examination of Mooney's athletic figure, her trim jumpsuit, and confident air, decided to heed her advice.

"All right," he said, signaling to the officer to help him carry Shores to her unit.

Mooney stood by as the two men lifted Shores then led them along the passageway back to her unit, the same passageway that only a few minutes before, she'd been herded and struck until finally flung over board.

At Shores' unit, the door was still open. Mooney entered first and, retrieving her ion pistol from the floor, slipped it discreetly somewhere into her jumpsuit.

The men deposited the still unconscious Shores onto a pneumacouch, arranging her so that she was comfortable, before turning back to Mooney.

Meanwhile, Mooney closed the door behind them, shutting out the gawking neighbors who had followed them from the deck.

"All right then," said the manager. "Here we are. Now can you explain what goes on here?"

Mooney nodded. "I'm a government agent in pursuit of an investigation. This woman is an important part of that investigation and as such, I've placed her under arrest."

"That's all very fine, but under who's authority are you operating?"

"I have my identification here..." began Mooney, reaching for her telcomm. But she stopped mid-sentence after discovering that it was gone!

"Damn!" she exclaimed. "I must have lost it in the river."

The manager and the officer exchanged glances.

"Very convenient," said the manager.

"Let me have your telcomm," ordered Mooney, holding out her hand to the officer.

The officer, startled at the demand, instinctively took a step back.

"I'm not going to steal it," chided Mooney. "I just want to use it to establish my credentials."

"Give it to her," said the manager.

The officer complied, still with reluctance.

"Thank you," said Mooney. "Can you shut down the voice activation function?"

She held out the device in the direction of the officer.

"Cancel voice recognition function," said the officer, speaking in the direction of his telcomm.

With that, Mooney was able to use the device choosing manual data entry to keep the two men as much in the dark as to her MI contact information as possible.

Deftly, she bypassed the public channels as well as those reserved for civil and police use, found the bandwidth meta level, and used her personal passcode to access the dedicated bandwidths reserved for military use. She further refined her accessibility to MI's bandwidth and then Leclerc's personal sub-routine.

Leclerc, of course, recognized that Mooney's incoming message was being made on an unsecure device and replied with caution.

"Mrs. Conroi," he acknowledged.

"I've lost my telcomm and have been forced to rely on an unsecure device," said Mooney, pointedly avoiding the use of Leclerc's name. "I've apprehended Shores and am awaiting pick up."

"Noted," was all Leclerc volunteered.

"But first, I need confirmation of my authorization."

There was a short delay before the telcomm projected a holo identifying in no uncertain terms Mooney's credentials.

"Military Intelligence!" gasped the manager. "I never would have guessed...I mean I didn't realize how high..."

"Never mind that," snapped Mooney, cutting off the holo and

watching as the officer's telcomm was wiped from afar.

"Sorry about that, officer," she said, handing the device back. "I'm afraid you'll need to take it in for servicing and reloading."

The officer took the device back, a glum look on his face.

"Anything we can do to help Military Intelligence in this situation will of course, be done," the manager was saying.

"Thank you," acknowledged Mooney. "Return the boat to the New Washington siding and wait there until agents arrive to collect the prisoner. The security officer can be posted outside the unit's door in the meantime. I'll remain in here to look the place over."

"Of course," agreed the manager, herding the officer out ahead of him.

When they were out, Mooney closed the door and secured it against entry. Her main concern now was to keep Shores out of contact with others. She was taking no chance of exposing her ideology to anyone else in the event she woke up before she could be bundled off.

Looking down at the prostrate Shores, Mooney preferred she remain unconscious in the meantime. The last thing she needed was to listen to more of her ravings.

But in case she did come to, it behooved Mooney to search her.

Quickly, expertly, Mooney patted Shores down from stem to stern. Nothing. Next, she fished in any pockets she could find in her form fitting attire and tutu overlay. Nothing. Next, look for hidden pockets. None of that either. Mooney left the next level of search to the MI experts.

Leaving Shores on the 'couch, Mooney took up where she left off in her previous visit to the living unit, before she was interrupted by Shores.

Stepping into the bedroom, she swept her gaze around. The bed was disheveled, and like the bathroom, clothes had been discarded on the floor.

Not a good housekeeper.

She began with the dressers, waving a hand at the showpiece handles, triggering sensors, and watching the drawers slide out one by one. Rummaging through them, she found nothing but dainties, tops, and slacks...all thrown in topsy turvy, not folded. Tsk.

The vanity table had the usual feminine articles, including items from The Ladies' Handmaid but that was all. To make sure, Mooney employed her poking and dipping trick again, sticking her fingers deep into creams and powders but this time came up empty.

Next came the iso-mattress. The bedside command console again, wasn't voice keyed so she was able to move the mattress and check underneath, inside, and all around as the child's game went. But her efforts were all in vain.

No book, no nothing.

"There must be something," Mooney mumbled. "She had to be at least coming or going from somewhere."

Next, she checked the floorboards and authentic looking but nonfunctional air vents, heating units, floor drains, all added as part of the historical accuracy of the recreated steamboat. None of that yielded anything except dust.

Mooney stood in the center of the living room, hands on hips, frustrated but not yet willing to give up.

Just then, the unit annunciator indicated visitors.

Mooney checked, recognizing one of the agents outside. She let them in.

The manager accompanied the agents and now was hanging back outside the door.

"There's your parcel," said Mooney, indicating Shores, who was just regaining consciousness.

"Where am I?" she asked, sitting up but still groggy,

"No need to worry about that, Miss," said one of the agents. "It's where you're going that you need to be concerned about."

"This is crazy," protested Shores. "I didn't do anything! It was her," pointing at Mooney. "I found her searching my unit. When I tried to get her out, she attacked me."

"She could be right," said the manager, swayed by Shores' protests of innocence. "Many of the other tenants and guests saw them fighting. Miss Shores' objections may be well founded. Your agent may have made a mistake, just made the wrong assumption..."

"The matter is out of your hands now," said the lead agent, cutting him off. "I'm sure it'll all be straightened out after we have this woman in custody."

"I did nothing wrong; I tell you," insisted Shores. "He's right! I saw this woman searching my unit. What was I supposed to think?"

"Yes, and what about the unit itself?" asked the manager. "What about Miss Shores' belongings? Her security deposit? What do I tell the owners?"

"You'll be contacted by social services," said the agent. "They'll let you know if your tenant will be coming back. If not, she forfeits whatever deposit you have on hand."

"You can't do that," insisted Shores. "That's my money! Tell them, Mr. Bandors. Insist on the rights of the owner. This is the real reason why I'm being arrested. Our whole society is rotten. We're ruled by elites who keep their power by soothing the masses with their stories of religion and morality. In reality, there is no objective morality. Each person is the measure of their own morality. No one can tell them what's right or wrong. That's what..."

But Shores was not allowed to finish her rant as the agent in charge quickly gagged her with a speech inhibitor.

"Why did you do that?" demanded Bandors, aghast. "She has a right to defend herself..."

"Yes, in a court of law," replied the agent, growing impatient.

It was unusual to gag a prisoner, but he had clear instructions from his superiors to silence Shores if necessary. Clearly her vocal protestations had become a distraction at the very least. Worse than that, the content of her protests struck him as bordering on the dangerously radical. Was that the reason for her being arrested? He knew of agent Mooney and her reputation within Military Intelligence and had been given specific instructions to do whatever she asked. Nevertheless, the whole situation had begun to disturb him. Better to secure the prisoner as quickly and efficiently as possible and be on his way.

"Don't worry," he told Bandors. "The prisoner will have access to legal representation and all the rights of the accused."

But was he sure about that? The way he and his men had been

assigned to secure the prisoner, with no background. Only instructions to gag her if necessary and deliver her directly to MI under the strongest security measures. It was all pretty much out of the ordinary.

Before the manager could raise further objections, the agents hustled Shores out of the room, still struggling to express herself over the effects of the inhibitor.

Mooney detained the lead agent a moment more, pulling him aside and speaking in low tones.

"Can you get a special retrieval team here as soon as possible? I'm afraid I lost my telcomm in the river. MI needs to recover it as soon as possible."

"I'll say," agreed the agent, looking as though he couldn't understand how a responsible agent could lose such a sensitive piece of equipment.

"It'll be somewhere between here and the boat's next scheduled berthing up river," said Mooney, slightly embarrassed about the situation herself.

"We'll get it," said the agent, following the others out of the room.

The manager and his security officer were making as if to leave as well when Mooney stopped them.

"Before you go, Mr. Bandors," she said, "can you tell me if Miss Shores had anywhere else that she might have left valuables? Does the boat for instance, have its own bank with safety deposit boxes where tenants can keep valuables? Did Shores have any friends aboard?"

Still shaken by the whole experience of what just happened, Bandors shook his balding head. "No. We don't offer such services. Every tenant is responsible for their own belongings. The corporate owners of the boat except no responsibility for lost or stolen items."

"And friends?"

Bandors shook his again. "I have no idea about that."

"From what I understand," said the security officer. "She kept pretty much to herself."

That made sense, thought Mooney. Even if Shores had been eager to spread her false gospel, she had an even more overriding concern in keeping her mission under wraps. Stealing *Elements of Humanism* was more important to her and whoever she worked with than a few immediate converts.

"All right," said Mooney. "I guess that's all. No need to tell the other tenants too much. And I'm speaking now with the full authority of Military Intelligence. Simply tell them Shores was arrested by the local bunko squad. Solicitation under false circumstances."

Which was true enough so far as it went.

"Give me a few more minutes here," she concluded.

Gulping, Bandors and the officer left Mooney alone, the unit's door closing shut behind them.

Alone again, she decided to take advantage of the living unit's amenities by throwing her soiled clothing into the garment cleanser while she stepped into the steam shower. A few minutes later, she emerged refreshed, her hair dry. Her jumpsuit was ready and after putting it on, she was ready to pick up where she left off. Now, where was that?

Oh, yes, she remembered, *I was getting nowhere*. Let's see, nothing in the unit, nothing on her person. But no one was ever without their personal telcomm.

A telcomm was an item of modern society that simply could not be done without. It connected each person to the super cloud. Every single item of business was conducted on it. It granted the user a worldwide reach, even to the Moon. Why, if a person had the patience, they could eventually reach Mars.

It didn't matter if that business was conducted here on Earth or on the Moon. It all worked on the principle that when messages were sent on the local network, they were shunted into sub-space on the quantum level where pre-positioned nanites picked up the signals and directed them where they were supposed to go.

What the public didn't know was that Military Intelligence's Science Division found a way to break the interstellar barrier allowing agents instantaneous communication to headquarters via a dedicated bandwidth through hyper-space.

That, however, was not at issue now. Only how such an essential personal item could not be found either on Shores or somewhere in her unit. Mooney immediately dismissed the idea that she could get along without it. How could she have paid for her living unit, travel expenses, provided identification, rented a 'car, or...that was it! Her air car. If she owned one, it would be out in the tenants' lot.

Swiftly, she exited the living unit, and caught up to Bandors, who was just disengaging himself from a gaggle of curious tenants. Mooney caught his eye. The look on his face told her that he was not happy to see her again.

"Can I help you, Mrs. Conroi?" he asked resignedly.

"You can," replied Mooney. "I assume that Shores owned a 'car? If so, can you show it to me?"

"Follow me," sighed Bandors.

By then, the steamboat had returned to its original berthing where it had met the MI agents and the gangplank lowered. The tenants parking area was adjacent and it didn't take long to find Shores' vehicle.

"Here it is," said the manager, pointing out a late model vehicle.

Now that she'd found the 'car, Mooney was presented with another problem: how to get in. That was usually done via the owner's telcomm. But of course, if she was right, Shores' telcomm was locked inside the 'car. How Shores could have left it behind was a mystery. Telcomm's were programmed with proximity alarms that beeped loudly if the keyed owner moved too far away from it. Had Shores shut the alarm off? Or had she been tipped off to Mooney's presence and left in such a fluster, that she not only forgot her telcomm but failed to heed its alarm? Thinking back, it occurred to Mooney that Shores may have been alerted to her presence by the guard at the gate. He likely told her someone had been asking for her and that he'd let her in. Since Mooney presumed Shores knew no one in the area save for Alfo Bikari, it stood to reason that her suspicions were immediately aroused, enough to take her mind completely off everything else, including her telcomm.

However, the locked 'car presented Mooney with a little problem. Her own telcomm with its unique MI provided features, could override any lock either by laser or voice key, or personal signal code. After finding the proper program, she could simply let it run through the untold millions of possibilities until it inevitably struck on the proper one. Unfortunately, none of that was possible as she'd lost her MI issued telcomm.

That left her fallback position, one that relied more on luck than skill.

Often 'car owners either forgot or never bothered to set locks on their vehicles. Sometimes they simply left the dealer's preset voice code. Mooney hoped that Shores was one of those or that in her haste, she simply neglected to reset the lock the same way she may have forgotten her telcomm.

Only one way to find out, thought Mooney.

"Open," she said, and was rewarded as the 'car hatch sprung open.

She breathed a sigh of relief.

She'd dismissed Bandors earlier to prevent him from observing her methods, such as they were, allowing her to get immediately to work. Eagerly, she slipped into the aircar's passenger seat and began poking around inside. There were various pockets and compartments she could have looked in but she didn't bother. Mostly because Shores' sling-purse was right there in the space between the front seats especially designed for such a use.

Mooney pulled it open and was immediately rewarded with the telcomm sitting atop the other feminine necessaries held within the purse.

Got it!

Using her MI override code, it was a routine matter to break past the telcomm's personal codes and in seconds, Mooney was privy to all of Shores' secrets. Or some of them anyway. Or maybe none?

As she soon discovered, there was precious little information available. Shores was at least clever if not completely sane. There was nothing about Bikari or the book or whoever else might be involved in the affair. Not even any personal notations beyond a record of purchases such as her visit to The Ladies' Handmaid.

But Mooney hadn't been a top agent for the Exterior Ministry and then MI for nothing. With little information in the obvious places, she immediately began to search in the less obvious ones. Her first choice was travel and immediately hit pay dirt.

Despite her professionalism, Mooney's heart began to race in mounting excitement. Shores forgot to erase one vital source of information. Her personal global positioning system tracking record showed everywhere she'd been almost since escaping from the Moon asylum. Consequently, Mooney was able to back track her movements from the time she arrived in New Washington.

Most were inconsequential local trips with a single aberration showing her visit some weeks before to Trans Stellar Rocketways at a small spaceport outside Baltimore. No information on what she was doing there. Keeping that in mind, Mooney completed her search of the telcomm but found nothing more.

Since she'd lost her own telcomm in the Potomac, she decided to keep Shores' for her own use. It would be an easy process to re-key the device, the only drawback being that it wouldn't have the programming tech needed to contact Leclerc. She'd have to do that indirectly using sub-space.

She did that now, calling MI's New Washington public affairs office. Realizing that Shores' telcomm would not have the interstellar communication tool that would allow her to keep in touch with Leclerc off world, she decided to leave him with as much information as she could. Hoping that Leclerc would be able to read between the lines, she informed him, and through him, Jules, that she was following a lead at the Baltimore spaceport. And if that led off world, she intended to stick with it. Briefly, she wondered what Jules would think about that. No doubt, he'd worry, but what could she do?

She stored Shores' telcomm, now her own, in a pocket of her jumpsuit then proceeded to look through the other items in the purse. The only other thing of interest was a badge, slipped into a hidden pocket. And a physical badge at that. Unusual! Most ID badges were holo-secured, projected from a telcomm. Examined more closely, Mooney saw that it was a freighter's union badge. Number 485766W. But where it had been issued and for what line, there was no indication. But so unusual an item being in Shores' purse was enough to arouse Mooney's suspicions. She pocketed the badge.

And since Shores wouldn't be needing the rented aircar anymore, Mooney decided to commandeer it for her own purposes. Slipping into the driver's seat, and having already overridden the 'car's personal signal code assigning it to herself, there was no problem commanding the 'car to transport her to the Baltimore spaceport. She wouldn't bother filling in the guard as she'd promised. Likely, he'd been the tattle tale who tipped off Shores and almost getting her drowned.

Dawn had long since broken and she was feeling hungry. Luckily, the smartway made traffic jams impossible and travel swift. It was only a matter of less than an hour before the 'car pulled up to the main lobby of the space port. Not sure if she would need it again, Mooney ordered it to a nearby lot as she made her way inside. There, she grabbed a quick coffee and bagel before presenting herself at the Trans Stellar Rocketways desk.

Unable to simply present her MI identification due to the loss of her telcomm, Mooney had to go the subterfuge route.

"My name is Constance Shores," she said to the clerk holding down the information desk. "I believe I have a reservation with Rocketways. Can you confirm that for me?"

"Just a moment, please," said the clerk, who began talking to her work station.

As she waited, Mooney felt the ground tremble beneath her feet. Looking up through the plas glass dome that protected the spaceport lobby, she saw a graceful rocket slowly lifting away on a plume of vapor. Its metallic skin glinting in the morning sunlight. Even as she watched, it adjusted its pitch to begin its sprint to the upper atmosphere where it would be released from the earth's pull.

The scene was interrupted however, by the voice of the clerk: "Identification?"

"Excuse me?"

"Identification," repeated the clerk. "I'll need to see your identification."

"Oh, of course," said Mooney, flashing Shores' holo-ID from her purloined telcomm.

A few seconds passed.

"Here it is," reported the clerk finally. "You have reservations for tonight's rocket to Wolf 359. That's unusual. We don't see many of those."

"Oh?"

"Wolf is mostly used as a way station for heavy construction and terraforming crews," explained the clerk. "Not much call for women travelers out that way."

"Guess that makes me an exception," said Mooney, before she turned and disappeared into the crowds.

Nothing to do but keep on the trail, she decided, then Jules won't like it.

Finding a quiet spot on the vast lobby floor, she pulled out her telcomm and left another message with the MI New Washington Office, expecting it to reach Leclerc and eventually Jules.

"Leaving on flight to Wolf 359 via Trans Stellar Rocketways this date."

Chapter Nine

Romak's Insurance

By coincidence, Jules was currently enroute to Earth's Moon via a rocket just like the one Mooney observed lifting off from the New Washington spaceport. The difference being that he caught his in Miami, located in the heart of the former United States from where the Constitutional armies once marched to sweep the Humanists from power.

The flight was expected to be a short one under the power of the ship's efficient fusion engines but long enough for Jules to sort out his thoughts.

So Romak and Shores had both been patients at Special Research Unit 6 and contrary to Leclerc's assertion, Jules didn't believe it was coincidental. Although what connection the two had beyond both being patients at the same facility was less clear.

"Romak was a university history professor before being removed to Special Research Unit 6," revealed Leclerc via MI's hyperspace bandwidth. "His field of expertise was pre-Consortium history with a concentration on Humanist government and ideology. You can see where this is going."

"The good professor became too caught up in his work?"

"Exactly. He wrote several well received books, hailed for their acumen and objectivity but it seems somewhere along the way, he stopped being objective and became subjective. That's the danger of doing work in this area. It's why any work on the Humanists is strictly regimented with peer over sight and review. Somehow, any signs of Romak's change of mind slipped past the overseers, or he was just clever enough to conceal his seduction."

"He needed special permission from an oversight committee to study the period, didn't he?"

"He did and it was given," reported Leclerc. "According to the records, there was nothing in Romak's background to suggest he was vulnerable to the dangerous ideology."

"Nobody's immune," said Jules, pessimistically.

"Be that as it may, concealment could only last so long," continued Leclerc. "Sooner or later, the seductee can't help but try to share his enthusiasms. That's where Romak slipped up. He began talking up aspects of the ideology in his lectures. Students reported their concerns and he was monitored by a committee of faculty members who swiftly became appalled at his behavior. He was removed from his classes and appeared before the university's review committee and questioned. Realizing he was caught; he chose to come clean. Then attempted to persuade the committee on the values of Humanist thought, if you can call it that. Needless to say, they were appalled, dismissed Romak from the faculty, and notified the oversight committee. He was found to be in gross violation of the New Social Compact, item 3..."

"All anti-social activity that threatens the peace and tranquility of the people shall be prohibited..." quoted Jules.

"The so-called anti-Humanist clause," completed Leclerc. "Well, the short of it is, he was judged tainted by Humanist ideology and recommended for treatment which, as you know, meant automatic detention at Special Research Unit 6 which was established to handle such hard core cases. It was located on the Moon both to make sure patients were kept as far away from the populace as possible and to prevent possible escape. Which obviously didn't work in Romak's case."

"Which begs the question: how?"

Jules could feel Lecrlec's shrug even across the one hundred forty million miles of space between Earth and MI headquarters on Mars. "Officials at the asylum are reluctant to talk about the escape. That's something you'll have to pry out of them in person."

"Who's in charge?"

"A Dr. Ludo Vecci."

"Has he been appraised of my visit?"

"Yes. He and his staff have been notified and full cooperation has been assured."

"What about the connection between Romak and Shores? Anything on that?"

"Only that they were both patients at the asylum at the same time," said Leclerc. "So, it is likely that they somehow met and were in on the escape together. How that was possible, I don't know. Asylum policy is to keep patients strictly isolated."

"Hm. If that's all, then I guess I'll sign off," said Jules. "I'll report in when I conclude my visit..."

"Just one more thing," interrupted Leclerc.

"What's that?"

"I have some news from 'Manda," said Leclerc. "It appears that her telcomm had been lost or disabled so I'm now only in intermittent contact with her. She apparently used a police telcomm to give me a progress report. For that reason, she couldn't be specific but reading between the lines, it seemed she was making some progress. Later, that was confirmed when she contacted me through our New Washington office, this time using a personal telcomm not her own. That was strange. I had it traced and it was identified as belonging to Constance Shores."

"Shores' telcomm?" Jules was alarmed. "How can you be sure it was her doing the contacting and not Shores?"

"Take it easy. A team from New Washington took Shores into custody. They reported 'Manda safe and sound if looking a little bedraggled. They learned from the manager of the steamboat where Shores was staying that she was thrown overboard at one point before finding her way back and subduing Shores. How she was able to do that, they didn't say. But it sounds to me like we don't have to worry about how she handles herself."

That last was for Jules' benefit as Leclerc sought to sooth his fears for Mooney's safety. His next words, however, defeated his purpose.

"The last I heard from her, 'Manda said she'd back tracked Shores movements to the Baltimore space port and then off world to Wolf 359."

"That's it?"

"That's it. MI does have an office on Wolf 359 and I've alerted them to her arrival. But you know the sensitivity of this operation. She won't contact the office directly and only if she needs to."

Jules knew Mooney. Her dedication to the mission as well as a native streak of independence would work against calling in help if at all possible. That personality quirk led her into tight spots in the past and he worried that it could do so again.

"Keep me posted if she contacts you again," was all he said to Leclerc.

"Will do.

Although he was pleased to find out what Mooney was up to, and had every confidence in her judgment and abilities, the fact that she was cut off from direct communication with Leclerc concerned him. Something he brooded over for the rest of the flight.

He only emerged from his thoughts after the pilot announced the rocket's imminent arrival at Heinlein Village, one of the many domed settlements that dotted the Moon's surface and the one closest to Special Research Unit 6.

There was a sensation of movement as the rocket righted itself and began its relatively slow descent to the formacrete pad reserved for it outside the dome. It being the dark side of the Moon, there was only starlight to indicate the surrounding terrain. Soon, however, floodlights were lit around the landing pad and the permanent glow of light from within the nearby dome shone brightly. Movement there indicated that the residents were up and about confirming Heinlein Village as a community that never slept. Which, in fact, it never did. 'Day' and 'night' were quite arbitrary here on the dark side. In fact, time on the Moon was based on Greenwich Mean Time and days divided in thirds. That worked best for the mining industry which was the biggest employer and the reason why Heinlein Village was situated just alongside the Mare Moscoviense, one of the few 'seas' located on the dark side.

As the rocket continued to right itself, passenger seats remained stable as the tubular interior slowly revealed itself as a central shaft running the length of the ship. In fully upright position, passenger seats were revealed to reside on multiple decks with Jules' holding a dozen passengers. The arrangement was considered inconvenient by modern standards but their durability and the public's sentimentality for the old fashioned rockets prevented all of them from having been retired long ago.

There was a dull roar as the rocket eased itself onto the pad and quickly came to rest. It would be some minutes before the escalator reached his deck, so Jules simply closed his eyes and rested. Before he knew it, there was a bump outside and a crew member opened a hatch so that passengers could begin to exit. Jules rose, fetched his travel bag from the overhead compartment, and followed the others out the hatch and let the escalator whisk him to the lobby at the bottom. Due to the vertical design of the rocket, the escalator had to be positioned at a hatch located at each of the vehicle's twenty decks, a lengthy but not interminable process. The escalator itself was enclosed in a plas-glass cover allowing passengers their first unobstructed view of the Moon. Due however, to the glare of lights from the space port and nearby dome, there wasn't much to see overhead. But beyond the space port, glimpses could be had of the satellite's rough and broken features.

Jules checked the public chronometer in the space port lobby and saw that the time here was mid-morning. Not feeling any sense of rocketlag, he decided to seek out Special Research Unit 6 immediately.

Although residents of the Moon in general and Heinlein Village in particular knew of the installation as simply Special Research Unit 6 and assumed it was some sort of private laboratory like any number of others, its real function was classified. Thus, there was no public means of contacting it. For that purpose, Leclerc provided him with a number to call. Using it now, Jules was immediately rewarded with a voice at the other end.

"Special Research Unit 6," stated the voice. "How may I direct your call?"

It was obvious whoever it was had been instructed to play up the fiction that the Unit was just another scientific research facility.

"This is Victor Conroi," replied Jules. "I have an appointment with Dr. Vecci."

There was a pause, then "Of course, Mr. Conroi. A 'car will be sent to you at once. I see you're at the space port. The 'car will arrive at the passenger pick up area in approximately ten minutes."

"Thank you."

It was always good when such appointments went smoothly without his having to identify himself and explain the purpose of his visit. Leclerc had cleared the way.

He'd hardly arrived at the pickup area when the aircar pulled up silently alongside the boarding platform. The door lifted with a slight hiss and he stepped inside. In another moment, without a word required, the 'car pulled out onto the covered smartway, merged into traffic, and darted toward an exit that peeled off before the smartway entered the Heinlein Village dome.

Now the 'car picked up speed and soon, it was out beyond the plas-glass covered stretch of smartway and into the rocky barrens of the lunar surface. The 'car itself of course, was sealed against the airless void of the Moon's surface so Jules had no concern in that regard. The smartway extended ahead for several miles toward a low ridge, the outer rim of Mare Moscoviense. There, it passed through a notch in the rocks and the ridge soon revealed itself as an old lava basin, on the far side, the ridge sloped down a few hundred yards to a relatively featureless bottom where an isolated dome complex had been reared.

The 'car began to slow just before slipping into an opening at the base of the main dome, one which closed shut as soon as the vehicle cleared the threshold. Jules found himself in a stall that doubled as an air lock. There was a bit of delay as the stall was pressurized and when the far wall slid up, the 'car pulled forward and stopped along a debarking platform.

There, a man in hospital whites stood apparently waiting to welcome him.

"Welcome to Special Research Unit 6, Mr. Conroi," he said.

Overhead, Jules recognized the motto of the Consortium's government: "Our Constitution was made only for a moral and religious people. It is wholly inadequate to the government of any other." A quote from John Adams, a founder of the old United States before Humanism tore it apart, an eventuality that proved the accuracy of the aphorism. Its prominent presence here was a reminder to visitors, staff, and inmates of the follies of Humanism.

"Dr. Vecci, I presume?" returned Jules, stepping from the 'car and taking the man's hand in greeting.

"Correct," replied Vecci. "I see you wasted no time in getting here. I'd just received word from Military Intelligence to expect you only yesterday."

"I'm not here on vacation, doctor," said Jules as Vecci motioned him to follow along. "I have very serious business. And sensitive as well."

"So I've been informed," said Vecci, aware the discovery by Military Intelligence that Romak and others had escaped from his institution months before and was never told about it placed him in a very delicate situation. At the very least, his job was at stake. "Shall we go to my office? We can talk privately there."

Vecci led the way from the receiving platform into the asylum proper where white, antiseptic corridors predominated. Rooms opening off the corridors however, did seem to sport a cheerier atmosphere with their multi-colored pastels and comfortable furniture.

Pausing by one of the rooms, Jules remarked on the living room aspect of its furniture and other accouterments.

"When our patients are up and about, we prefer to place them at ease," explained Vecci. "It soothes their anxieties. It assures them that their stay here should not be considered punishment but for their own good. We offer them a relaxed atmosphere conducive to talk, verbal give and take between patient and therapist that brings out the issues for which they were sentenced here. Once out in the open, the two can begin to work them out hopefully to society's satisfaction."

Jules nodded, psychiatry not being his field.

"All that doesn't sound problematic enough to require an institution as isolated as this one is, nor its misleading name."

"Well, you have to remember, although these techniques may be standard in psychiatry, our patients are far from the ordinary type handled in your earthbound hospitals," said Vecci. "Here, we treat patients who have become infected with the Humanist ideology which, as you know, is extremely dangerous. When identified, it must be isolated and treated immediately lest it spread any farther than the affected party. The less the general public is aware that there are even such cases at all, the better."

"Are there many such cases?"

"Thankfully, no. At the moment, we here have only a few hundred. Most of these were seduced by Humanism while in educatory capacities. Citizens of the Consortium, in the ordinary course of their lives, rarely, if ever encounter elements of Humanism. The only times they do, is when they learn of its horrors in history classes at the college and university level. In that environment, educators are careful not to present the ideology in any kind of favorable light. Most students leave unaffected, especially when teachers keep to their guidelines. It's when teachers go beyond the guardrails, are themselves seduced by the ideology, that trouble starts."

"And what about the staff here?" wondered Jules. "Isn't there a danger that they themselves could be infected?"

"There certainly is," admitted Vecci. "For that reason, all staff are required to go through a regular review process to make sure they remain unaffected. If any doubts are raised during the reviews, they're transferred back to Earth for evaluation."

As they proceeded, Jules noticed that most of the staff were maintenance and tech workers. He mentioned the disparity to Vecci.

"Despite the misleading name of our institution, no actual research is done here," explained Vecci. "Except, of course, some gathering of behavioral data which is used to help identify cases that require the kind of intensive treatment we offer. But don't get the wrong impression. Although we offer psychiatric service as in ordinary asylums, we are essentially a prison. Our special...clientele...represent the most extreme cases of Humanist infection who are judged too dangerous to be let out into society even in a hospital environment. The hope is, of course, that they all can eventually be safely released."

"What is your success rate on that basis?" asked Jules.

"We have a fifty-two percent success rate," revealed Vecci, who was unable to suppress an element of professional pride. "Which is very encouraging."

"It is," agreed Jules, impressed. "How is it achieved exactly?":

"Through what we call virtual therapy," said Vecci. "Of course, you've heard of virtual reality in the entertainment sector..."

Jules nodded.

"Well, some years ago, decades actually, when the technology was refined to the point where reality and fantasy could not be distinguished, psychologists began to use it on an experimental basis. The results were encouraging with many patients benefiting from its use. There was some talk of applying it to criminal reform, but because the Consortium values free will, even for criminals, its use has been discouraged in ordinary penal environments. But because the cases we handle here are deemed some of the most difficult and most dangerous for society at large, we have been cleared for unrestricted use."

By this time, they had entered a completely different wing of the institution. Familiar environments featuring pneuma-couches and synth carpeting gave way to colder, technological surroundings. They had clearly entered the domain of the virtual engineers and world builders.

Vecci ushered Jules into a large room where a few techs sat at consoles as they monitored brain waves, heartbeat, and other biological reactions of a patient who had been strapped to a padded chair. His bare chest was covered with EKG stickers and from his shaved head, similar stickers included small, WIFI antennas. Otherwise, there seemed no particular precautions as one might find in an operating room or other antiseptic environments.

"Dr. Andreus," said Vecci to a white coveralled man that had been hovering over the patient. "Can you explain to Mr. Conroi here, how virtual reality is applied to cases like Carl here?"

"Certainly," said Andreus, apparently unruffled speaking openly to a total stranger.

Had everyone in the asylum been told of my visit? wondered Jules. *And if so, how much were they told?*

"The basis of virtual therapy," began Andreus, "is the emersion of the patient into a reality that corresponds as closely as possible to his background. His deep background that is. By that I mean, his childhood and young adulthood; the years before he was infected by Humanism. To do that, the patient is first diagnosed through extensive sessions with the institute's psychiatric staff. Over time, details of his life are teased out as the patient relaxes and develops a personal relationship with his therapist. With that information, virtual technicians such as myself and staff can begin rebuilding the world the patient lived. From there, the patient is slowly introduced into that world in the manner you see here. Naturally, at first, the subject resists what he sees in that world, but gradually, through repeated sessions, his reticence breaks down as he learns to enjoy being back in that simpler, happier time. Between visits, he continues to visit his therapist from which more information is gleaned which is then added to the virtual scenario making it more and more realistic and convincing. When we sense that the patient has accepted the virtual world, we can begin to manipulate his experience there, steering him along paths of our own choosing. For example, if he did not receive enough supportive affection from his parents, we can change that so that they did. You see? Later, we might weave incidents among his genuine memories that speak against elements of Humanism. Nostalgia and the yearning for a simpler time in our past even if it never existed, is a powerful urge in all human beings. We use that impulse to counteract the patient's Humanist beliefs. There comes a point when the patient cannot reconcile Humanist values with those of the family and friends with whom he now more strongly identifies. That's the point where either the patient is cured or virtual therapy must continue usually by starting the process all over again."

"Fascinating," admitted Jules. "I was aware of the use of virtual therapy in some criminal cases, but didn't realize it had become as advanced and nuanced as you describe here."

"When you come right down to it," said Andreus, "it's the most humane approach to psychiatry in the treatment of anti-social behavior yet devised...and the most successful in its results."

"So Dr. Vecci has told me. It's all very encouraging."

Andreus beamed at the compliment, which kept him talking.

"Of course, virtual therapy has proven helpful in other contexts including sexual deviancy and dysphoria," said Andreus. "It's only to be regretted that the technology wasn't available immediately following the war with the Humanists. So many of its victims might have been treated instead of ending up in re-education programs that often did little to help.

Many Humanists, as you may know, ended up spending the rest of their lives in such programs."

"The Constitutionalists and then the Consortium had little choice in that," said Jules. "Execution was out of the question but they couldn't just set them free to continue undermining society. There were medicines that helped restore chemical imbalances in the brain. That helped some but not all. However, you're right, virtual therapy would have been a Godsend at the time."

"Well, I think we should let Dr. Andreus return to his work now," interjected Vecci.

Jules was glad for the timely interruption. As interesting as the subject might have been, he didn't come all the way to the Moon to discuss recent advances in psychology.

"Thank you for your insights, doctor," said Jules to Andreus. "You and your colleagues are doing valuable work here."

Together, Jules and Vecci left the room and a few moments later, were in Vecci's office, the door firmly shut behind them, assuring privacy.

Vecci waved Jules to a chair as he took his place behind his work station, clear plas windows over his shoulders giving a view of Mare Moscoviense, or what could be seen of it in lighting immediately around the institute. Being on the dark side of the Moon, there was little more than weak starlight beyond the range of the fusion powered lights so that the 'sea' beyond and the distant rim, were indicated only in limited detail.

To relieve the tedium of lunar living, the walls of the office were hung with stereopticals which, just then, were programmed for cheerier scenes from Earth's forests and lakes.

"Scenes of my native, Latinium," said Vecci, noticing Jules' interest in the stereopticals, "I miss the countryside dearly but my term here at the facility goes for another two years."

"Then it's not a permanent employment?"

"Oh, no. Studies have shown that extended life on the Moon, barren as it is, can be oppressive to many people, never mind living on the dark side. Of course, for others, it has no effect. Their nature allows them to live in this environment indefinitely. But I'm not one of them, I assure you."

"I've visited many worlds," revealed Jules, "most of them more appealing than our own Moon. So I can understand the feeling."

"It's hard to believe that such a beautiful world had once been dominated by such a poisonous culture as Humanism," said the doctor. "Gender reassignment surgery, gender dysphoria suffered by a major portion of the population, disastrous energy policies that left millions freezing in winter and power rationing, schools altered to become indoctrination platforms rather than learning centers where racism, gender confusion, and self-contempt were instilled in impressionable minds. It Balkanized society; turned people against each other. Group against group: race, gender, religion, and more."

Vecci visibly shuddered.

"Even as a professional, I find it difficult to accept such violations of both conscience and common sense," he continued. "It was as if three quarters of the Earth's population went insane. They promoted racism and the worst kinds of sexual abnormalities, promoting them directly to children. I can't imagine a more toxic mix of corrupting forces designed to bring society to the point of meltdown."

"It's hard to believe that the Humanists couldn't see that it all couldn't end any other way," said Jules. "These people weren't stupid or even ignorant. They simply refused to accept that their Humanist policies were unworkable. It became like a religion to them. Its dogma couldn't be questioned. Even more insidious, was the fact that many of its most attractive qualities were based on traditional Christian values but without the peskiness of Christ Himself. That's why, inevitably, the only place it could lead was to the gulag."

"It was a melange of age old hatreds and resentments that once unleashed, plunged most of the world into chaos and war," concluded Vecci. "Humanism played up to people's worst instincts, their selfishness and suspicions."

"A specter that threatens the world again," warned Jules.

"What's that you say?" asked Vecci, startled.

"Your former patient," reminded Jules. "Morgul Romak."

"What of him?"

"There's no need to beat around the bush, doctor," said Jules. "You've been informed of the reason why I've come. Romak successfully resisted treatment, escaped, and has stolen the movement's holiest text, The *Elements of Humanism*."

Vecci gulped.

"Should he use that text to spread the virus further, the Consortium could find itself plunged into the same war it fought to free the world from the scourge of Humanism once before. Except this time, the war will not be confined to the Earth but likely spread over dozens of worlds."

"I realize the danger, after all, it's the whole reason this institution exists..."

"Then how was it that Romak escaped?" demanded Jules. "Was he being treated with virtual therapy?"

"No, we hadn't reached that stage yet," replied Vecci. "We were still collating data being gathered from in person sessions."

"I'll need to review the records of those sessions, doctor," said Jules. "There might be some hint about Romak's plans, where he intended to go once he was free."

Vecci shifted uncomfortably in his chair.

"And then there's Constance Shores," pressed Jules. "She also escaped. Coincidence?"

"I don't know if her escape was due to Romak or if she simply seized an opportunity when it presented itself," speculated Vecci. "She and the others..."

"Others?" This was the first Jules had heard of other patients aside from Romak and Shores that had escaped. "There were others who escaped with Romak? How many? Why weren't they mentioned when MI contacted you on this subject?"

"They didn't ask," was all Vecci could muster. "Mr. Conroi, this is not the sort of thing the institution likes to see bandied about..."

"You of all people, doctor, should realize the gravity of a situation like this," reprimanded Jules. "This information is of crucial importance to my investigation. The lack of your being completely candid has already placed the life of one of our agents in jeopardy." Jules felt a rising anger as he thought of Mooney's encounter with Shores. "How many of your patients escaped with Romak?"

"Thirteen," admitted Vecci.

"Thirteen! And do you believe they too escaped only as a matter of opportunity? That they weren't influenced by Romak at all? From what we've learned, that was not the case with Shores, who has expressed Humanist beliefs with conviction."

"I don't know what to say," said a humbled Vecci. "If Romak was able to influence them, it was in a manner that no one here was able to detect."

Getting his anger under control, Jules tried a different tack.

"Are patients allowed to commiserate with one another?" he asked. "Did they socialize at meal times, exercise periods, before lights out etcetera?"

"We try to minimize the penal nature of the institution," said Vecci. "The object is always to put patients at their ease, the better to conduct their in person sessions you see..."

"So they were allowed to talk to each other?"

"Yes, but under strict supervision," insisted Vecci. "We realize those sent here by the courts, are most difficult cases involving Humanist influences. We isolate them as much as possible and those times they're allowed to socialize, we carefully monitor and record their interactions."

"I see. Then there are more records I can review?"

"Yes."

"Are patients allowed to communicate with anyone outside the institution? Family for instance?"

"Absolutely not," insisted Vecci. "Such communication poses the danger of contradicting the virtual reality we attempt to build for each patient. They might cast doubt in the mind of the patient about the scenario we build for him."

Jules nodded. "What about inside the institution? Whom did Romak speak to?"

"His fellow inmates mostly. Occasionally a guard or two."

"Was there anything in what he said or did that might have raised suspicion that he was planning an escape?"

"We always assume patients are looking for any opportunity to escape but none have ever been successful," said Vecci. "Being on the Moon and some distance from the nearest settlement makes escape from here more unlikely than the remote spots on Earth used for penal purposes. In addition, ground transportation is secured with voice codes and redundancy blocks to assure against any unauthorized use. As for Romak, no, we never detected any open planning of escape from him. In fact, we have reason to believe that Romak himself was taken by surprise when the attempt was made."

Jules perked up at that. "What do you mean? Tell me more."

"Well, this is somewhat embarrassing..."

"Never mind that," said Jules. "What do you mean that Romak may not have known about the escape?"

"I...well, let me call in the head of our security team," offered Vecci, referring to his work station and asking for Lindis Fairweather to come to his office.

A few minutes later, a large man crowded the opening to the office.

"You wanted to see me, doctor?" he asked.

"I did. Lindis, this is Victor Conroi, of Military Intelligence. The man we were expecting."

"I heard you'd arrived," said Fairweather, taking Jules' hand.

"I've been filling Mr. Conroi in on our work with Morgul Romak but thought you might better explain the details of his escape."

"Not much to tell, but I'll do my best," said Fairweather. "I'd like to show you something, Mr. Conroi. We can talk along the way."

"Fine by me," replied Jules, wondering what it was that Fairweather wanted him to see.

"No need to accompany us, doctor," said Fairweather, turning to Vecci. "I'll deliver Mr. Conroi back to you in short order."

"Very well," said Vecci, relieved to be free of Jules' questioning. "I have some work to do here anyway."

Outside Vecci's office, the corridors seemed barely wide enough to permit Jules and Fairweather to walk side by side but they managed.

"Just how did Romak make his escape," asked Jules, not wasting any time. "Dr. Vecci believed that Romak may not even have been aware that a plan existed?"

"We believe that's true," confirmed Fairweather. "The plan was devised and executed by some of his own students from Dodering University where he was teaching prior to his arrest."

"Students? Acting on their own?"

"Exactly," said Fairweather as they entered a down capsule. "Young people often look for something to rebel against; their parents, society, the university they attend. They're naturally restless and questioning, making them easy prey for ideologues. These students, about a dozen of them as near as we can figure, were especially susceptible to the seductive nature of Humanism. Because of their limited experience in the world outside academia and their own naive optimism, the qualities of socialism appealed to them. In short, these students were looking for a cause, even if it was one they couldn't identify on their own, but one Romak was able and willing to supply them. Romak's arrest only confirmed what he'd told them about an unjust society with all of its inequalities and unfairness."

They exited the down capsule in the very bowels of the institution below even the level containing its life support systems and power grid. This far down, Jules guessed, could hold only one thing, the dome's artificial gravity control system and its particle of dwarf-matter.

What are we doing down here? Jules wondered. Did it have anything to do with how the students were able to spring Romak?

"But just how were these students able to accomplish the rescue?" he asked, as Fairweather motioned him forward.

Just ahead of them was the smooth sided, concave pit where the dwarf-matter particle was restrained within a specialized electro-magnetic field. Overhead, pipes and conduits gave the whole room a claustrophobic feel. "Even more, how did they know this Special Research Unit 6 even existed?"

"A good question," acknowledged Fairweather. "There was no way that ordinary college students could know of this place, never mind doing anything to help Romak escape. The remote location and our own security measures would be enough to prevent that."

"Hm. That leaves only one other possibility," mused Jules.

"What's that?"

"They must have had inside help."

"That's exactly right, Mr. Conroi," agreed Fairweather.

Jules turned to face the security man. Something in his voice warning him of danger.

"In fact, it was me who did the helping."

With that, Fairweather lunged toward Jules.

Chapter Ten

The Screw Tightens

Luckily, Jules wasn't taken completely by surprise.

His suspicions had already been aroused when Fairweather led him to the institution's sub-basement, a place that clearly would have had little to do with any escape attempt. As a result, he was able to avoid the main thrust of Fairweather's attack, dodging to the side and tripping him with his legs.

Being somewhat top heavy, the big Fairweather couldn't stop himself from toppling forward into the well of the inverted cone at the bottom of which the dwarf-matter rested. But the reprieve would only be a short one as he recovered and immediately began scrambling back up the slope.

Thinking quickly, Jules realized he needed an equalizer. Casting his gaze about, he spotted the room's control surfaces. Dashing over, he swiped a hand over the surfaces, engaging the holo-menu. Running out of time, he found the item he wanted, indicated it, and the dwarf-matter stasis board sprang up. It was no problem to recognize the button that managed the electro-magnetic field that surrounded the particle and he wasted no time in readjusting it.

Immediately, the pull of the dwarf-matter was altered and gravity in Special Research Unit 6 was reduced by five sixths slowing Fairweather's climb and making it more difficult to negotiate the featureless slope leading up to where Jules stood.

Jules had just turned to check on Fairweather when something struck him on the shoulder, numbing his left arm.

Grabbing his injured arm, he turned and saw Dr Vecci standing in the opening of the down capsule.

Is he in on this too? thought Jules. Had Romak really been that persuasive? How far had Humanism penetrated among the staff?

There was no time for more speculation as Vecci, a heavy armature in his raised hand, prepared to strike again.

Jules surmised that Vecci's first blow had been intended for his head but when the gravity was cut, he was thrown off balance and the blow missed. This time, he took a more deliberate approach and it gave Jules his chance.

In the end, Vecci had no combat training nor much experience with gravity less than Earth normal. Thus, his method was awkward, his approach easily avoided by Jules who, even with a near useless left arm, was able to avoid Vecci's attack and place a fist in his gut.

Vecci doubled over, the breath knocked out of him. Jules grabbed the armature from his hand and shoved him over with a knee. The doctor flew backward easily in the lessened gravity and struck his head against the wall rendering him momentarily dazed.

It was a good thing Jules had taken the armature as, turning, he saw Fairweather had reached the top of the incline and had reared up preparatory to launching his own assault. But, like Vecci, he wasn't used to the lesser gravity of the Moon and his movements tended to lift him from the floor, his arms outspread, windmilling, seeking balance.

Jules wasted no time moving in and giving the man a good tap on the head with the armature, sending him to the floor and into unconsciousness.

Using his good arm, Jules dug out his telcomm and contacting Leclerc.

"Acknowledged," came Leclerc's voice over the hyper-space bandwidth.

"Request for an MI security team for Special Research Unit 6," said Jules. "Reason to believe institute's staff has been infected but no idea yet how far the infection has spread."

There was no need for Jules to be more specific. Leclerc would certainly recognize the danger.

"Entire installation must be quarantined until extent of the danger can be identified and quantified."

"Acknowledged. Security team on its way."

"Unit's director also contaminated," continued Jules. "Intend to question him as to target Romack's next moves."

"Let me know what you find out," said Leclerc. "This is one genie that has to be put back in its bottle."

Jules signed off before realizing that he'd forgotten to ask Leclerc if there had been any news regarding Mooney. But there was no time to reestablish contact as Vecci was recovering from his fall and Jules didn't intend to give him time to rally his thoughts.

First however, he needed to secure Fairweather before he also woke up. Taking advantage of the lighter gravity, it was easy for Jules to haul the big man over to a standing conduit, wrap his arms around it and secure them together with a pair of DNA nodules.

That should hold him.

Next, he restored the electro-magnetic field that neutralized the effects of the dwarf-matter, reestablishing Earth normal gravity to the institution and, picking Vecci up from the floor, directed him into the up capsule.

At the proper floor, Vecci was walking with a stagger while Jules steered him in the direction of his office. Around them, there was still consternation among the staff at the recent cut in gravity and it was only with some fast talking that Jules was able to stave off questioning by the maintenance supervisor who'd been trying to access the down capsule to the basement level.

Safe in Vecci's office, Jules dumped the director into a chair and secured the door against entry.

"I have to admit that you were very convincing in our earlier interview," said Jules. "But now you're going to explain yourself, doctor."

Jules made sure there was the proper amount of menace in his voice.

"My attack on you was perfectly obvious, wasn't it? We needed to stop you, and Military Intelligence, from interfering with Romak's great work."

"Great work?" questioned Jules. "The work of reintroducing fear and hate and suspicion into the world? To set men against each other based on race and religion?"

Vecci waved such concerns aside. "Hyperbole. Wild accusations intended to impune the pure philosophy of Humanism whose goal is to set men free from the moral strictures of society. How can more freedom hurt anything?"

"Did Romak bother telling you about the other side of Humanism? The side that set groups against each other? The side that shut down free speech, even free thought? The side that crushed rights, rights granted men by God, not government? The side that always leads to the gulag?"

"How much different is that from what we do here?" countered Vecci. "Yes, the Consortium does not abide the gulag but it achieves the same purpose in its virtual therapies."

"Only in the most extreme cases as you yourself pointed out not long ago," reminded Jules. "The Consortium respects free will, even for criminals. Isn't that so?"

Vecci remained silent.

"Is that how Romak reached you? Pointing out inconsistencies in the Consortium without considering the lengths it goes to in order to preserve human dignity? Are you aware at all about the horrors committed by the old Humanists before the Constitutional wars?"

Again, Vecci remained silent.

Jules decided to weaken Vecci's resistance with another, more oblique approach.

"How did Romak make his escape?" he asked. "How do his former students fit into the plan?"

Vecci grunted. "That was simplest of all. Romak was allowed to contact his former pupils, talk to them, gain their sympathy, refortify their Humanist convictions, until they agreed to try and free him. They were told where the institution was located and instructed to gather in Heinlein Village and there to await contact. They did and Fairweather was sent to meet them."

"Fairweather," reiterated Jules. "How many other staff members were turned by Romak?"

Vecci shrugged. "I have no intention of betraying them to

Military Intelligence."

"Well then, what was Fairweather's weak spot," pressed Jules. "What was it that Romak used to turn him?"

"Romak didn't need to use any subterfuge to 'turn' anyone," replied Vecci. "He simply pointed out truths that were self-evident."

"And in Fairweather's case?"

"Fairweather is descended from what used to be called Native Americans, the Indian tribes of North America," said Vecci. "Romak simply reminded him how his ancestral culture was crushed and obliterated by Europeans and ultimately the Consortium. Anyone under the same circumstances would be angry at that."

"But you can see how dangerous Humanist ideology can be?" replied Jules. "Native American culture had been dead and gone for hundreds of years. No one alive had anything to do with its eventual disappearance, nor the Consortium as a government. In fact, whatever anyone knows of the culture of the Indians is from records written by Europeans from Indian testimony that itself could only be a few generations old. That, and scraps of information gleaned from anthropological research."

He was getting the idea now of how Romak operated. It didn't matter what the facts were, only how people felt. It was the heart of what made Humanism so dangerous, how it set people against each other over trifles.

"So what about the students?" asked Jules again, deciding to keep to his original interrogation plan.

Vecci shrugged. "Fairweather arranged for a private rocket in the name of one of the students then returned to the institution. Romak was given false identification as a patient prepared to reenter society and taken to one of the institution's aircars. He was transported without incident to the Village and given into the custody of his students. From there, he was taken aboard the rocket and removed from the Moon."

"And what about the thirteen other patients who escaped with him?"

"Oh, of course. They were also taken from the institute with normalization documentation," explained Vecci. "They're presence added verisimilitude for reservation of the rocket. It wouldn't have done to reserve a full rocket for only a handful of passengers, especially mere students. It all fell together nicely, you see?"

"I do," admitted Jules. No wonder there were no reports of escapes from the institute. Vecci and who knew how many others had all been in on it.

"And what were Romak's plans for the future?" asked Jules.

He kept the question purposely vague, choosing not to reveal that the raid in Zululand failed to apprehend Romak. It was just possible that Vecci hadn't heard from Romak, giving Jules some room to maneuver.

"Why should I tell you that?"

"Because Romak's escape and all your plans have come to nothing," said Jules. "Soon, this institution will be under the control of Military Intelligence and on a personal level, the tables will be turned on you. Are you ready to become an inmate in your own institution, doctor?"

The question seemed to take Vecci aback. It was plain, he'd never considered such an outcome.

"Why, I..."

Now's the time to spring the trap, thought Jules. While he was confused, threatened by a loss of personal freedom.

"At this moment, a special MI unit is closing in on Romak," said Jules. "His headquarters building in Zululand is surrounded and I expect to hear of his capture at any moment."

"Zululand? You know about that?"

"Romak made one mistake," pressed Jules. "One was all it took. He left the manufacturer's name and address on a device he used to trap me in New Washington. They had his order information for the device leading us straight to his hideout in Zululand."

Suddenly, Vecci's self-confidence seemed to deflate. He realized that the only way Jules could know of Zululand was if the operation was real. That Romak was defeated. Now it was a matter of saving his own skin. To come clean, denouncing his dalliance with Humanism.

"It's all over then," he sighed. "The dream never had a chance to become real."

"Don't you mean the nightmare?" asked Jules.

"Oh...yes, of course," replied Vecci quickly, cognizant of the need to rehabilitate himself and prevent consignment into his own institution. "It was all a nightmare, as you say. I don't know what came over me. It was Romak's fault! He was so persuasive. Like no other patient I ever dealt with."

"Of course," soothed Jules. "That's what made him so dangerous."

Jules was careful to talk of Romak in the past tense. After all, the man was still on the loose with no leads as to his whereabouts.

"Have you heard from Romak since his escape?" asked Jules. "And what of the other escapees and the students? Were they with him? We need to know in order to keep casualties to a minimum in our raid in Zululand."

Vecci saw another way to add to his defense. Cooperation. If lives could be saved, it would be a credit to him, wouldn't it?

"So far as I know, all of the escapees and students are with Romak," he said. "There wasn't enough time to build an organization. On the other hand, Romak thought it might not have been necessary. He said he'd found another way."

"Another way?" asked Jules. "To spread the ideology of Humanism?"

"Yes. When I spoke to him only two days ago, he said that he'd come into possession of the *Elements of Humanism*, and in it, discovered something that could change everything."

"He said that? Those are his exact words? Change everything?"

Vecci nodded, all in now. "Yes. It could not only shift the balance of power in the Consortium, it could transform all of society as well!"

Chapter Eleven

Back to Earth

Once again, Jules found himself on a rocket this time heading in the opposite direction, back to Earth.

Special Research Unit 6 had been secured by MI before he left; the extent of the corrupting influence of Humanism at the institute still unknown. Jules was happy to leave that rabbit hole to others. In fact, fear that the personnel of the institute may have contacted other Research Units under cover of the routine exchange of information, was cause for concern and Leclerc moved quickly to warn oversight committees to conduct thorough examinations of their respective Units.

In the meantime, Jules had other things to be concerned about, chief among them finding out what this discovery Vecci talked about could be and keeping Romak from getting his hands on it.

Where to start though? Earth was a big place and Romak could have gone anywhere.

However, Jules thought he had one thing going for him that could narrow the search considerably. He believed that whatever the secret was, it was likely located within the former Humanist stronghold located roughly in the eastern to midwestern portions of the old United States. Still a lot of territory to cover. To further narrow his search, he decided to go back to the beginning of his investigation and sift through what he had in hopes of being inspired. And what he had mostly, was *Elements of Humanism* itself.

First, why did the book even exist in hardcopy format? Even by the standards of the Humanist state, it was an inefficient method of storing information. On the other hand, it was also a stable one. More stable than a data version? The answer was yes. Data could be erased and if someone knew their way around artificial intelligences, ways could always be found to delete information permanently. From their point of view, *Elements of Humanism* was akin to the Christian Bible and something like that would not be trusted to the cloud or any digital format.

Furthermore, the book wasn't simply a manifesto of Humanist principles. It was written in the closing days of the war when even the most diehard Humanists, despite the fanaticism of the rainbow brigades, realized that the backwardness of their technology made victory impossible. For that reason, *Elements of Humanism* was intended to preserve the fundamentals of the ideology against the day when they could again become a valid alternative to the moral order. Its purpose was to record and justify Humanist principles and become a blueprint for an underground resistance that would keep the movement alive until a dissatisfied population was again ready to receive it. Luckily, the Humanists did such a bad job of governance, proving that Humanism was fundamentally unworkable, that people quickly abandoned it and a thorough job by the new Consortium of rooting out any resistance made its return highly unlikely...but not, as Romak was proving, impossible.

So where did all that review leave Jules?

It left him with only one possibility he could think of, and that was a long shot.

That whatever Romak found in the book, might likely be located back where the stolen book was first discovered. Jules hoped that his search could be narrowed further by finding out where Romak's rocket landed when it returned to Earth. That was easy enough. It berthed at the Buffalo field but from there, he could have gone anywhere in the Northern Hemisphere. Not only that, but Buffalo was nowhere near the place where the book was found. That place was in Boston, on the grounds of the former Harvard College, the old Humanist stronghold where its most fanatical theorists worked and taught. It was the intellectual nerve center of the movement and the place from which government activists and gulag officers were recruited.

Romak, however, was nothing if not clever. He would have avoided coming in a rocket that landed exactly where he intended to go. Or at least so Jules theorized. In that case, its landing in Buffalo didn't negate the possibility that Boston was Romak's true destination. At least that was what Jules hoped.

Thus, Jules found himself aboard another stratoliner. This time, one whose flight path took it over the northeast metropolitan area to the district of Boston.

In the city proper, Jules took a robocab directly to the Harvard Remains. On the way, he was surprised that many of the streets still conformed to the narrow, twisting paths they followed from pre-Humanist times which must have greatly frustrated the smart street planners. In the Cambridge part of the city, it was even worse until the 'cab arrived in the vicinity of the Remains, which weren't remains at all. On the site were several glassite towers that left little of the former campus in evidence. However, a small building in the style of the region's colonial past stood where the school's green used to be and directly over the entrance to a subterranean lair where the Humanists held their last stand at the conclusion of the war. Now, preserved for historical purposes, it served as a tourist destination and local curiosity.

Just then however, what was happening at the site was anything but what anyone would expect of idle touristry.

"Stop," commanded Jules of the 'cab.

Immediately, the vehicle halted and settled lightly onto the smartway just a few yards from the Remains and behind a line of police vehicles, some with lights flashing.

Outside the building, a crowd was milling, hiding the entrance from view. A small knot of police was holding people back, keeping the doors clear.

Suspecting the worst, Jules ran up to the officer in charge and managed to catch his attention.

"Officer, I need to speak with you," he said.

"Keep back sir," was the reply. "I have no time to talk right now."

"Officer," persisted Jules. "I have business here."

With that, he flashed the holo of his Military Intelligence identification before the officer's eyes.

Unable to avoid seeing the identification, the man's demeanor changed immediately.

"What do you mean you have business here?"

"Circumstances of an investigation I'm working on has led me here," said Jules. "Whatever happened here isn't a coincidence. I believe it's directly related to the case I'm working on. I need to get inside to make sure. If it is related, I can help clear up some of the questions authorities might have about it."

The officer was silent a moment, thinking over what Jules had said. Finally, he stepped aside to let him past the cordon.

"Ask for detective Ryan," he said. "He's in charge."

"Thanks."

Jules passed through the entrance doors that slid aside to admit him and then swished silently closed behind him shutting out the tumult outdoors. Inside, plex-glass display cases and stereopticals constituted a modest museum with information kiosk in the center. A number of small paned windows allowed natural light to suffuse the room and decorative molding evoked architectural styles of colonial Boston.

But Jules wasn't in a position to appreciate such details as another uniformed officer approached to ask his business.

Again, Jules was obliged to flash his identification with another brief explanation of his possible value to investigators.

This time, the officer pulled out his own telcomm to contact Detective Ryan who was with the museum curator somewhere in the tunnels beneath the building.

"Who is it that wants to come down?" asked Ryan's voice from the telcomm's speaker.

"Victor Conroi," said Jules in the direction of the telcomm. "Military Intelligence. I'm working on a case that I think will have bearing on what happened here."

"Come on down," invited Ryan.

"This way," said the officer, pointing to a down capsule at the rear of the room.

In moments, Jules emerged into the cool, semi-darkness of the tunnel system which once served the Harvard campus buildings that stood all around the green back in Humanist times. Rooms and doorways lined the corridors which branched off in different directions ultimately to dead end in closures made when the new spires were constructed. The system had been preserved in the interests of historical preservation, consequently, many of the walls still included pocked and marred surfaces where exchanges of gunfire struck in the final, desperate battle with Humanist holdouts.

There was obviously a hubbub of activity going on in a large open space where corridors intersected. There, several officers stood about with a pair of suit jacketed individuals the center of attention. One was asking questions, the other, answering. When the officer who escorted Jules into the tunnels interrupted, it was to the man asking the questions to whom he spoke.

"Detective Ryan, I presume?" asked Jules, extending a hand.

Ryan took it. "I am. You're Conroi? What does MI have to do with all this?"

"I'm on the trail of a suspect and it's led me here," said Jules guardedly. "Can I speak with you privately?"

Ryan nodded and motioned Jules to follow him into a nearby room. It was completely empty except for an informational plaque on one of the four walls stating something about the Humanist last stand.

Ryan took hold of the antique door knob and closed the room's door manually. He twisted it to make sure it was secure. "Now what's this all about?"

Jules told him.

"And I can't stress it too much that the information I've just given you must remain secret," concluded Jules. "Keep all of it out of your reports. You'll be informed when and how much can be divulged when my own investigation has been completed."

Ryan didn't need to answer, his face said it all. He didn't like the admonition but with Military Intelligence involved, knew he had no choice.

"So, do you know what exactly this Romak character was looking for here?" he asked.

"Not exactly," replied Jules. "I just know that whatever it is, it's highly dangerous to the Consortium. What does the curator have to say? Anything missing?"

"As a matter of fact, there is," said Ryan. "And since nothing else has been disturbed down here except a single display case, I think your man knew exactly what he was looking for."

"And that was...?"

"Why don't you ask the curator," suggested Ryan. "I'll refer to you as Detective Dorrity, all right?"

Jules nodded.

Together, they exited the room and returned to the small knot of people gathered at the intersection. For the first time, Jules noticed numbers of wall mounted and floor displays containing various artifacts found in the tunnels after the ancient battle and in subsequent archeological study. Clothing, books, weapons, and other gear were on exhibition along with explanatory plaques and stereopticals. But what really captured Jules' attention was the small group of young people to the side, all secured with DNA nodules.

What are they doing here? Jules wondered, but knew the answer. These were some of Romak's students who helped him escape from the Moon. Were they too left behind to foil anyone coming after their mentor? Jules decided to concentrate on what the curator had to say first before tackling the students, all of whom had a certain arrogance about them that suggested he'd find no cooperation there.

"Detective Dorrity," Ryan was saying, "this is Mr. Kovsky, the museum's curator."

"Hello Mr. Kovsky," greeted Jules.

Kovsky said nothing, perspiration beading his high forehead.

"Detective Dorrity will be working with me on this case," said Ryan. "Tell him what you've told me."

Kovsky cleared his throat nervously. "Well, as I told Detective Ryan here, a gentleman arrived at the museum a few hours ago. He said he was a history teacher and was accompanying some students..." he glanced over at the half dozen young people standing nearby, "...on a field trip. They bought their tickets and while some of the students asked me questions upstairs, the others, including their teacher, took the down capsule."

"Was that allowed?" asked Jules. "To have visitors go into the tunnels unaccompanied by a guide?"

"Certainly not," insisted Kovsky. "But I couldn't pull away from the group I was with and the others were downstairs before I could object."

"How long were you delayed?"

"I'd say it was about fifteen minutes before I insisted on breaking away and going downstairs," said Kovsky. "By the time I arrived there, the theft had already occurred and the teacher must have taken the up capsule while I was headed down with his students."

"You said there had been a theft," asked Jules. "What was taken?"

Kovsky stepped aside to reveal one of the display cases. A hole had been melted through the plas-glass shielding. The obvious sign of an ion pistol on high mag. The resultant hole was big enough for a hand to reach inside.

And inside rested an ancient hand weapon and a row of four cartridges. The weapon was a pistol to be sure, but the kind that hadn't been used, at least not by anyone except collectors of antique firearms, for almost two hundred years. According to a readout below the display, the gun was a 38 Special, issued by Smith and Wesson, that fired up to five projectiles. Jules was surprised. His own ion pistol was a Smith and Wesson product. The revolver, however, looked somehow crueler and more brutal even though, outwardly, it looked much like his own weapon. He thought of the kind of massive damage a projectile fired from such a gun might do and shuddered inwardly. Ion weapons could be just as deadly of course, but their beams cauterized even killing wounds so there was never an unsightly mess.

Continuing to scan the informational readout about the gun, Jules then learned that it was used by the last holdout of the tunnel firefight to kill himself, a man named Samuel Pimdale.

Pimdale! The thought screamed in Jules' mind. The author of *Elements of Humanism*.

Was it a coincidence?

His mind worked quickly to put the pieces together: for months before the end, the Humanists knew the war was lost. Pimdale then writes *The Elements of Humanism*, a primer as well as a manifesto of the movement that includes a clue to a secret weapon whose intention is to somehow revive the evil ideology and again curse mankind with it. There were multiple chambers in the ancient revolver and yet, instead of saving the final round for himself, Pimdale uses the first leaving the others unused...yes! The secret device must have been hidden in one of the extra cartridges.

"...a single one of the unspent rounds that were found in the revolver after Pimdale used it to end his life," Kovsky was saying.

"That's all?" asked Ryan.

"So far as I've been able to tell amid all the excitement."

"And these young people?"

"They tried to leave while I was distracted with the evidence of theft but when they were still in the up capsule, I called the lobby to warn the museum guard to stop them before they could leave the building. He held them until the police arrived."

Jules looked over to the students who showed no sign of concern about being caught. The arrogance of the initiated still clouded their faces, even the lone female, where it seemed out of place.

Considering, Jules wondered if the same kind of bluff he'd pulled on Vecci might work here.

"Detective Ryan," he said. "Do you mind if I speak to your prisoners?"

Ryan shrugged. "Be my guest. But I have to warn you, we haven't been able to get them to talk much."

Jules went over to the students. Up close, their youthfulness became even more apparent. He could understand how easy it must have been for Romak to influence them. He decided to get right to the point.

"You're students of Prof. Romak?" he asked, choosing to use Romak's formal title thinking if he indicated some respect for their teacher, it might weaken their resistance.

It did. Most of them nodded.

"What did you think of his classes?"

No answer, just stony smiles.

"Pretty ambitious of you to try and rescue him from that institution on the Moon."

Would a compliment to their ingenuity loosen them up?

"How did you know about that?" asked one of the boys, startled.

"There was nothing to it," said another.

Jackpot!

"I wouldn't say that," encouraged Jules. "Took some real planning to pull that off."

"The hard part was getting the rocket."

"But you had some inside help, right?"

The boy shrugged.

"Did you come straight to Boston after leaving the Moon?"

Nothing.

"Oh, come on. You're not telling me anything I don't know. I'm here, aren't I? Right on your heels. You landed in Buffalo then set out from there."

That information seemed to take them by surprise.

"You didn't have time to stop anywhere else before coming here."

"Think you know it all, don't you?" challenged one of the boys.

"Shh!" shushed the girl.

"Ah, he doesn't know anything," said the boy. "Anyway, it's too late for anyone to do anything now. The professor has won."

"How's that?" challenged Jules. "Seems to me we have him on the run."

The seeming attack on their mentor's abilities was intended as an insult to their group pride. Jules hit a sensitive spot.

"It's the other way around, agent of order," declared the boy. "The professor's plan is unfolding exactly the way he wants."

There was a general consensus on this by the rest of the group. Except for the girl.

"Bim!" she warned.

Bim shrugged her off. "It's too late for anyone to stop him, Jill. Doesn't even matter that we're being arrested. By the time Prof Romak is done, we'll be heroes!"

"What do you mean by that?" asked Jules, alarmed.

"The professor's left Earth by now," said Bim. "The Consortium will never find him among the infinite worlds of the galaxy!"

Chapter Twelve

Intuition

"The Consortium will never find him among the infinite worlds of the galaxy," recalled Jules of Bim's claim to Romak's whereabouts.

Certainly, the Milky Way galaxy was a big place but the worlds claimed by the Consortium weren't infinite and neither did it make any claim on the entire galaxy. In fact, the Consortium occupied only a small portion of the Orion-Cygnus Arm and even that had to be shared with the Outer Arm Coalition.

It placed a limit on the places where Romak could be hiding. At the very least, they were within Consortium space and somewhere that was either conducive to human life or had facilities to support it in an otherwise hostile environment. Still, all that represented many worlds and lots of possibilities. How to narrow down the search?

Since the events at the Harvard Remains, the students had been taken into custody (and no doubt were even now being processed for consignment to Special Research Units to undergo deprogramming) and police cooperation secured. That left Jules with the problem of how to proceed next. By comparison, figuring out where Romak might have gone with the device he'd stolen would be like looking for a needle in a haystack.

The situation, however, wasn't hopeless.

Along with the disposition of the students and police cooperation, Jules asked Leclerc to send out an all points alert to security on Consortium worlds to look out for Romak. Retinal scans, fingerprints, and DNA had been beamed to security agencies both public and private throughout the Consortium. Meanwhile, voice and face recognition were being 'cast on commercial entertainment networks as well as individual telcomms. All, of course, without exact details as to why Romak was wanted. In addition, it was also stated that Romak may be traveling with a small entourage...his fellow escapees from Special Research Unit 6.

So, while Jules held out hope Romak would be recognized somewhere, perhaps even apprehended, he wasn't counting on it. It was in his nature to be proactive and not to sit idly by waiting for something to happen.

In that regard, he had what he believed to be an ace up his sleeve.

It was called Bayes' Theorem.

Related to probability theory and statistics, Bayes' theorem works to describe the likelihood of an event based on known conditions that could be related to the event. While the resulting equations could balance and deliver a near certain outcome, the probabilities themselves might involve different probability interpretations.

Jules was willing to take that risk.

But he'd need a tool with far more number crunching capability than even his MI issued telcomm.

Luckily, it was with the aid of his telcomm that he could access some of the most powerful computing tools in existence.

Accessing MI's reserved bandwidth, he contacted Leclerc.

"Nothing yet," was the first thing Leclerc said, anticipating Jules' question.

"Okay, then I've got something else we can work on in the meantime," replied Jules.

Leclerc perked up.

"I'll need Winnie in on this though, can you bring him in?"

"Winthrop?" queried Leclerc, puzzled. "Dr. Winthrop?"

"That's right. Link him in on this call."

A few seconds later, the familiar face of Winthrop Docha appeared beside that of Leclerc on Jules' telcomm screen.

"What can the director of computing sciences do for you, Jules?" he asked.

"No offense, but it's really your Q7000 that I need."

Winthrop rolled his eyes. "It's not very flattering when that computer is more popular than I am."

"Can't be helped this time," smiled Jules. "Listen, I need you to run a program 92 on the system. You know which one I mean?"

Winthrop nodded. "The Bayes' Theorem? Sure."

"Okay. Can you set it up so that I can feed the information directly to the Q7000 from here?"

"No problem." There was a moment's silence, then, "You're all set. Fire away."

"Hold on," chimed in Leclerc. "I'm not clear on this Bayes Theorem..."

"Sorry, sir," said Jules. "Bayes Theorem was first formulated by Thomas Bayes, an English clergyman of the eighteenth century who developed a formula that described how the probability of possible causes for an observed outcome could be computed from what was known of the probability of each cause and the probability of the outcome of each cause. Here's the formula..."

Jules textized the formula manually on his telcomm which was transmitted in nano-seconds to Leclerc. It looked like this:

$P(A|B)$ – the probability of event A occurring, given event B has occurred

$P(B|A)$ – the probability of event B occurring, given event A has occurred

$P(A)$ – the probability of event A

$P(B)$ – the probability of event B

"After I've fed it the statistics involved and the known facts of Romak's movements and intentions, the Q7000 will do the heavy lifting using this formula," continued Jules. "Built into its calculations will be certain assumptions I've made, the human factor if you will. Hopefully, between the facts and the assumptions, the resulting equation will balance out and we'll have a good estimate as to where Romak went."

"It sounds farfetched to me..." mused Leclerc.

"This theorem has proven its efficacy over the hundreds of years since Bayes first formulated it in many different contexts," assured Jules. "May I proceed?"

"Go ahead."

Quickly, Jules textized MI's super-fast diamond quantum based Q7000 with direct input of known statistics including the number of known planets within the Orion-Cygnus Arm of the galaxy as well as those known but not yet explored on the peripheries. He balanced the equation with the number of known worlds that were uninhabitable. That left considerably fewer places where Romak could have gone. Next, he inputted the assumption that Romak went to a planet that was habitable or at least that boasted facilities to support human life. Add in Romak's desire not to be found while subtracting those worlds claimed by the Outer Arm Coalition. Combining the law of averages, statistics, and a dash of human instinct (assumptions made by Jules), the Q7000 would take no more than a few seconds to run billions of probabilities, explore millions of options, before supplying the answer Jules was looking for.

In the end, that's exactly what happened but not without some surprise.

"Tobanikoganabagin?" wondered Winthrop. "What's that?

"Sounds like a Zhapoologani word," guessed Jules as he looked up the word on his telcomm.

But before the information appeared, Leclerc spoke up.

"It is Zhapoologani," he said. "It's a frontier world on our border with the Coalition. The Zhapoologani have claimed it but the Consortium hasn't recognized it yet. Although negotiations are in progress, it hasn't stopped the Zhapoologani from going ahead with terraforming activities."

"The Q7000 estimates the probability that your man is on this...Tobanikoganabagin...as 98 percent probability," noted Winthrop.

"What are the conditions on this..." Jules stumbled over pronunciation of the word. "...Zhapoologani world? You said they're terraforming it? I assume for the Zhapoologani or their allied worlds, not necessarily for Terrans?"

"Right the first time," said Leclerc. "The finished product will be too dry for human comfort. Right now, it's even worse. Breathing masks are recommended although not necessary. Prolonged exposure to the atmosphere however, will damage the lungs."

"I assume the Zhapoologani aren't interested in the tourist trade at the moment," said Jules.

"They aren't," confirmed Leclerc. "They haven't locked out visitors completely. After they lost the use of their black hole tech, the Zhapoologani knew they couldn't win a long war with us. But they had an out. Our diplomats left them an exit ramp and they took it. As a result, the Coalition allows some cooperation between themselves and the Consortium, albeit grudgingly."

"Including this...Tobanikoganabagin...let's just call it Toba for short!"

"Yes, including...Toba. In fact, there are some Terrans working there I understand."

"Good. That'll make it easier for me," said Jules. "Can you arrange it?"

"You'll need a cover story. I'll see what I can do."

"And transportation," reminded Jules.

"We'll get you there as quickly as it can be arranged," promised Leclerc before signing off.

All right, breathed Jules in relief. Now the only question was how reliable Bayes Theorem proved to be and...*Damn!*

Jules struck his forehead with the palm of his hand.

I forgot to ask Leclerc about Mooney again!

Chapter Thirteen

Wolf 359

As it turned out, the clerk at Rocketways had been right: Wolf 359 was a strange place for a woman to be traveling to.

Or, rather, 359b, the outer of the system's two planets.

Nearly eight light years from Earth, it had taken the Rocketways flight about three weeks to reach Wolf which featured a low mass star subject to infrequent flareups resulting in the inner planet being bathed in stellar radiation about three times the amount Earth received from Sol making it uninhabitable.

Not that the outer planet was much better, but at least human life could exist there under strict conditions, which was why 359b had never been more than a way station to other, more habitable worlds.

As it was, 359b featured only the bare minimum of facilities: a handful of rocket cradles and shuttle landing pads; a half dozen living domes for the few thousand semi-permanent residents, overwhelmingly male; and an assortment of construction vehicles for some limited mining operations in the hinterland surrounding the colony.

There was no atmosphere to speak of and no native life of any sort.

Not someplace Mooney would ever consider spending any time, not even for a layover. But here she was, stepping out of the receiving tunnel into what passed for a terminal. Overhead, through the clear plas of the dome, the dark sky was dominated by Wolf's sun, now quiescent but being closer to 359b than Sol was to Earth, appeared much larger, wiping out hope of seeing any other stars.

Most of her fellow passengers had been men bound for 359b or points beyond; all dusty, dirty, mining operations or freighting assignments. All would have signed three to five year contracts for wages that would take them nearly twenty years to earn back among the habitable worlds. She'd been the only female aboard and as such, earned much attention not only from her fellow passengers, but from the crew as well.

Traveling as Constance Shores, she took advantage of the attention to slowly build up a credible resume as an accounting or personnel professional so that by the time she arrived, there'd be few questions about her reasons for being on Wolf.

Not that she expected to be here for long.

On the long flight out, when she wasn't fending off clumsy advances by the male passengers, she'd had plenty of time to think things through. The union badge she'd retrieved from Shores' handbag rested safely in one of the pockets of her jumpsuit. It included a badge number suggesting it had been issued to a particular person. Mooney assumed, and hoped she was right, that the person had been Constance Shores. But the lack of any other information on the badge indicated that it wasn't tied to any particular employment...giving the holder freedom of movement on the frontier? She didn't know. What she had to do was check around, flash the badge, and find out if its number matched up with any outbound rocket or duty station. Could Shores' compatriots be right there on Wolf 359b? Or did they move on, requiring her to catch another flight? Mooney didn't know.

Hoisting the small kit bag she bought and filled up with necessaries back at the Baltimore rocket field, she decided to check at the offices of the union local. Directions from a holo kiosk showed that it was located in dome four so that's where she headed. All around her were rough characters in mining and construction uniforms that mostly meant coveralls in company colors with insignia denoting to which outfit they belonged. All of them stared, but Mooney was used to that by now.

One feature that did arrest her attention was the fact that some of the men wore union badges attached to their overalls. Deciding to make herself less conspicuous, Mooney withdrew Shores' badge from her pocket and affixed it to her jumpsuit.

Stepping out of the terminal tripped a robocab signal and in a few seconds, one pulled up to her. It was battered and scratched but apparently serviceable.

"Union local offices, dome four," she instructed as the hatch snapped shut beside her.

Immediately, there was a lurch, some grinding of gears, and the 'cab entered the smartway heading for a tube entrance only a few hundred yards away. Glancing out the clear plas walls of the tube, Mooney saw nothing much to interest her: some idle construction vehicles, a flat, rocky landscape that extended off to the horizon on either side. Not exactly a vacation spot. Idly, she allowed her thoughts to drift to Callisto, where she and Jules had gone for their honeymoon. Now there was a beautiful world with its spectacular views of Jupiter every night!

She was still lost in memory when the 'cab came to a jolting halt at a siding beneath dome four. She quickly transferred some credit to the 'cab's meter via her telcomm and exited.

Around her, high risers were reserved to various corporations, used for offices and living quarters for workers. Others were dedicated to enterprising local businesses and restaurants, all likely over charging and scheming to part workers from their hard earned credits. Not that prices could be kept low this far off the regular rocket lanes anyway. Transport rates must have been exorbitant.

Well, I didn't come here for the shopping, thought Mooney as she headed for the union offices.

With nothing on her badge to indicate which union it represented, nor what sort of employment, she hoped to get the information without revealing her ignorance. If she'd still had her own telcomm, this would not be a problem. She'd simply flash her MI identification and be done with it. But she had to go and lose it in that river. Now she had to do things the hard way.

Plas-glass doors slid aside as she entered the offices of the Exo Mining and Construction Workers local. Mooney was pleasantly surprised to find a fellow female holding down the courtesy desk.

"Nice to see I'm not the only woman on this dust ball of a planet," she said as she walked up to the work station.

The woman saw her coming and had already placed a welcoming

smile on her face.

"There's not many of us on Wolf so we have to stick together," said the woman. "But we do muster enough warm bodies to hold a dance now and then."

"Enough for a union of our own?" joked Mooney.

"Believe it or not, that subject has come up now and then."

"We'd have all the power."

"You can say that again, sister!"

They laughed.

"So, what can I do for you? Checking in?"

Mooney nodded. "What do I do next?"

She hoped she wouldn't have to volunteer any more information and she didn't. The woman, noting Mooney's badge number, was already talking to her work station, calling up the related information.

"Constance Shores?" she asked.

"That's me."

"Says here you've got a unit reserved in building 12; that's the women's quarters."

"Fine."

"Data entry? We can use someone like that here. Want to switch over?"

Data entry? Mooney thought about it a second before deciding she could do that.

She shook her head and tried to look crestfallen.

"Sorry."

"You prefer those dirty old freighters? With mineral dust all over the place? It'll wreak havoc with that nice red hair you've got."

"A contract is a contract."

The woman shrugged her shoulders. "We can break it if you want."

Mooney made a show of considering the offer before turning it down.

"No, I think I'll stick with what I've got. At least for the first trip. Maybe I'll change my mind by the time I get back."

"You will. Says here you ship on the *Tarsus*. Whoa! Leaves

tomorrow! You sure cut it close."

"There aren't many ships running this far out," explained Mooney, relieved that she'd decided to take up Shore's trail as soon as she did. "You have to take the ones that are available."

"I've entered your badge number into the system," said the woman. "You can use it to access the *Tarsus* logs and scheduling. You're all set. Good luck."

"Thanks."

Outside the office, Mooney wasted no time in looking up the *Tarsus* specs: a short haul freighter run by Mills-Dexter Corp between Wolf and a world called Tobanikoganabagin.

Hm, a Zhaboologani name, wondered Mooney. Language skills might come in handy.

The *Tarsus* included a crew of twenty-two, mostly handlers. Current assignment: running pumlite to Tobanikoganabagin in exchange for water that was then sold to the corporations working Wolf for short profits.

Mooney knew that pumlite was a key element in the manufacture of formacrete, an important feature of all modern construction. The Zhapoologani must be doing something big on Tobanikoganabagin.

Looking further, Mooney found that Tobanikoganabagin was in the register. A frontier world that the Outer Arm Coalition claimed and that the Consortium conceded in the interests of promoting amity with the Zhapoologani. A description of Tobanikoganabagin seemed to show that it would have been useless to the Consortium anyway. No prized minerals, uninhabitable for Terrans, too far out.

That last, Mooney could agree with. This sector was certainly the butt end of the Consortium.

It seemed that the *Tarsus* would be ready to leave for Tobanikoganabagin in thirty-six hours, Terran time. Mooney decided to seek out her assigned berth and grab a few hours' sleep before reporting for duty.

Nine hours later, wearing Mills-Dexter issued coveralls, Mooney stepped into the company's dispatch office.

"About time you showed up," said a pot-bellied, half shaven man behind a grimy work station. "Thought you weren't goin' to make it. Wouldn't have been surprised. We lose a lot of the ladies as soon as they catch sight of Wolf."

"It was a flight scheduling issue," explained Mooney, unruffled. "Not many come out this way."

"That's true," said the man, mollified. "Let's see that badge number."

Mooney stepped closer. Leaning in, the man squinted to read the numbers.

"485766W," he read aloud.

His work station picked up the reading and immediately displayed the relevant information with a holo projection that flickered a bit.

"Damn this 'station," swore the man, banging a fist on its surface. It did no good. "Been waitin' weeks for a tech to come look at it."

Despite his complaints, the man managed to work with the program.

"Okay. You're official. Report for crew call with the *Tarsus*. You're data entry. That's a bridge function. Report directly to Captain Wah."

"Right. Thanks."

"Uh..."

"Yes?"

Mooney was about to head out the door labeled 'crewmen only' that presumably led onto the prep area for the short drive across the apron to the freighter.

"If you ever come through here again..."

"I'll be sure to look you up," she finished, recognizing the routine.

The man brightened immediately. Mooney left him that way.

Chapter Fourteen

Tobanikoganabagin

With the ship's sub-photon drive fully engaged, the *Tarsus* only took a week to travel through the hyper-void and complete the short hop to Tobanikoganabagin.

Not that it was smooth sailing all the way. At least for Mooney.

The *Tarsus* wasn't exactly a pleasure rocket. In fact, it was just about the ugliest, most ungainly thing she'd ever seen. For sure the rusty, worn out hulk had taken a few more trips than its manufacturer guaranteed in its sales literature.

Streamlining was the last thing its designers considered in engineering it. All bump outs, extensions, and sensor pods, it was a wonder that it could make planetfall without a hard landing. But it did. Its massive holds had been filled to capacity with crushed pumlite and when Mooney first saw the payload, she expressed her doubts to the load master that the ship would be able to handle it.

"She'll take it," he said. "She's a tough ole bird. Got plenty of life left in her."

Mooney had her doubts. When the solid state engines blasted against the blackened launch pad, it felt as if the pull of Wolf 359b would never let it go. Eventually, however, after a heart stopping thirty seconds, the *Tarsus* began to win the tug of war, slowly lifting away from the surface and into orbit.

Good thing 359b had no atmosphere, Mooney thought at the time, otherwise the *Tarsus* would never have gotten away.

Once in freefall, the captain didn't waste any time engaging the main sub-photon drive. He simply had the pilot aim the ship straight for Tobanikoganabagin and disappeared into the hyper-void. For her part, Mooney held her breath during the entire process. Used to smooth sailing with military transports and modern civilian craft, the rumble and sudden clunk that echoed through the *Tarsus* when the drive was engaged rattled her. It must have shown on her face, because the other members of the bridge crew had a good time at her expense.

Well, at least her discomfort broke the ice with her fellow crewmen. The only female aboard ship, she was either leered at or treated with excessive caution. She preferred to be considered just one of the boys and by the time she settled down in the data entry cabin, she was. Even so, she made sure to muss up her looks some by stuffing her hair up into her cap and donning a pair of thick rimmed glasses she'd picked up on Wolf. Together with the shapeless coveralls, she looked a sight.

She found that she was more than capable to hold down the data entry job. Not that there was much to enter. Mostly it was monitoring the holds and making sure a time stamp was placed on the hourly readings proving that a human being looked at the readings and not simply relied on the sensors. It was a boring job but one that allowed her plenty of time to plan her next moves once on Tobanikoganabagin.

Surely, the Zhapoologani or any of their allied races, the Drool and the Sangi, would require permitting before allowing anyone else to roam about. Anyone else being Terrans as there weren't any other intelligent races among the worlds of the Consortium or the Coalition. Then again, it shouldn't be too difficult to get the permitting seeing as how Terran commercial establishments had been approved for business. Not many to be sure, but Tobanikoganabagin did boast several bars and flop houses that catered to Terran workers on layover. Also, from what she'd been able to learn from her crewmates, all there was to do on layover was getting drunk and sleeping it off. The fact that there were never more than a hundred or so Terrans on Tobanikoganabagin at any given time, should make her task of finding Shores' contact easy.

Which left the question: how to approach her, or him, or them?

On Tobanikoganabagin, with nowhere to go, whoever they turned out to be, they'd be backed into a corner. They'd feel desperate. Might lash out. She had to be ready for that. Unknown to Mills-Dexter or its employees aboard the *Tarsus*, she'd secreted her ion pistol aboard ship by the simple expedient of disassembling it and scattering the pieces about her person and her kit bag, pieces that were designed to look like other things than parts to an ion pistol. It would be a simple matter to reassemble the weapon once she was permitted by the Zhapoologani.

Mooney had still not figured out how to approach Shores' contact once she'd found them when the *Tarsus* emerged from the hyper-void just outside the ten planetary system of Tobanikoganabagin. Two days later, they were ordered into their crash couches and under two Earth Gs of thrust, Captain Wah managed to guide the ungainly vessel to a soft landing.

What followed were weeks of unloading cargo, with the most data entry work Mooney had done on the whole trip, before the empty holds were turned over to the load master and his cleanup crew. Everything had to be ship shape before the *Tarsus* could be refilled with the giant bladders holding water from Tobanikoganabagin's oceans, which were all subterranean.

It was during that down time after the pumlite had been removed and before the water was loaded, that Mooney could get away to prowl what passed as the planet's social scene.

But first, she had to deal with local Zhapoologani authorities.

Luckily, she had a bit of an advantage, When the Zhapoologani permitting official learned that she could speak his people's language with no need for her telcomm translator function, he was impressed. The stand offish nature of the Zhapoologani eased off and he became downright friendly. At least Mooney guessed it was a he. Although she learned the language as part of her duties as a translator for the Exterior Ministry, one thing she could never master was how to tell the difference between a male Zhapoologani and a female.

They looked alike, they dressed alike.

For one thing, the Zhapoologani weren't mammals so there were no distinguishing features such as breasts, or at least nothing so obvious. Both genders featured squat, bullet shaped heads with little or no neck. Pinched features rested in something that was more grayish hide than skin. Their upper torsos were heavy and broad tapering down to heavily muscled legs. Their arms were as thin as a human female's.

They dressed alike too: fancy breech clouts with heraldic sashes across their chests adorned with family or military insignia.

From her own experience, Mooney could sometimes tell a female Zhapoologani from a male when they used more colorful tones for their breech clouts. At the moment, the official facing her was sporting earth tones so she proceeded from there.

The environment on Tobanikoganabagin was dry and dusty, just the way the Zhapoologani liked it. And with their terraforming activity, they hoped to make it more so. Just the same, the atmosphere was still breathable for Terrans, at least in short exposures. Too much of it though would result in lung disease. As a result, outdoors, Terrans used breathing masks such as the one Mooney had been wearing when she stepped into the permitting office. Now she removed it in order to make herself better understood.

"I just came in on the *Tarsus*," she said. "I need a drink to wash the dust of this waste out of my throat."

"Want a drink, eh?" growled the Zhapoologani. "Try Zhapoologani drink. That put you all right for sure."

Mooney shook her head. "None of that rotgut stuff. I want one hundred per cent proof Terran alcohol."

The Zhapoologani snorted his disgust before punching a few buttons on an ancient looking control console.

"You give telcomm address?" he asked.

Mooney flashed it manually on her telcomm screen, keeping it simple.

"Done," said the Zhapoologani. "Go get your drink. Be back on ship no later than three days from now."

"Don't worry," said Mooney. "The less time I need to spend on this world, the better."

Armed with her pass, she decided to waste no time with her search.

First things first though.

Outside the permitting office, Mooney looked around at the pitiful conglomeration of formacrete huts, barracks buildings, and thrown together business establishments and picked a space between two of them that looked dark enough in the harsh, unyielding light of

Tobanikoganabagin's sun. There, she set down her kit bag and began to reassemble her ion pistol. Finished, she slipped it into one of the pockets in her all weather jacket, the one that could be reached easily if there was trouble.

Stepping out of the shadows, she scanned what passed for a street, the big formacrete mixing plants looming in the distance, and made her way to the first barroom she saw, a stinkeroo named Toba's Last Stand. Bracing herself, she barged in as if she'd done it before on a dozen different worlds and called out to the bartender.

"A whiskey, bartender," she ordered. "With a beer chaser."

While putting on her act, she took in her surroundings: glow walls gave only a dim amount of light over the bare bones room where furniture cobbled together with spare parts gathered around a battered set of tables. Sitting at some of them were crewmen between hauls and to her surprise, a couple of Zhapoologani and one of their Sangi allies.

The bar was simply a sheet of metallicus balanced on some shipping containers. The shelves behind the bar looked well stocked though.

The proprietor began to pour her drink well before she reached the bar.

"Scan our prices before you order any more, crewman," he warned, gesturing to a light board overhead where drinks and prices flickered in the uncertain power train.

Mooney had to fight to keep a straight face. The prices were unbelievably high. But then, the cost of shipping genuine Terran liquors across multiple hops through the hyper-void, way out to this butt end of the galaxy had to really cost. Likely the proprietor was himself an ex-crewman who saw more profit in overcharging thirsty workers than working the Wolf/ Tobanikoganabagin hop.

Giving a mental thanks to her MI expense account, Mooney held up her telcomm. "Sky's the limit, my friend. Sky's the limit."

"That's what I like to hear," said the bartender, clumping down a vacuum bottle of Rocketman's Ale.

"What's your name, crewman?" asked what appeared to be a grizzled veteran of the spaceways as he moved from one of the tables to

Mooney's side at the bar.

Mooney had no intention of giving the man any encouragement, but did welcome the opportunity to speak her name aloud. Hopefully, if anyone who was to meet Shores was hanging around, they'd hear her or at least that her presence here might spread through the small Terran community.

"Shores, crewman," she said. "Constance Shores. But you can call me Shores."

"I prefer Constance," leered the fellow.

"I prefer arm's length," returned Mooney, downing her whiskey in a single gulp.

"That's not very friendly, crewman," persisted the man. "Especially since I aim to pay for that drink you're havin'.'"

"Too late," said Mooney, taking up her beer. "I pay my own way."

"I like that in my women," said the man. "Independence."

"That's what I am, independent. No attachments. Sorry buster."

Since there had been no reactions among the rest of the patrons, Mooney assumed whoever she was looking for wasn't present or wasn't making their presence known. Time to move on.

"Just wanna be friends," said her erstwhile companion.

"Try one of the Zhapoologani over there," indicated Mooney. "I have it under good authority one of 'em's a female!"

"No kiddin'?"

While the man was thinking that over, Mooney took the opportunity to get away and back outdoors. It was day outside but the planet's thin atmosphere permitted stars to show through the wispy atmosphere where the sun didn't outshine them. Nevertheless, the street was empty of pedestrians as she made her way to the next bar, which seemed slightly more upscale than The Last Stand.

There, prices were even more outrageous but at least patrons could nurse their drinks under better conditions with real furniture, office cast offs from the Zhapoologani mostly, and some food basics. Enjoying the ambiance, were a bigger crowd which seemed to be made up of ship's officers and other professionals rather than simple crewmen.

Once again, Mooney went to the bar and ordered the same as

before. She could hold her liquor but only to a point. She hoped to find whomever she was looking for before it began to tell.

Also like the last time, it didn't take long for the men to take notice of her. Soon, she had a number of them offering to buy her drinks or show her the town, such as it was. She fended them off with a combination of firm refusal and the light hearted brush off. It all ended well with her leaving the bar without any recriminations and with her name having been bandied about a bit.

So far so good.

Deciding to walk off her drinks before heading to the next dive, she went over to the crewman's barracks to arrange a bunk for the night while at the same time, hoping to leave her name with the clerk.

She had no difficulty finding the single floor 'crete structure located on the edge of the settlement. Grey and featureless, it looked more like a prison stockade than a barracks. Dust stirred in the spaces between the buildings, testament to the improving environment under the Zhapoologani terraformers.

The entranceway acted more like an airlock than a doorway, the better to keep the dusty atmosphere outdoors where it belonged. Inside, Mooney wasted no time in removing her mask, appreciating the climate controlled indoors.

The front desk was a simple podium at the head of a double rank of doors extending for the length of the barracks behind it. From what she could see, the place looked tidy enough, indicating some pride on the part of the management.

"Lookin' for a cubicle?" asked a man standing behind the podium.

"What else would anyone come in here for?" she asked with falsified irritation. "Got anything for women?"

The man looked at her dusty, rumpled clothing as if confirming she was indeed a woman.

"The cubicles got doors, if that's what you want," he said. "Haven't got much call for woman boarders."

"What about toiletries?" asked Mooney, dropping her kit bag onto the shiny floor.

"We got two. Take one person at a time."

"Guess I haven't got much choice," grumped Mooney. "Where do I sign in?"

"What's your handle?" asked the man, his fingers poised over his work station.

A manual? How far off the regular space lanes were they?

"Shores," she said.

"Full name?"

Mooney sighed as if with impatience.

"Constance Shores."

"How long you expect to be on layover?"

"A few days. Not sure how many."

"You'll have cubicle twenty-one," said the man. "Just follow the numbers."

"I know how to count."

The man didn't seem to appreciate the humor. "And I don't like any hanky panky. Women mean trouble so far as I'm concerned. Last time we had one, there were fights. One guy was shivved."

"I'll do the shivving if anybody tries to put the moves on me uninvited," said Mooney, and meant it.

The man seemed to reappraise her before asking "Telcomm account?"

Mooney gave it.

"I'll be back later. Going to leave my kit bag in the room. Will it be safe?"

"Crewmen don't steal," said the man, insulted.

She'd forgotten about the union code. She nodded and went to her cubicle. It was bare bones: a bunk, a night table, a window with a wonderful view of the pumlite refineries. It might as well have been a prison cell. Locking her bag inside, she left. Might as well take in the last two bars. So far, there had been no evidence that Shores knew anyone on Tobanikoganabagin. Could she have been wrong? Had her trip all the way out here been a waste of time?

She had no sooner stepped outside again, when she was met by the same man who'd tried to pick her up at The Last Stand.

"Still not interested, crewman," she said by way of brushing him off.

"You're Constance Shores, right? Late of Special Research Unit 6?"

Mooney stopped short.

"Thought so," said the man. "Follow me. I'll take you to the others."

He sauntered off toward the rear of the barracks building. Mooney followed, making sure her ion pistol was still where she could reach it in a hurry. She'd hoped there would be only a single contact but if there were more than one, well, it would just make things a little more difficult than she anticipated.

At the back of the building, the man first led the way into the emergency exit then to a cubicle down a side corridor from the main hall where her own cubicle was located.

The man removed his breathing mask and brushed a hand against a door, activating sensors that swished it aside.

Zhapoologani design, noted Mooney, just like the rest of the building.

Removing her own mask, she stepped inside the cubicle where several others were waiting for them.

"She the one?" asked one of the women.

"Yes. She identified herself as Constance," said the man, joining the others on the opposite side of the cubicle.

Mooney remained silent. Preferring to let the others do the talking. With luck, she could learn enough to continue her bluff.

"So, you're Constance Shores?" asked one of the men.

"That's right," replied Mooney.

"Wrong!" The man stepped forward suddenly and knocked the hat off Mooney's head, allowing her crimson tresses to tumble free. "And those glasses don't help either."

"What goes on here?" demanded Mooney.

"We should be the ones asking that," said the woman. "Who are you? You're not Shores."

"Of course I am," insisted Mooney. "Got my union badge right here..."

Some in the group laughed.

"Don't you think we'd know a woman we spent years with in that asylum on the Moon?"

One of them produced an ion pistol before Mooney could move.

"Search her, Ronny," said the man holding the pistol.

Ronny, the man she'd met in the bar, patted her down, soon finding her telcomm and pistol.

I'm in a real fix now, thought Mooney. Apparently, she'd fooled no one with her disguise allowing them to get the drop on her.

"I asked you before, who are you?" said one of the women.

Mooney chose not to answer.

"Doesn't matter, anyway," said another. "Take 'er out to the plant and throw 'er in to the pumlite mixer. No one'll ever find the body."

"Wait a minute," said the woman. "Maybe we should wait until Romak gets here? He might find her useful."

"What for?"

The woman shrugged. "Hostage or something."

"That's all?"

"I agree. No rush to kill her. She isn't goin' anywhere."

The man who wanted to kill her shrugged. "Okay. So what do you want to do with her?"

"Lock her in here until Romak arrives. He should be here soon."

With that, they shoved Mooney into a corner and retreated from the room, securing the door behind them.

Finally, Mooney allowed herself a sigh of relief before she was struck by a wave of nausea. Holding her stomach, she fell onto the bunk and fought off the feeling, just as she'd done a few times before over the last weeks.

I have no time for this, she chided herself. *Have to concentrate on the job. There'll be enough time to worry about it later.*

She just had time to master herself when the door swished open again and another prisoner was shoved into the room.

His presence gave her the shock of her life.

"Jules!"

Chapter Fifteen

Escape

Even before the door had closed behind him, Mooney was in Jules' arms, laughing with relief but also with concern. It was good to see him safe again, even if they were both prisoners. But she had faith that with the two of them together, they would find a way out and even save the day.

But something was wrong. She could feel it through Jules' embrace. There was something tentative about it, lacking warmth. She pulled away and there was a look of recognition in his eyes that should not have been there.

"Mooney!" he exclaimed. "What are you doing here?"

"I followed Shores' trail and it led here," replied Mooney, hesitantly.

"Shores?"

Instantly, she was on alert. Something was wrong here.

"Constance Shores? The woman who was involved with Bikari?"

"Bikari?"

"Yes, Bikari. Don't you remember?"

"I never heard of either of those people." He lowered his voice. "Are you here on a mission for the Exterior Ministry?"

Now she was sure of it. This wasn't her Jules, this was Jules-prime, the other Jules that came into existence after she and her Jules saved the galaxy from the dangers of black hole technology. Part of Jules' solution to the crisis involved a rewind of time resulting in there being two of him, both exactly the same in every respect. But her Jules was the one who knew of the duplication, Jules-prime was ignorant of it. As a result, Jules chose not to reveal his existence to Jules-prime and chose to let him proceed thinking all was right with the galaxy and to return to his wife, Joan, back on Mars. Since then, her Jules went on with his new life which included marriage to her and no contact with Jules-prime. None of it came without a price; Jules had been plagued by his conscience for several years until finally learning to live with his decision.

All that, however, left Mooney with a problem right now. Jules-prime was beginning to suspect something wasn't right. Being the exact same person as her own Jules, she knew how brilliant he was. How quickly he could grasp any situation. He knew!

As a result, before she could reply to his last question, he went on to the next.

"The way you flew at me," he began. "That was more than relief at seeing an old friend. You expected me to know about Shores and Bikari. Who did you think I was?"

"I..."

"Come clean."

Mooney thought quick but there was no way around it. She couldn't explain why she expected him to know Shores and Bikari. Considering their situation, and the need to act together...quickly, she decided to tell him the truth and hope her Jules would understand.

"It's a long story..."

"Give me the condensed version," said Jules-prime.

She told him.

"Whew," he sighed when she'd finished. "I've always suspected such a thing was possible and even wondered why it didn't happen. Nice to know that I was right. Still, your Jules ultimately made the right choice keeping me in the dark. One of us had to and since he was in the know it only made sense for him to be the one to make the sacrifice.

"But then, maybe things turned out all right for him after all," he concluded, staring at Mooney.

"It didn't come easy for him," she said, feeling somewhat awkward. After all, this was literally the same man she married. "For a long time, he felt guilty with feelings of abandoning Joan."

"I can understand that."

"He told me he had a long talk with his...I mean, your brother, Andrew...and it helped to straighten things out for him..."

"He met Andrew? When?"

"Last year."

"How do you like that? I saw Andrew only a few months ago before Joan and I came out here. He never mentioned anything about your Jules."

"I think that was part of an agreement between the two of them. You'll have to take it up with Jules whether it was the right thing to do or not."

"I won't make a fuss, I promise, but I am eager to meet your Jules."

"But how did you wind up here on Tobanikoganabagin? You said Joan is with you?"

Jules-prime nodded. "The Survey received a permit from the Zhapoologani to do some geological work here before the planet is fully terraformed. We've got a base camp about fifty miles north of here. That's where I left Joan to come in to the settlement for some supplies. We've got our shuttle grounded and it has some survival gear but we were getting tired of the same menu of prepared foods. Thought one of the Terran's doing business here might sell us some foodstuffs to diversify our meals. Unfortunately, I approached the wrong people. I was taken aback when they started talking about Humanism. Thought that thing died over a hundred years ago. They were pretty animated about it. Kept talking about how soon it was going to sweep through the Consortium, turn the tables on the establishment. I tried to back away but my efforts to patronize them, keep them calm, may have been too obvious. Suddenly there were ion pistols pointed at me and they were arguing about whether they should kill me right away or hold me over until somebody named Romak turned up. Overall, I thought none of them were too stable."

"You were right," said Mooney. "All of them are refugees from an insane asylum on the Moon called Special Research Unit 6."

"Really? Say, what goes on here, anyway? How are you involved?"

"Leclerc called us in on a different kind of mission than the science division usually handles," explained Mooney. "More political

158

than scientific."

"Oh?"

"It seemed Leclerc said he needed agents whom he could absolutely trust to keep the whole thing quiet. It was a compliment, I guess." Mooney thought a moment before proceeding. "I suppose I'm breaking that trust now by filling you in. Then again, you are the same Jules as my Jules so I suppose, technically, I'm not betraying any confidences."

"No wonder I haven't heard much from Leclerc the last couple of years," said Jules-Prime. "He's been taking his assignments to you and your Jules."

"And because of that, we've hardly been able to enjoy our new home in Nevada."

"Nevada? Not around Joshua Tree? Would love to get a place out there."

"Of course, you would," laughed Mooney, before filling in Jules-prime on the whole situation beginning with the theft of the *Elements of Humanism* and ending with their current situation.

"Tobanikoganabagin is the perfect hiding place," Mooney concluded. "They joined the union back on earth before traveling to Wolf and the badges fooled Zhapoologani officials into letting them stay."

"Makes sense," agreed Jules-prime. "What worries me though, is your presence here. All that Jules or Leclerc know about what you've been up to, is that you left Wolf to come here?"

"Afraid so."

"That means we're on our own."

"We?"

"Of course. Now, first thing is to get out of here."

"My thoughts exactly."

"Well, then, have you given any thought on how to escape?" asked Jules-prime.

"Not yet. I was hardly in here for a few minutes before you showed up."

Mooney felt there was no need to tell him that she had spent those few minutes combating a spell of nausea.

"Well," said Jules-prime, looking over the cubicle, "the good thing is that these rooms weren't designed as prison cells. That makes them inherently insecure."

"Can't use this door," observed Mooney, running a hand along its surface, and getting no response. "It's been secured and no doubt, the group left someone on watch."

"Which leaves this window," said Jules-prime, walking over to it and checking its fastenings. "Not made to open."

"With climate control, there's no need to. In fact, with the atmospheric conditions outside, there's no reason to open it."

"Doesn't mean we can't use it," said Jules-prime, absently digging his fingernails into the seal that secured the unbreakable plex pane in place.

Mooney joined him at the window. By then, Jules-prime had begun to pry the seal off the pane.

"If we can remove the seal, we should be able to remove the pane too," he said.

Together, they both began to work over the seal and soon, it pulled away neatly and had been thrown aside.

Next, Jules-prime tapped vigorously against the pane until it jogged loose near the top. From there, it was an easy thing to take hold and pull out of the frame. Immediately, the weak, dusty atmosphere from outside, swept into the room.

"Better put on our masks," said Jules-prime.

"Doesn't seem to be a long drop," observed Mooney, leaning out of the window.

"Ladies first," said Jules-prime.

Mooney threw herself onto the sill and wormed her way to the outside. Then, hanging from her fingers, dropped the few feet to the ground.

Jules-prime followed suit.

"We need to get to a telcomm," said Mooney. "Then contact Leclerc for back up."

"That's good so far as it goes," agreed Jules-prime. "But help won't get here for days, maybe weeks, even if a naval cruiser was in the area."

"We'll have to keep the group under observation and find some way to keep them here until it does," said Mooney.

"I think the best move would be for you to go back to the freighter you came in on and get one of the crewmen to lend you their telcomm," suggested Jules-prime. "I'll stay here and snoop around, find out where all the players are."

"Sounds good," agreed Mooney. "I'll get back as soon as I can. We'll meet back here?"

"Okay, but you better keep away from the hub of the settlement. Less likely you'll be spotted. We don't know yet if all the members of the group are inside the barracks or not."

"Good idea."

Leaving Jules-prime, Mooney took the long way through and around various outbuildings, storage sheds, equipment parks, and pumlite dumps until she came into sight of the landing fields where the *Tarsus* still rested at the far end. It had grown dark but lights around the ship indicated that cleanup and loading operations were still going on.

Feeling safer away from the possible prying eyes of the Humanists, she came out into the open and approached the *Tarsus*. There, Mooney wasted no time in going inside, seeking the load master. She found him in the near empty hold as the first bladders of water were being brought aboard by Zhapoologani drivers.

"Darye," said Mooney, raising her voice over all the noise. "Can I use your telcomm for a minute?"

Darye turned, surprised to see Mooney during actual operations.

"What're you doin' ere, Shores? Why aren't ya draggin' the bars with the others?"

"Got some business to attend to," said Mooney. "But some grifter lifted my telcomm. Can I use yours to make a call?"

The man frowned, as if to register his disapproval of Mooney's carelessness, but pulled out his device anyway. He canceled the voice recognition function before handing it over to Mooney.

"Thanks," said Mooney, turning and walking away out of earshot.

Quickly, she followed the same protocol in bypassing the unit's civil functions and accessing the dedicated MI bandwidth and from there logged onto Leclerc's personal sub-routine.

"Manda!" was the first thing Leclerc said after recognizing her own personal passcode. "Where have you been? Why haven't you reported in?"

"I can't go into detail now," said Mooney, stepping over Leclerc's last words. "I'm on an outworld called Tobanikoganabagin. The Humanist group is hiding out here waiting for someone called Romak whom I think is their leader and the mastermind behind everything that's happened since the theft of the book..."

"He is," interrupted Leclerc, not bothering to ask any more about how Mooney ended up right in the middle of the Humanist nest. "Jules is on the way there now to arrest him."

Though she was surprised and delighted to hear that her Jules was on the way, Mooney didn't ask for details. "How soon will he be here?"

"At any time," said Leclerc. "He's aboard a naval cruiser, the fastest transport I could arrange."

"Fine. We'll do what we can to keep the Humanists under observation until he gets here."

"Who's we?" asked Leclerc, suspicious.

"No time for that now," said Mooney quickly. "Mooney out."

Mooney hardly had time to register her relief that Jules might arrive at any minute before she felt a tap on the shoulder.

It was Darye.

"Couldn't help overhearing what you were saying," he said.

Mooney noticed then that the noise in the hold was gone. Operations ceased while she was reporting with Leclerc. As a result, she hadn't retreated far enough away to keep Darye from eavesdropping.

"You some kind of police woman?" he asked.

Mooney decided that the best policy at the moment was to come clean. "Something like that."

"And you're in trouble?"

"Sort of. It's under control though."

"Didn't sound like it to me. Sounded as if you're gonna need help keeping an eye on these people you were talking about. You can't do it by yourself."

"Well, I..."

"That union badge," said Darye, pointing at the badge Mooney still wore attached to her coveralls, "represents solidarity. Means members stick together no matter the situation."

"Like you said, I'm a...policewoman...not a real union member."

"Doesn't matter. You wear the badge."

"Are you volunteering to help?"

Darye nodded. "Yeah, and the first thing I'm gonna do is get the word out to the other crewmen. We'll have a dozen men here in no time."

Before Mooney could object, Darye reengaged his voice code on his telcomm and sounded the alarm. In a few minutes, true to his word, a dozen *Tarsus* crewmen gathered in the hold and were listening to Darye's explanations.

Resigned to the well-meaning load master's actions, Mooney told the group as much as she thought they needed to know including her status as an agent for Military Intelligence, the presence of Jules-prime, and the danger posed to the Consortium by the Humanist gang that she believed were holed up in the Terran barracks building.

By the time she finished, the group were fired up and anxious to get going. In fact, when she'd finished, Mooney also felt buoyed by their presence. Darye might have had a good idea after all. With so many extra eyes, she and Jules-prime would be able to keep the entire building under surveillance and could even spare people to follow anyone that left it.

After cautioning the crewmen to silence, she led them back the way she'd come, arriving at the rear of the barracks where Jules-prime was waiting.

His eyes widened when he saw the large group of space veterans in Mooney's wake.

"What's this? Playing pied piper?"

"They volunteered to help and after thinking it over, I thought we could use them," said Mooney.

"I think so too," agreed Jules-prime. "There are a number of entrances to this building and we couldn't have watched them all with just the two of us."

After a hurried consultation, they spread the crewmen around the building, hopefully with most out of sight. Not without a word of caution from Jules-prime however.

"These people are armed," he said. "We know that they have at least two ion pistols. So don't take any chances with them. Don't confront them. Just keep an eye on the entrances and if anyone leaves, follow at a discreet distance. You got that?"

They all nodded in agreement, still somewhat dazed that they found themselves involved in an important government operation.

Jules-prime then led them around the building, depositing a few at every entrance and rank of windows. When he'd finished and completed the circuit, he returned to Mooney, who waited across the avenue from the building's main entrance.

"All set?" she asked.

Jules-prime nodded. "So far as I can tell, they're all inside, toward the rear."

"You sure?" asked Mooney, looking around the empty street.

"Positive. While you were gone, a man I didn't see with the rest of the gang showed up and went inside. I have a feeling it was this Romak character they said they were waiting for."

"Perfect," said Mooney. "Leclerc told me that he's the mastermind behind all this and that the other Jules was right behind him."

"Let's hope so," said Jules-prime. "Because if they choose to start something, I don't know if we'll be able to stop them. And I don't want to see any of these volunteers hurt."

"Neither do I," agreed Mooney, looking up to the dusky sky as if expecting to see Jules' shuttle coming in to the rescue, "so do I."

Chapter Sixteen

Siege

Leclerc was as good as his word.

The naval K-class cruiser he arranged for Jules, brought them to Tobanikoganabagin in near record time. As a result, Jules was confident they would either beat Romak here or at least be hard on his heels.

But as they approached the Zhapoologani world, complications arose.

Despite the recent entente between the Consortium and the Coalition, relations could still be a bit frosty. It would take time for either side to let their respective guard down and become true neighbors. As a result, the Zhapoologani would still be nervous if a Consortium fighting ship suddenly appeared in orbit.

For that reason, Jules judged it expedient to stand off and make the final approach in a less ostentatious style.

Conferring with the ship's captain, it was decided to replace the markings on the ship's descent shuttle with some suggesting it belonged to a local shipping line complete with company slogan: "No job too small!"

Inside, of course, would be Jules and an MI tac team, the same that had accompanied him to Africa.

Then came the thunderbolt from Leclerc: Mooney would be on the surface to welcome them.

"You're kidding!" was all Jules could muster.

His wife never ceased to surprise him which, of course, was par for the course for women, wasn't it?

Still, this was an incredible coincidence, or was it? Mooney's last communication stated she was following a trail left by Shores that led off world; all the way out to Wolf 359 which, of course, was in this sector.

Jules shook his head in disbelief as Leclerc filled him in on Mooney's plan. Apparently, she'd found Romak's group holed up in a barracks used by Terrans when planetside. With the help of others, she'd managed to recruit, they were keeping the place under observation. He and the tac team were to meet her there, get updated on the situation, and proceed as Jules saw fit. Preferably without the need for violence.

Jules had his doubts about that. Romak was a fanatic, as Humanists tended to evolve into, and with the device he retrieved from the Harvard Remains, believed he had the winning hand. To just give up when he was so close to success seemed unlikely.

Thus, when Jules joined Daly and his tac team in the shuttle's personnel bay, he made sure they were fully loaded.

"Ready?" he asked Daly.

"All set."

"Remember, the priority is keeping things peaceful," reminded Jules. "I'm told the Zhapoologani won't interfere, even if there's some shooting. So long as the Consortium supports their claim to Toba, they're inclined to cooperate with us."

"Enough to turn a blind eye?"

"Yes. They have zero interest in the affairs of the Consortium. We could blow ourselves up for all they care."

"Feeling's mutual," mumbled one of the team members.

Jules chose to ignore the sentiment. "On the ground, I'm in charge. But if they refuse to surrender, we'll have to force the issue. If they resist, we're authorized to use whatever level of persuasion we want commensurate with the occasion.

"All right, pilot," called Jules, strapping himself in. "Take us down."

There was a sharp clang as the bay doors opened beneath them, a roar as the atmosphere trapped in the bay whooshed into space, a momentary sense of weightlessness as the shuttle fell through into freefall.

The rest of the ride was uneventful until the whine of Tobanikoganabagin's thin atmosphere began to warm the deck plates. But before the temperature rose to anything like an uncomfortable level, they were slowing down and on approach to the Zhapoologani terra forming base with its accompanying settlement. There was a sudden jar as the pilot applied reverse thrust, more roaring, more whining from protesting deck plates and then they were down; so softly Jules hardly felt a thing.

That pilot is good, he thought, as he swiftly undid his safety harness along with the rest of the tac team.

"Set you down at the edge of the landing area, Mr. Conroi," called the pilot from over his shoulder. "The barracks are north by northeast. As ordered, we'll wait for you here."

"Roger that," replied Jules, waiting for the exit ramp to come down amid swirling dust.

Mooney telcommed the directions to the barracks and using his own device, he could follow them unerringly.

The tac team consisted of eight men including Daly and all followed Jules in single file, with plenty of space in between each. Most were armed with rapid fire ion rifles with the anchor man carrying a portable pulse cannon in case of barricade.

But they had hardly left the area when Mooney was there to meet them.

"Over here, Jules," she called, her words muffled beneath a breathing mask.

After giving him a quick, businesslike hug, Mooney stayed close to say:

"There's something you should know before we go any farther."

"What's that?" asked Jules, suddenly concerned.

"By sheer coincidence, Jules-prime is here too!"

She didn't have to say any more. Jules-prime was the name they'd always used in referring to the other Jules.

"He's here with Joan on a mission for the Survey," continued Mooney. "I was forced to tell him about you and what happened on the black hole mission."

"How did he take it?"

Mooney shrugged. "Very well. He seemed to have deduced something like that might have happened so he wasn't surprised. His attitude reminded me a lot of you, actually."

"Of course. Well, we'll have to deal with this later. Where is he now?"

"We've kind of teamed up," said Mooney. "He's watching the main entrance to the barracks. We'll join him there...unless you want to cover another part of the building for now...?"

"That's okay. We might as well start getting used to each other. We're going to have to have a long talk afterward."

Joan was something else though, thought Jules. After so many years, he wondered what he'd say to her, how could he explain? What would he feel when he met her again? He dreaded the return of the complicated emotions he'd had to deal with when he first made the decision to let Jules-prime go back to her and later, marrying Mooney. Would all the old feelings of guilt rise up again?

"Come on," urged Mooney, having moved off a few steps.

With an effort, Jules shook off his concerns and concentrated on the job at hand. He hoped the Humanists would surrender peaceably. If so, it would be just a matter of transporting them back to Special Research Unit 6...if it had been placed under new management in the meantime. As for Romak himself...well, he'd been responsible for many deaths already so his fate was more problematical. That left the question: would he give himself up?

And what about the device he'd found? Did Romak still have it in his possession?

Jules was still wrestling with those questions when they arrived at the main entrance to the barracks building, where Jules-prime took cover around the corner of a warehouse across the way. Everyone quickly followed suit and a conference held to determine next steps.

Jules tried to discern himself behind the breathing mask worn by his counterpart, but failed. There was no doubt however, it was him all right. Jules-prime said nothing, as did he. As if by unspoken agreement, they simply nodded in recognition and proceeded with the work at hand.

"There's been no activity around the building since you left," reported Jules-prime. "The *Tarsus* crewmen are still posted around the building and report no movement."

"Crewmen?" wondered Jules.

"My fellow crewmates from the *Tarsus*," explained Mooney. "They volunteered to help."

"I'm not even going to ask," said Jules, smiling, then: "Have you been able to determine how many of them are in there?"

Jules-prime shrugged. "There were over half a dozen in sight when they captured me and since then, one man has slipped inside."

"Thirteen of Romak's fellow inmates of Special Research Unit 6 escaped with him and one has been apprehended," said Jules. "There hasn't been any evidence that they've split up so, with Romak, that leaves as many as thirteen holed up in there."

"What about weapons?" asked Jules-prime. "Any information about that?"

"They have at least one ion pistol of their own," confirmed Mooney. "Plus, the one they took from me. Of course, it was DNA coded so they can't use that."

"Still, we can't rely on the fact that they might have only a single gun," said Daly.

"We'll proceed as if they're fully armed," said Jules. "Daly, spread your men around the building. Have them join whatever crewmen who are already on post. But no shooting unless they get the order directly from me."

Daly nodded and began to disperse his men, retaining the team member armed with the pulse cannon with Jules.

No sooner had the tac team been dispersed than a message from one of the crewmen on watch came in to Jules-prime.

"There seems to be some activity inside the barracks," he reported. "Some shouting and moving around."

"They must have finally noticed that Jules and I have escaped," guessed Mooney.

"Then this is as good a time as ever to demand their surrender," said Jules. "While they're off balance."

Using the public address feature among the tac team's equipment, he stepped out and addressed the Humanists.

"Romak!" Jules paused to allow the thunder of his voice to carry over to the barracks. No doubt anyone inside heard him. "Romak!" he said again. "This is Military Intelligence agent Victor Conroi. For your safety and those of the others, I'm asking you to throw down your weapons and come out peaceably. No harm will come to you."

There was a pause and Jules was surprised when the whole group emerged from the front entrance. They came out with their hands up, Romak in the rear.

Relieved with the cooperation, Jules again spoke into the public address device. "Throw down your weapons."

A single ion pistol was tossed onto the ground.

"It doesn't work anyway," said one of the women in the group.

"We know you have another weapon," insisted Jules.

"Listen to me," shouted Romak, suddenly, pushing himself to the front of the crowd. "What we're doing, we're doing for you. All of you! We're fighting for your freedom! Freedom from the oppression of the Consortium and its deadening rules. It gives you no control over your own bodies! No control over your own identities! Anyone who disagrees is labeled insane and confined to asylums for brainwashing! I urge you to lay down your arms and join us! Together, we can be the catalysts for fundamental change in the Consortium!"

"You're a fool, Romak," returned Jules. "You've read about humanism in Pimdale's book, but that's only theory. What's more, it's theory that can't and didn't work in the real world. You're a college professor, you know history. History is concerned only with facts, not the flights of fancy the old Humanists believed in. All their beliefs, their policies, every one turned out to not only be wrong, but harmful to everyone who embraced them. They turned ordinary people into heartless oppressors, the same way the old Nazis turned ordinary shop keepers into rabid haters. The ultimate result of unfettered humanism, is the gulag. There is no true freedom without a matching morality. After the Constitutional wars, the Consortium rededicated itself to the ancient values of Western culture which in turn, was the creation of Christianity. The Consortium already offers freedom for all, but without guardrails, that same freedom can turn to oppression."

Jules dared to hope that maybe his argument might strike a chord in Romak, prompt him to rethink his positions, but it was a forlorn hope and he knew it. By now, Romak was too far gone. Secondarily, he wanted to combat any influence Romak might have had among the tac team and the crewmen. As it was, they'd all have to be placed in isolation following the conclusion of the mission until experts could determine whether their minds had been affected by Romak's words.

In the meantime, Romak wasn't wasting any time.

At his word, his followers rushed forward, directly toward Jules and the others. In no time, they were among them and there was a general melee of flying fists and struggling forms as the Humanists threatened to overwhelm their outnumbered opponents.

Chapter Seventeen

Data Bomb

Jules felt the weight of the charge throw him back as he sought to defend himself against a pair of attackers and even as he did so, he sensed more than saw that Mooney was holding her own, using judo moves to convert her opponents' momentum against them. But he knew that following the initial rush, the odds would increasingly be against her as the weight and height of bigger, heavier male opponents took their toll.

They needed reinforcements and quick.

Suddenly; just like that, they were there!

A mix of tac team members and *Tarsus* crewmen flanked the Humanists, taking them by surprise and as the tide turned, Jules caught Romak beating a retreat into the barracks building.

"Stop where you are, Romak!" he ordered.

He really didn't expect Romak to listen and was confirmed in his belief as the former college professor ducked inside the barracks.

Drawing his ion pistol, Jules lit out after him, followed closely by Mooney. Together, they threw themselves to either side of the entranceway.

Jules tried again. "Romak, surrender! It's all over!"

No reply. He'd have to do it the hard way.

Mooney was still unarmed so he signaled her to hang back.

Counting to three, Jules threw himself inside, rolling on the floor into a prone position and firing his pistol as he did, hoping to keep Romak under cover. It seemed to work as there was no return fire.

"He's in the fourth cubicle on the right," said Mooney from the entranceway. "I saw him duck inside out of the way when you fired."

Seeing how Romak was still out of view, Jules resumed shooting in the direction of the occupied cubicle even as he threw himself into another directly opposite.

"Romak," he tried again. "You're trapped. You have no way out. Throw down your weapon and come out with your hands in the air."

In response, there was a searing sound and Jules saw the results of an invisible ion beam as it scoured across the door frame and into the near wall of the cubicle that he'd sought shelter in. As Romak, like any amateur, waited to discover the effect of his shot, Jules fired back.

Instantly, Romak flew back, out of sight.

Jules knew he hadn't missed and chanced a dash across the corridor. His shoulder struck the door jamb across the way, his arm raised in readiness, pistol poised to shoot instantly with any sign of danger.

There was none.

Romak lay sprawled across a bunk, a hand covering the wound in his chest. Jules had missed the heart but the damage was no less mortal.

He kicked Romak's fallen pistol out of the room before approaching him, his own weapon still at the ready.

Romak was still breathing, still conscious, but no longer a threat.

"Mooney!" he called.

Instantly, Mooney was at the door, taking in the scene.

"We need a medic," said Jules. "Find one."

Without a word, Mooney left.

"You're too late, agent man," coughed Romak who was apparently not so bad off that he could not resist taunting Jules. "The information contained in the device has already been uploaded to the super cloud. It will reach to every corner of the Consortium. With enlightenment in their hands, the people will soon begin to question themselves, second guess the so-called values that they've always taken for granted. They will see things in a different light until at last, realize that they've been duped all along. There will be revolution in thought and then in deed. There's nothing you can do to stop it now. Freedom, at last, will prevail over the entire Consortium!"

With Romak's words, Jules' blood froze.

Talk of uploading and the super cloud, could only mean a data bomb. A single, massive dump of information that could instantly permeate the bandwidths of sub-space communications, overload the nanite network that policed them, and insinuate itself into the billions of personal telcomms that were indispensable to modern society. Humanist poison would spread everywhere, unstoppable, uncontrollable, dangerous in the extreme!

Jules forced himself to remain calm.

If there was still a chance to stop the looming disaster; if perhaps, Romak was exaggerating when he said it was too late, then there might still be time to act.

Just then, Mooney reappeared.

"The only person I could find qualified to treat Terrans was the medico assigned to the *Tarsus*," she explained.

"Matto Cohen..." was all the man had time to say before Jules interrupted him.

"No time for introductions," said Jules. "I need this man to talk. No matter if he dies afterward. He must be made to talk. All I can tell you is that the whole Consortium is at stake. Millions could die."

But Cohen hadn't paused to listen to Jules' explanations, he was already bending over Romak, examining the wound.

"An ion burn?" he asked.

It was a rhetorical question.

"Do you need help removing his tunic?" asked Mooney.

"No need," said Cohen, opening a flat case he'd brought with him.

Inside, was a simple control panel with most of the rest of the space given over to the storage of several prepared osmotic syringes.

"Open," he told the case, and a holo bounced into the air before him.

Taking one of the syringes, he injected its contents into Romak's arm, through the fabric of his tunic.

Next, he began to speak to the hologram as it responded to his commands. It showed what was obviously the interior of Romak's body, the scene shifting, magnifying, resolving to Cohen's spoken directions.

In the meantime, Mooney signaled Jules to join her outside the room.

"What is it?" he asked, irritated.

"I found this in one of the other cubicles," said Mooney, holding up an old hard covered book.

"*Elements of Humanism*?" asked Jules, unnecessarily.

Mooney nodded. "He must have taken it from Shores' unit; between my first search when I was interrupted by Shores and my second after she was taken into custody."

"Well then, technically, retrieval of the book makes our assignment a success."

"Leclerc will be happy to hear that."

"I should be glad the way it all turned out, but I'm not," said Jules. "If Romak succeeded in dropping his data bomb into the sub-space communications network, it won't make any difference."

With not a little trepidation, Jules took out his telcomm, accessed the holo function, checked various bandwidths and found to his relief, that there was yet no sign of contamination. What did it mean? Was something delaying full implementation of the data dump? If so, it meant there was still a chance of stopping it. However, every second counted. Who knew how close the Consortium was to final disaster.

As he pondered the possibilities, the corridor outside Romak's cubicle had begun to fill with tac team members and curious crewmen.

"What's the situation?" asked Daly, reaching Jules' side.

"Still up in the air," said Jules. "I had to shoot Romak and a doctor is in there with him now. As soon as he's able to, and even if he's not, he has to talk. I need more information."

Daly didn't ask what information that was or, indeed, what the whole mission was about. It was not his business.

"Well, we've got the rest of the gang secured," he reported. "They're all pretty cocky. Like they still expect to come out on top. No injuries except some skinned knuckles. They've also been talking about some wild stuff..."

"Ignore them," said Jules. "And make sure they're gagged. Use the speech inhibitors we brought. You heard what Romak was saying outside?"

Daly nodded but kept his speculations to himself.

"Look," said Jules. "I need to get back inside. You and the tac team can take the prisoners back to the shuttle, okay?"

"Yes, sir," acknowledged Daly. "And sir? Good luck with whatever it is you're up to."

"Thanks, Daly. We'll need it."

Squeezing past the onlookers, Jules reentered the cubicle to find that not much had changed. He joined Mooney where she stood by looking over Cohen's shoulder at the holo of the insides of Romak's chest cavity.

Answering Jules and Mooney's unspoken questions, Cohen said "The syringe I used on the patient contained pre-programmed nanites. In this case, nanites programmed to treat burn injuries similar to those caused by an ion pistol. Through visuals relayed to the holo, I can follow their progress and direct them when necessary. No need for any kind of intrusive surgery."

"Can you get him in shape to talk?" was all Jules wanted to know.

"Yes," said Cohen. "Injury caused by the ion beam wasn't extensive and as you can see, the wound is already being closed."

As Jules watched, he sighed with relief. Cohen opened the tunic some and the wound did indeed appear smaller, less fearful, than it was.

Just then, Romak heaved with the intake of a sudden breath.

Jules was immediately on the alert.

"Can he talk, doctor?"

Cohen shook his head, his eyes leaving the holo to look at the wound in real time. "The lung has been healed as well as most of the surrounding musculature, but as you can see, the wound itself is still open..."

"Can he talk? Is he conscious?"

"I'm conscious," came the weak reply from Romak's own lips. "I expect the Consortium is already feeling the effects of the upload?"

Jules held his hands up, silently cautioning Mooney and the doctor to silence.

"Get those people away from here and close the door," he whispered to Mooney.

He decided to humor Romak in his mistaken belief that the data bomb had succeeded. If he believed victory was achieved, he'd be more willing to talk. Or at least Jules hoped so.

"You haven't won yet," said Jules, hoping to make his story sound more believable. "We have the best men in quantum communications working on the problem. If there's a way to stop the spread, they'll find it."

Romak tried to laugh, but it was still too painful. "Not likely. You know as well as I do that once uploaded to sub-space, the program can never be recalled. It's just too widespread. Wherever it's allowed to remain unmolested, it'll grow, it'll expand. You'll never be rid of it."

Wasn't that the truth, worried Jules. Still, his telcomm had shown that for some reason, the data had not yet been distributed. Something had held it up and if he could just find out what it was...

"If you're that confident, then you can tell me how you did it," said Jules, very cautiously. He didn't want to spook Romak. Give him any suspicions.

There was no need to worry. Romak wanted to talk. Wanted to gloat.

"Simplicity itself," he said, weakly. "I used Shores' telcomm...or should I say, that woman standing with you. A fellow agent, I presume?"

"Yes," acknowledged Mooney.

"Enchanted," returned Romak, courteously. "I'm sorry I was not able to make your acquaintance earlier. I was told you are quite a formidable woman."

Mooney disregarded the compliment, preferring instead to ask Romak what he meant by Shores' telcomm.

"Well not exactly the telcomm you brought with you when you were taken by my associates," said Romak.

"This one," he continued, holding up a telcomm that had been out of sight beneath his prone form. "The one you so handily dropped in your altercation with Shores aboard that river boat."

"What?" cried Mooney, grabbing the telcomm from Romak's hand. "What do you mean? My telcomm was lost in the river..."

"Ah! Is that what you assumed?" Romak smiled. "If so, you were wrong. You must have dropped it on the ship's deck during your fight with Shores. At least, that's where we found it later when my students and I went aboard to collect Shores before heading to the museum.

"It was that telcomm that allowed my plans for the ancient humanist device to be accomplished in the most efficient manner. How ironic, how delicious would it be if the doom of the Consortium could be accomplished with a device belonging to an organization dedicated to maintaining its authority!"

With the words, Jules could almost feel Mooney's blood run cold with the realization that her carelessness may have contributed to the end of their civilization. He gave her arm a reassuring squeeze as his own mind raced with possibilities and then dismissed them as quickly as they occurred to him. At the same time, running at the edge of his consciousness, was the concern that if it wasn't stopped, the humanist ideology could reach every corner of the Consortium, spreading its message of division, greed, and hatred. The law of the jungle would prevail as Christian values were abandoned in favor of every man for himself. The only way it could all end was in violence and war just as it did the last time when it cost the lives of millions of people.

Now, on the brink of disaster, prayer seemed to be his only hope, indeed, mankind's only hope.

And then, as his mind continued to search for a solution, his prayers were answered!

Romak had made a mistake.

In using Mooney's MI issued telcomm, Romak did not realize that it operated on a different, classified, bandwidth. Instead of accessing the public uplinks, he must have unknowingly used the dedicated MI bandwidth so that the program only went to MI storage units and not immediately uploaded to the super cloud. If he was right, it gave Jules a chance to locate it, corral it, and reel it back in.

Eagerly, with shaking hands, he contacted Winthrop back at MI headquarters on Mars.

"Jules?" came Winthrop's questioning voice.

Jules gave Winthrop no time for more. "Winthrop, I need you to do a search through MI's information storage units. Anything identified as ancient. Pre-Consortium era tech."

"Pre...? You're kidding!"

"Do it! Do it now! No time for discussion."

Noting the seriousness in Jules' voice, Winthrop conducted the search, which took only seconds.

"Found something," he said. "Dated...well, dated only 73 minutes ago..."

"That's it! Now I want you to reroute and sequester it to a sub routine in the Q7000."

It was a strange request, but Winthrop didn't ask any questions. He just did it.

"Done."

Jules almost laughed with relief.

Sequestered as it was within the labyrinthine matrices of the Q7000, the program was rendered harmless. It could be deleted with a simple command from Winthrop, one that Jules asked him to give now.

"Done," was all Winthrop said, which seemed to Jules far too anti-climactic to mark the enormity of the occasion.

"Can I breathe now?" asked Mooney, breaking the tension of the moment.

"One more thing," said Jules, plucking the data bomb device itself from where it had been inserted into Mooney's telcomm. Dropping it to the floor, he put his heel to it.

Only then did he allow a smile to crease his face.

"Now you can breathe," he said. "We did it!"

He explained what happened but it wasn't until there was a cry of despair from the bunk that he realized Romak heard as well.

"No!" he shouted. "No! The device worked! The Consortium is doomed!"

It was all Cohen could do to restrain him, holding him down on the bunk, the nanites in his body completing the last stages of healing. The final irony being, thought Jules, that Romak would soon find himself back under virtual therapy if not at Special Research Unit 6 then at some other secure facility.

"Do you mind leaving the room," pleaded Cohen. "For some

reason, your presence here is aggravating the patient."

"No problem, doctor," laughed Jules, his arm around Mooney's waist. "He's all yours now."

They left the room, Romak's protestations still ringing in their ears.

Outside, the crowd gathered cheered the end of the episode, for all they knew, a simple arrest of a gang of outlaws. Jules did not disabuse them of the notion.

When the cheering crewmen had finally been convinced their help was no longer needed, and had been dispersed back to the local bars for celebratory drinks, Jules found himself once more facing his other self. This time, though, he was doubly surprised.

With Jules-prime, his arm around her waist just as Jules' was around Mooney's, was Joan.

If he'd thought meeting Jules-prime was strange, seeing Joan again was merely awkward. He found himself without anything to say so Jules-prime said it for him.

"I've already explained the situation to her," he told Jules. "She understands."

Jules looked at Joan.

"Can you forgive me?"

Joan smiled then, and it was as if none of the years since he'd seen her last had happened. He knew her Jules was just as much Jules as he was. That she hadn't been cheated out of anything. Since that day when Jules made the decision to let Jules-prime go back to her, subsequent events further altered their personalities. He and Jules-prime were no longer exactly the same and Joan had grown alongside Jules-prime. She could no sooner re-attach herself to Jules than she could with a stranger. In other words, it was all right now. There would no longer be any need for secrecy. No longer any need to masquerade as Victor Conroi.

"Of course, dear," Joan was saying. "Now, if I'd have known about this from the beginning..."

She left the sentence unfinished as they all burst into laughter.

It was cut short however, when Mooney suddenly stopped,

holding her abdomen.

"What's wrong?" asked Jules, reaching out to her, concerned.

"What time is it back on Earth?" managed Mooney.

"What?" asked Jules, confused. What did that have to do with...?

"What time is it back on earth?" Mooney asked again.

Puzzled, Jules checked his telcomm.

"9:33 AM Terran standard time," he said. "That is, back home in Nevada."

"Then it's morning sickness," concluded Mooney, getting over the attack of nausea.

"Huh?"

"She's pregnant, Jules," laughed Joan. "You're going to be a father!"

Epilogue

"So, it was you who brought in those reinforcements in the nick of time?"

They were sitting in the living room of Jules and Mooney's Nevada home. It had been a year since the conclusion of their last case, the one that saved the Consortium from a resurgent humanist nightmare. A year full of surprises and delights. A year of retirement from Military Intelligence, or at least from active service as science agents. For Mooney it had been mandatory on her part. Like most women, she chose to raise her own children when they began to arrive instead of handing them over to strangers. Jules worked from home, finally solving the nitinol problem before taking a few months off. Currently he was working as a consultant to the science division.

Julian Santros had been born on time and in good health a few months before, none the worse for wear following his mother's exertions during their last case, much to Jules' relief. In fact, it was due to Julian that they were now hosting his brother Fr. Andrew Santros, and Jules-prime and his wife Joan. The former had flown in from Anglia to preside over Julian's baptism while the latter were present as its godparents. And Jules wouldn't have had it any other way.

The past year had given him plenty of time to reconcile himself to the new reality. It was agreed that he and Jules-prime should consider themselves brothers and the ritual of baptism had cemented their new relationship. Jules even found it good to be in Joan's presence again; no longer the awkward situation that it had at first seemed. In fact, as Joan now revealed, it was she who had directed the cavalry charge that had saved the outnumbered tac team and crewmembers that day on Tobanikoganabagin when they were charged by the humanist gang.

"Who did you think?" Joan was saying. "When my Jules failed to return to our base camp in time, I gave him a grace period before going into the settlement to look for him. I thought for sure he'd got into some trouble with the local Zhapoologani authorities. Then someone told me he was at the barracks. I went there and saw there were guys with guns all around. I've been with Jules long enough to recognize MI's Tactical Team when I see it so knew something was up. I kept looking and finally spotted my Jules or maybe it was the other Jules...who knew? Anyway, I saw you just as the charge began. I saw right away you were outnumbered and ran back to get help."

"And I'm glad you did," said Mooney.

"Me too," agreed Joan, giving her new friend a squeeze. "Wouldn't have wanted to see you roughed up, not while carrying my godchild!"

Mooney laughed. "The roughest part of the whole adventure was the deprogramming we had to go through before we were released."

"You'd think Leclerc could have made an exception, especially for you two," remarked Joan.

"I think he was just getting back at Mooney's slip ups," said Jules, with a wink. "It was ironic that due to her losing both her ion pistol and her telcomm, she placed first my life and then the life of the Consortium at risk."

Jules had to duck to avoid being struck by a pillow that Mooney sent his way.

"The deprogramming sessions were unavoidable," said Jules, getting back to the question. "It was mostly pro forma anyway. We were in and out in no time."

"I only feel sorry for Cohen and my *Tarsus* crewmates," said Mooney. "I'm sure they didn't see that coming."

"Well, I for one am glad to know that MI was so thorough," said Andrew. "I'd hate to see them take any chances of letting such a hateful ideology get loose into the world again."

"Amen," said the two Jules in unison.

"You know, this is really a lovely area," observed Joan, changing the subject. "There's something about the open desert. The wide open vistas."

"It was Jules' idea to look into the area," revealed Mooney. "Have you given it any thought, Jules?"

It was Jules-prime whom she addressed.

"Naturally," he replied. "Didn't we both come through the southwest in the process of investigating that black hole affair?"

"Jules mentioned moving here once or twice," admitted Joan.

"Except that she wasn't ready yet to settle down," he said, smiling.

"I remember that being a sticking point," recalled Jules.

"Now don't start ganging up on Joan, you two," said Mooney.

Just then, there was the sound of a baby awakening from sleep coming from somewhere in the house.

"Will you excuse me?" said Mooney. "Duty calls."

"Which reminds me, 'Manda," said Joan, following her out back. "Weren't you concerned about being pregnant when you were given the mission?"

"I really wasn't sure I was pregnant until later," said Mooney, her voice diminishing with distance.

After the two disappeared toward the nursery, Jules cocked a questioning eyebrow at Jules-prime.

"I'm working on it," he said. "I think she's coming around, especially after meeting Julian."

"I know how much Joan was caught up in her work," said Jules. "Always putting off having a family."

"I'm keeping my fingers crossed. Good to see she likes the area here. So do I."

"If you're really interested, I can put you in touch with a real estate agent. Plenty of lots available. Of course, I'd hate to see the neighborhood get too crowded..."

"It'd make it easier for me when I visit," said Andrew. "Convenient to have both of you in one place."

"See there?" said Jules. "We could make it a Santros compound."

Jules had time to refill the others' drinks before the women returned. They were about to resume their places when a chime sounded indicating that a 'car had stopped outside.

"Who could that be?" wondered Mooney.

Going over to the front doorway, she peeked outside.

"Oh, no!" she exclaimed.

"What is it?" asked Jules, as they all rushed to look outside too.

It was Leclerc!

"What do we do?" asked Mooney.

"What do you suppose he wants?" asked Joan.

"I'm afraid to find out," said Mooney.

"Do we have to let him in?" asked Jules-prime.

"How about we act as if no one's home?" suggested Jules.

They were still undecided, when the door chime sounded...

Although not strictly related to the novel above, "The Cursive Code" might, in retrospect, serve as a background piece to the events recounted there. It was written several years before I had any idea of writing a third chapter in the Science Agents series but looking back, does anticipate life behind the Humanist lines during the Constitutional wars as I describe them in the novel.

A funny thing though is that at the time I wrote "The Cursive Code," political correctness seemed to me to have gone far in its outright insanity. Here, I exaggerated a few points but not, I think, so as to make them unbelievable. Now, only a few years later, I find that I was too conservative in my predictions! As anyone who has followed current events over the past decade, there seems to be no limit to the lunacy of the left and I fully expect that after the novel has been published, the movement will have gone even farther. But to the point where the United States as we know it, will disappear? Who knows?

"The Cursive Code" is presented here to give the reader the sense of a more complete background history to the world of the Consortium.

The Cursive Code

"After many years of debate and controversy, plans by the Federal government to destroy the Constitution of the former United States of America have been set for March 20, the great anniversary which gave birth to the Green States of a Diverse America," read Anomie Whitney.

Around her, stood the other members of the resistance comprising the northern sector. The cell had gathered that day after an emergency message was flashed earlier in the week via sub-wave. That message was ordered by commander Vince Norwood immediately after the news about the Constitution broke in local newsvids.

"The Constitution, the original and sole surviving copy of the document that had been used to found the old USA, had been condemned as racist and oppressive at the Second Convention of Detroit in Year 1. Replaced by the Declaration of American Diversity, the original Constitution has continued to inform the political basis of the GSDA and consulted from time to time when a question of rights arose.

"However, in the decades since the Second Convention, many have argued that the Constitution was tainted due to the lack of diversity among its framers and had, like the remainder of unreconstructed citizens of European descent gathered in the Special Enclaves, become an anachronism.

"With the Law of Year 26, it became illegal to possess copies of the Constitution and a program of eradication succeeded in eliminating all physical copies and blocking it from the govnet. The last remaining copy then, is the original once housed in the former National Archives but since the Revolution, has been kept under guard at the Institute for Green Impositions and Diverse Rectification. There, government approved experts in its arcane language have had sole access to it when questions of political structure and authorization have arisen. That time, when reference needed to be made however, has been deemed passed and in May of this year, the Supreme Revolutionary Court deemed it proper to have the last remaining copy destroyed."

"Destroyed!" exclaimed Disda Pondatti. "We can't let that happen!"

"We won't," assured Vince from where he sat at the head of the long conference table. "The Constitution is too important a document to allow it to be destroyed. Our ancestors regarded it with reverence even building a vault powerful enough to withstand a nuclear attack in order to protect it."

"But it hasn't been in that vault for over a hundred years," objected Flannery Distib. "The GSDA government removed it and has had it under lock and key at the GIDR offices where only its own experts are allowed to read it."

"That's ancient history at this point, Flann," said Anomie.

"Which is exactly what we've been fighting for all these years, isn't it? The true history of America and not a fantasy of the past fabricated by the government's liars. If we can prove what we believe about the history of the old USA it will help support our other claims of freedoms guaranteed to the people that were lost in the Revolution."

"You're just stating the obvious now, Flann," said Vince. "We all know what the resistance has been fighting for and unfortunately, with little success. The lies perpetuated by the government have been repeated too long and too often so that the scraps of evidence we've managed to retrieve from the cloud, even from old newspapers and books have not been convincing enough to the general population. However, for decades, the government has told people that its mandate to rule and the basis of its promulgations were justified in the wording of the Constitution, a document whose interpretation the government has monopolized for itself."

"Thus, this news about its impending destruction is doubly serious," broke in Piers Fenroke, chief historian of the resistance. "Not only can we not allow such a key historical artifact to be destroyed, but we must seize this opportunity to rescue it for ourselves. Only with it in our possession can we read it for ourselves and discover the rights it is rumored to contain. Once we have its text in our possession, we can post it everywhere in the cloud. Am I right Denn?"

Denn Fiole nodded. "I've managed to crack the cloud supra-text. With that kind of control, I can post whatever we want on every website and mail box on Earth instantaneously. Within seconds, every person on the planet will have the information placed before their collective eyes."

The affirmation was greeted by a murmur of approval from the assembled leaders around the table.

"If we can do it," Vince reminded everyone, "we can start a new revolution, one aimed at restoring the freedoms Americans have lost and reestablishing the old USA."

"Imagine the shock and delight that will sweep the public when we make the Constitution available to everyone!" exclaimed Anomie. "There will be such an uproar that the present government will be swept from power."

"Let's not get over excited," cautioned Vince. "The current government will not give up power so easily. It still controls the electoral process. It can change the rules as it has done in the past to ensure whatever outcome it wants."

"But surely, once its methods are exposed as lies, the people will not tolerate any more such deceitful practices?" said Flann hopefully.

"They will not but no revolution has ever gone unopposed by those it aims to overthrow."

"You forget, Vince, that the GSDA came to power with no such opposition."

"True. That happened because its divisive positions were promulgated slowly over many decades sugar coated in a secular humanism that made it difficult for anyone to oppose them," replied Vince. "With many useful idiots to back them up, the revolutionaries implanted those of European descent with a self-loathing that stripped them of the ability to defend themselves. From there, it was a simple thing to demand changes in society that reversed the power structure and ended with the establishment of the special enclaves for those of European descent and others who refused to conform to the new dynamic."

"We know all that," said Flann. "Most of us here have escaped from the enclaves and joined with others to pose as useful idiots so that we would be unsuspected as members of the resistance."

"And I for one am tired of it," declared Anomie. "It's beneath our dignity to continue to espouse the illogical and hateful positions of the GSDA just so we can live normal lives. If there's any chance that exposure of the contents of the Constitution can change all that, I for one, refuse to wait another minute."

"Here, here!" agreed those gathered around the table.

When the tumult had died down, Vince lit the table top to display a street map of Tubman D.C.

"All right. Since we're all agreed on what needs to be done, here's my plan..."

~ * ~

Flannery Distib stood in the shadow cast by one of the columns of the Martin Luthor King Memorial. Once it housed the seated figure of Abraham Lincoln before the sixteenth president fell out of favor for his racist views and was replaced. Still, he had fared better than Thomas Jefferson whose own memorial had long since been razed. The race neutral words of Lincoln's Gettysburg Address still adorned the rear wall of his former memorial however.

But sightseeing was not on Flann's mind now. It was the mission. The Constitution was scheduled to be ceremonially burned in exactly one half hour and a huge crowd had gathered on the Mall to witness what the government had billed as a symbolic renunciation of an oppressive past.

Still, Flann could not help feeling disgust at the festive mood among the crowds with peddlers moving up and down selling everything from balloons to the rainbow flag of the GSDA. Here and there, groups had broken out into song, their voices ringing with tunes first made famous during the revolutionary years with "Hands Up, Don't Shoot," and "I Can't Breathe" prominent among the cheery throng.

Overhead, the sky was blue and clear and a slight breeze fluttered the world flags ringing the towering Tubman Monument. The green of the Mall itself could hardly be seen beneath the crowds that filled the open space between the Monument and the Capitol Building in the distance. As such, nearly every single member of the D.C. Police Department as well as Capitol security forces had been called in for crowd control and possible terrorist threat. Not that there was much likelihood of that after the surrender of the West to the Caliphate but it served the government's purposes to stoke the public's fears with warnings of Christian diehards and racial supremacists that it imagined peopled the resistance. Which, of course, was not the truth at all. Although the underground movement was made up predominantly of those of European descent, it included a fair share both Christians and Muslims as well as other racial groups all united in their faith in the admittedly human Founding Fathers and the form of government they founded.

Which was why the mission was so important. Preservation of the Constitution was crucial if the resistance was to expose the current government for the sham it was. How it divided people and fostered hate and suspicion over the enlightened principles of the founding document. At least such was what the underground leaders believed to be enshrined in the Constitution. Every evidence at hand indicated that it was so. If it was allowed to be destroyed, that certain knowledge would be lost to Americans forever and the climb back to a sane world where every man would be clothed in dignity would be extended indefinitely or maybe made impossible to recapture.

Flann shuddered at that possibility, recalling the indignity of the special enclaves for those who refused to accept the thirteen articles of green-diverse certainty. A thinly veiled excuse to segregate unreconstructed Americans of European descent from the majority, the enclaves had their share of other races as well. Anyone, in fact, who refused to accept the counter intuitive positions of the GSDA.

Unbidden, Flann recalled his childhood in the Pittsburgh Enclave, the re-education seminars everyone was required to attend, the talks and speeches that sought to convince people of their never ending racial guilt, the need to save the planet from the ravages of their ancestors, and the forgiving nature of their fellow Americans to welcome them into their midst despite their historic crimes. To be sure, some became convinced of the arguments and were joyously received into the bosom of the GSDA while others, to the disgust of those who refused to admit guilt, simply lied about their conversion in order to be released from the enclave. It was with a bit of self-loathing that Flann thought of his own false acceptance of the thirteen articles in order to leave the Pittsburgh Enclave to join the underground. He did it after being told to do it by outside recruiters, but he still blushed in shame when he recalled friends and family who did not know why he had done it. Well, he told himself, after today's successful operation, they will.

"Freedom Team, are you all in position?" he asked through the implanted nanophone in his throat.

Instantly, reports began to come in. Team members were spread throughout the Mall waiting on his orders. He gave them.

"Proceed to point Alpha," he said as he left the shadow of the column and descended the stone stairway to the street. Everywhere along the Mall, the dozen members of Freedom Team would also be on the move, slowly congregating in the neighborhood of the Institute for Green Impositions and Diverse Rectification where it was known that the Constitution had been removed from its vault in readiness for the ceremony before the Tubman Monument.

Ahead of him, the street was lined with horse drawn coaches and a lane down the center kept clear for the limousines that only high government officials were permitted to use. At the edges of the green space, long lines of both men and women waited patiently to use the unisex porto-potties provided for the occasion. Flann's attention was not on his immediate area however, but fixed on the GIDR building in the distance.

Casually, he looked around. Outwardly, he seemed like a typical visitor dressed in the drab woolens expected of the working classes. Hidden on his person, up his arm actually, was the extensile length of a staser which could deliver a stunning shock to the nervous system rendering its human target unconscious. He would need it once he reached the entrance to the GIDR where, hopefully, security would be light.

He arrived in the vicinity of the department's service door away from the crowds that stood about the main entrance. Guardedly, he noticed passersby across the narrow side street, ostensibly on their way to the ceremony but really timing their movements so that they would be ready to rush inside the service entrance as soon as Flann had cleared it of security personnel.

With a barely perceptible nod to the team members across the street, he turned his steps to the side entrance exactly the way a visitor to DC might approach thinking it was open to the public. Pushing the heavy glass door inward, he was confronted by a uniformed officer.

"Sorry, sir, but the building is closed to visitors today," said the guard.

Flann was quick to note with satisfaction that the man was alone in the short hallway leading inside and reaching up as if to remove his hat, allowed the staser to slide from his sleeve into his hand. In another moment, he felt the familiar tingle run up his arm as the guard collapsed to the floor.

Instantly, other members of the team were inside the door, and while a pair worked to remove the guard to a small ante-room just off the entrance, Flann and three others moved quickly down the corridor to a junction connecting the front part of the building on one hand, and the rear areas on the other. Floor plans had shown that the vault room was accessed by a bank of elevators in that rear area. With only a few minutes remaining before the start of the ceremony, it was expected that the Constitution would already have been removed from the vault and if not located in the ground floor elevator foyer, then in its counterpart downstairs.

Dashing to the foyer, Flann saw that it was empty and leaving the two men who had disposed of the guard behind in case the document was transported up before it could be stopped, he and the others took to the stairs.

"Jefter, Stilg, follow me," he ordered.

The buzz of voices filled the empty stairwell as they reached a door giving access to the downstairs foyer beyond. Peeking through a vertical slit in the door, Flann could see several figures standing around on the opposite side with not a guard among them. In their midst was a wheeled cart upon which a half dozen plexiglass slabs protected what he was sure was the document.

Being so close to it, Flann felt a thrill of anticipation, of eagerness to set his eyes on it, to read its legended words and sensed the same air of expectancy from his comrades. With hand signals, he indicated to the others which of those on the other side of the door they would target upon entering the foyer and after confirming that they were ready, whispered a count of three before bursting out of the stairwell and stasering his first target. In seconds, it was over. Achieving complete surprise, the government people froze in fear and confusion and before any of them could move, the well trained team members immobilized them all.

Quickly, they all gathered around the plexiglass slabs and looking down, laid their eyes on the first page of the Constitution. For his part, Flann had certain expectations but now it was his turn to be surprised.

"There's more than one document here," he said.

"Was the Constitution that long?" asked one of the men. "I thought it would be only a single page."

"Me too," admitted Flann.

"And what kind of language is that?" said Jefter.

"I can't read it," said Stilg, clearly disappointed.

"Whatever it is, it's not English," said Flann.

"Then how can we be sure this is the Constitution or not?"

"It must be," insisted Flann. "They were getting it ready to take upstairs."

"But if we can't read it, the mission is a failure. The government claims were right. It can't be read without an interpreter."

"If they can read it, then we'll discover some way of doing it ourselves and find out what's really written down here. Do you trust the government to tell us what all this means? My guess is they didn't know how to read it either and just made up whatever they wanted the people to think."

"Anyway, the document itself seems old enough. Look at how that parchment has yellowed."

"Okay, let's get to work. Jefter, you got the roll?"

"Right here," said Jefter, removing something from inside his coat that proved to be a collapsible tube.

Searching the fallen officials, Flann found the tool he needed to release the documents from their plexiglass prisons and carefully rolled up the brittle parchments and slid them into the tube.

"It'll be a tight fit but we can't afford to leave any of them behind," said Flann. "Any one of them could end up being the Constitution."

Quickly, they made their exit the way they came, emerging in the upstairs foyer and rejoining the other members of the team. After a brief pause by the doorway they had entered from to make sure the street outside was still quiet, they slipped out and dispersed again, the precious tube hidden on Jefter in such a way as to be completely unnoticeable on a cursory inspection.

~ * ~

When news of the successful mission reached the underground's northern sector, members wasted little time in meeting again around the long conference table. Those gathering for the important conclave had little fear of discovery by government agents located as it was somewhere within the no go zone of the Midwest Caliphate.

Anomie Whitney was just removing the chador she wore when operating within the Caliphate when Flann and the rest of the team that had rescued the Constitution joined Vince and the others in the crowded room.

After the initial hubbub died down, Jefter handed Vince the tube he had been carrying. Vince in turn, handed it to Piers who carefully removed its contents and spread them over the length of the table. Instantly, everyone closed ranks in order to get a better look at the documents, one of which they fervently hoped would prove to be the Constitution itself.

But immediately, the same problem that confronted Flann and his team was met by the other members of the resistance: none of the documents could be read.

"We told you, they're written in some kind of code," said Flann.

"What about it, Piers?" asked Vince.

"It's not a code exactly," said Piers looking over the text with an old fashioned magnifying glass. "It's just a different manner of writing than the alphabetic letters we use in our electronic devices. It's how people communicated over long distances before the digital age. At one time, every school child learned how to write in such a manner but with the rise of personal digital devices, it was abandoned so that today, very few people can even read it anymore. A circumstance, of course, that played into the hands of the government. Since most of the original documents of western civilization were written in such fashion through letters, legal papers, manuscripts, contracts, etc., all proved inaccessible to the general population. That left it to the government to set itself up as the sole custodian of the past. History became whatever the government said it was including of course, the history of the old United States as encapsulated within the wording of the Constitution."

Piers pondered a moment more before continuing, as if thinking aloud. "The writing appears to be an early form of what used to be called cursive, using the alphabet we know in a linked manner in order to make it faster and easier to create messages by hand. Once you realize that, it's easy to recognize many of the letters." Pointing, he continued. "See here, that's an e and that is an o. I think that with careful study, we might be able to piece enough of the cursive together to read the writing. It'll take some time though."

There was silence then for a moment before Vince spoke again. "But now we have the key, right? If we can learn the cursive code, we not only can know the contents of the Constitution, but the true history of the West through any of the old documents we can find in the future?"

Without waiting for an answer, he shot a further question to Denn. "If you can drill deep down enough into the old cloud, do you think you can retrieve any original documents that may have been scanned at one time or another?"

"If they were scanned, they can be retrieved," said Denn with confidence.

At that point, everyone looked to Piers hopefully.

"I'd like a few volunteers to work with me to break the cursive code as you called it," said Piers. "I don't foresee too much trouble in recognizing most of the alphabet and context will likely help with the rest. What will take a little longer is translating the actual wording into the alphabet we recognize today. Once that's done, it can be placed before the eyes of every person on the planet if Denn's earlier assurances still hold."

"They do," said Denn.

"Then let's get started."

~ * ~

"There were some surprises," said Piers when the group gathered again some weeks later.

"Now there's an understatement," said Anomie, grinning.

"Then surprise us," challenged Vince.

"The cracking of the cursive code proved easier than I anticipated and daresay that it's easy enough to learn that any child can do it."

"We foresee a follow-up project designing an online program that would teach how to read and write the cursive code to anyone who is interested," said Anomie. "Along with any original documents that Denn can retrieve and make accessible, the combination could prove to be the most explosive development since the revolution that spawned the GSDA."

"It could make all our efforts so far pale into insignificance," added Flann.

"That sounds great," enthused Vince to nods all around. "Let's not get ahead of ourselves though. You spoke of surprises? They're not the kind that will interfere with our plans for the Constitution, are they?"

"To the contrary," said Piers. "These surprises will only enhance the presentation."

"Then by all means, let's hear them."

Piers pointed to the set of parchments that had been carefully laid across the surface of the table. "As you'll recall, Flann and his teammates were taken by surprise when they rescued the Constitution by the number of pages there were. Until then, we were under the impression that the document comprised only a single sheet. We were wrong. The Constitution itself includes four separate pages as you can see here concluding with a signatory document."

Eagerly, everyone in the room save those that had been on the cursive interpretive team leaned in to observe more closely what was written on that final sheet. There, signatures were plainly listed. Piers read them aloud: "This one belongs to George Washington and this to Alexander Hamilton. Here is James Madison and there Benjamin Franklin."

"The Founders..." whispered Vince, chills running through his body. Placing his hand hesitantly over the list of names, he seemed to absorb the mythic qualities of that pantheon of legendary figures whose existence until that moment, had to be taken on faith. But now, preserved in fading ink and on crumbling parchment, they became real. "They really existed. They lived and breathed, just like we do."

"Yes," agreed Piers. "But don't hagiography them. They were only men just as we are. But they had the good chance of being in the right place and the right time and in the right frames of mind to rise above the thinking of their day and see into the future. Unlike others who may have had the same opportunity in times past or since, they chose to take advantage of the fact."

"Granted, but if only our ancestors heeded their words and intentions more closely, maybe the world would not have turned out as it did," said Vince.

"Who can say?"

"Tell them about the other surprise," reminded Anomie.

"Right. I'm sure you've noticed that although I said that the Constitution had four pages, these others are separate and comprise the Bill of Rights."

"What!" cried Vince, immediately focusing his attention on something no one had anticipated. "It exists?"

"That's correct. For decades it was assumed the Bill of Rights was only a legend. That there was no such thing. No government would ever put in writing something that would deliberately limit its power. But this document proves otherwise and proves conclusively the wisdom and courage of the Founders. Those men, it seems, were even greater than we imagined."

"This means we have the means at last to counter any claim by the GSDA about what rights the people have. They'll no longer be able to say and do whatever they want pointing to a document that they alone have access to."

"Indeed, here is the right to freedom of religion, speech, and the press, the right to bear arms, freedom against unreasonable searches and seizures, a fair trial, and perhaps the most important, the assurance that all issues not addressed in the Constitution or Bill of Rights are assumed to belong to the states," enumerated Piers.

There was stunned silence in the room for many minutes before someone said something and then there was shouting, and laughter, and back slapping as everyone realized the enormity of the discovery.

Even Anomie broke with protocol to accept a kiss and an embrace by Flann in the enthusiasm of the moment.

Finally, after Vince had restored order, he asked Piers if the translation of the Constitution and Bill of Rights was ready for Denn to take over.

In reply, Piers produced a mem-stick and handed it over to Vince. "Here's the complete translation as well as a scan of the original documents. Anomie is prepared to work with Denn in producing an instructional program in the cursive code so that those interested can teach themselves how to read it. That way, anyone who knows how, can study the original documents and verify that our translation is correct."

Holding out the mem-stick to Denn, Vince instructed the tech agent to proceed immediately with uploading the documents and to do the same with the instructional program as soon as it was ready.

~ * ~

"What happened?" demanded Vince. "Why has there been no reaction? No upheaval? Where are the crowds in the streets? The demands for freedom and liberty?"

It was some six months after the initial release of the Constitution and Bill of Rights and members of the underground leadership had gathered in emergency session at their hidden headquarters. Now, an angry Vince stood at the head of the table.

Vince's questions were echoed by others gathered around the table.

"To tell you the truth, this eventuality has not been unexpected," admitted Piers. "I suspected our expectations upon release of the historic documents might have been too rosy."

In the months since their release into the cloud, Denn verified the documents had reached every corner of the world, had found themselves posted to every website, overriding every program and protocol so that every person that accessed the cloud could not help but see it. The phenomenon had been noted by the media which quickly dismissed the mass posting as a prank and not to be taken seriously while away from public scrutiny, the authorities scrambled to find those who had stolen the original documents, luckily with no success. Failing that, the government concentrated its efforts in denouncing the posting, calling it a sham, and an attempt to undermine its legitimacy by anti-green, colonialist forces who would like nothing better than to regain their former position of dominance over the non-European citizens of the GSDA.

That kind of flack however, had been expected with the indisputable truth as revealed by the scans of the original documents (whose authenticity was supported by a vast number of circumstantial evidence as compiled by the underground and added to the download in the form of hyper-links) easily countering them.

However, the expected outrage at the discovery the government had been lying to the people for decades, claiming that it alone had the ability to interpret the Constitution, and never even revealing the fact that it also had the Bill of Rights in its possession, had not come to pass.

The dreams of counter-revolution, of angry citizens gathering in the streets, marching on Tubman demanding freedom and liberty faded as the months passed with no such activity happening anywhere. As a result, it was a disappointed group of revolutionaries who gathered around the meeting table somewhere in the Midwest Caliphate, one that Vince had a very difficult time keeping together. Many were becoming resigned to the fact that it was too late to change anything in the GSDA. That the time of the old USA and its values of freedom and liberty had passed. It was as some had begun to say, that a new dark age had descended the length of which no one could predict. The pessimists were now being heard and they were doubtful of any possibility that when the dark time finally passed, there was no guarantee that the light of the Founders would be re-embraced.

"What do you mean when you say that you expected this result, Piers?" asked Vince.

Piers thought a moment before replying.

"There used to be an old saying," he began. "'You can lead a horse to water, but you can't make him drink.' It was not enough to simply present the people with the truth and expect them all to immediately see things our way. They have been the victims of decades of indoctrination. From the cradle to the grave, they have only heard one side of the argument, the government's side. Their faculties for critical thinking have been dulled, even blocked by years spent in an educational system that values what is politically correct over common sense. We see the evidence of that all around us: the slow decomposition of our technological civilization, the failure to inspire the most creative scientists and thinkers in our society, the embracing of theories that have set aspects of our civilization back to the nineteenth century. But most of all, the people have lost faith both in God and the freedoms that God made inalienable. Today, their faith is in the government and like any faith, it cannot be questioned. All of those factors made it incredibly difficult to break through the training even with the diamond drill of truth."

"So, what you're saying is that our dreams of freedom are impossible?" asked Flann, holding hands with Anomie beneath the table.

"Not impossible, merely delayed," said Piers. "Unless a seed is thrown onto fertile soil, it will not take root. That soil must first be made ready to receive the seed. A process that can take many years as any farmer knows. Eventually, the soil could be made fertile again. But it will take time, and patience, and hard work."

"What kind of work?" Disda Pondatti asked. "Already, many of our members are giving up the struggle as hopeless. How can we convince them that they must persevere? How can we ask them to continue to make the necessary sacrifices? Take the risks?"

"The work I'm speaking of will not involve the same kinds of risk or physical actions the resistance has taken in the past."

"What then?" asked Vince.

"We must fight smarter. Improve our tech skills. Learn to use the cloud to our advantage and then moving our message into the virtual public square and keep it there. We must create programs that people can access to learn about the truth. Create entertainment venues catching the attention of bored trollers that can in turn lure users to news sites where they can be informed. If we do all this, we can slowly build a more educated and aware populace until critical mass can be reached. At that point, someday, our dream of restoring the values of the Founders can come true."

Silence descended on the room then as everyone contemplated the new course to be followed and the diligence it would demand of each of them.

Finally, Disda broke the silence.

"If we do all that you advise, Piers, how long do you think it will be before there are results?"

Piers sighed. "Do not expect it within the lifetimes of anyone gathered here today. Of course, with the pace technology gives to communication, there is no telling exactly when the tide might begin to turn; but I would hesitate to predict that anything short of a hundred years would be too soon. This is a project for the long term. Not to be embarked on lightly. Anyone who does so, must be prepared to commit themselves without possibility of being rewarded with success in their own lifetimes."

"That leaves us with much to think upon," said Vince, looking into the uncertain faces of his colleagues.

Then, one by one, they left the room, each with their own thoughts.

The last to leave was Anomie, who paused first to turn out the lights...

Also by the Author
at
Rogue Phoenix Press

Talismanic

Glenn Springer could hardly believe his good luck. After moving to Maine to escape the Boston rat race, he bought a farm, was successful, and became the envy of his neighbors. Then, he fell in love with the beautiful and bewitching Grizelle Beaumarchais. Was his good fortune all due to a locket he found inside the walls of his old farmhouse? And why was Grizelle so interested in it? Could it have anything to do with her being descended from an Indian shaman? Why were there things about herself that Grizelle wasn't telling him? Was his love for her genuine or was he being subtly manipulated? His luck, it seemed, had its price, and as Glenn began to realize, the bill was coming due.

Prologue

Hugging his muzzle-loading, long rifle close to his chest, Nathanael Winsor walked through the misty Maine woods with a number of his fellows detached from General Benedict Arnold's army that was headed north to invade Canada.

A Groton resident, he'd arrived too late to help out against the British troops that retreated from Concord earlier in the year, but earned his veteran's status at the Battle of Breed's Hill. Afterward, he'd discovered he had a taste for battle and when Arnold asked for volunteers to accompany him on a bold move to capture Canada from the British, he fancied the adventure.

Unfortunately, adventure took a back seat in the buggy to the sheer drudgery of marching through unmarked wilderness and the onset of winter. That had been bad enough, but poor planning and inexperience made things worse. First, the boats used to get the army up the Kennebec River leaked, spoiling both gunpowder and food supplies. As cold weather set in the men began to go hungry and many turned back. Maybe he should have too, but Nathanael always had a stubborn streak and once he'd set his mind on something, it was seldom he changed it.

Not that he didn't have second thoughts at times. Just now, for instance, with his stomach growling, he couldn't decide which was worse, hunger or the constant, discomforting cold.

To add to his misery, a light snow fell during the night, crusting the surface of the ground in patches of white. Feet crunching as he walked, Natty reached a big tree and took a moment to rest against it.

Behind him, the rest of the hunting party caught up. There were a dozen of them, chosen, like himself, because they were all good shots, to range afield in search of game which was desperately needed to feed Arnold's dwindling army and fuel its passage over the final leg of the march to the Chaudiere River.

They had left the army a few days before as it huddled around its meagre campfires and moved up along the Kennebec. One good thing about the snowfall, it made tracking game easier and signs had pointed away from the river. Wary of local Indians, the hunting party spread out along the trail with Natty in the lead. Now, pausing behind the tree, he watched the others as they drew up to him.

"Find anything, Natty?" asked Homer Lawton, a volunteer from Pepperell.

"Just resting a bit, but it can't be long now."

"Sure is cold," said Homer, his breath steaming on the frigid air.

Nathanael didn't reply.

"All right," he said finally, as the rest of the party gathered around the tree. "We must be close now. Spread out and let's see if we can flush something out."

Slowly, the ragged figures moved off to left and right of the tree and when all were in a rough line, Nathanael stepped out and led the way forward.

As he walked, Nathanael could not help noticing how quiet the forest was. All around him, leafless, lifeless trees stood motionless and overhead a slate grey sky hung featureless and lowering. Along the ground, the morning mist still clung, revealing the game trail only a few feet at a time.

Suddenly, Nathanael stopped.

The deer sign they had been following was still present, but now there were other prints, human prints.

"Hold it," he whispered; a command that was passed along the line of men to the right and left.

Pointing, Nathanael signaled danger ahead. The others understood. They'd wait and follow his lead in silence.

Warily he continued, until a shot rang out.

Instantly, Nathanael threw himself to the ground as did many of the others. Some scooted behind nearby trees. But nothing else happened. There were no other shots. Maybe it was not aimed at them? If so, the hunting party had not been discovered. It still held the element of surprise.

Cautiously, Nathanael regained his feet and moved slowly forward, followed by the others. Soon, shapes began to take form in the mist, shapes he recognized as the kind of temporary structures used by Indians. Instantly, he halted and waved his fellows in.

With furtive movements, they drew themselves together until the entire band crouched among a stand of white pine.

"What do we do now?" asked someone.

"They must know we're here."

"Don't look like it to me..."

"What about that shot?"

"Hold on," said Nathanael. "There's nothing to suggest they were shooting at us. Otherwise, there would have been more."

"Natty's right," began Homer before being interrupted by a second shot, this one no doubt aimed at them as a ball shredded its way through the clustered pine branches overhead.

"Quick, spread out and return fire," advised Nathanael as he unlimbered his own rifle and took aim at a figure standing amid the bark structures.

Boom! His gun unloaded and for a few seconds there was too

much powder smoke to tell if he'd hit his target.

When the smoke cleared, however, he had the satisfaction of seeing the figure lying in a crumpled heap on the frozen ground. By then, the air was filled with the loud retorts of other guns as the hunting party fired on the village. With a shout, the little band of soldiers advanced, some stopping to reload their muskets and firing again.

To add to the confusion, some of the men set fire to the lodges whose bark walls and thatched roofs went up quickly.

Nathanael was reloading his rifle when he spotted the Indian sitting at a campfire at the edge of the village. Throughout all the noise, commotion and flying balls, he continued to sit, smoking a long-stemmed pipe just as if nothing was happening.

Suddenly, determined to shatter the old man's tranquility and to see him hop to his feet in alarm, Natty aimed his rifle and shot. The old man didn't move. Still he sat there smoking. Unsure of how he'd missed, Natty loaded again, took more careful aim, this time squarely at the old man's form and fired.

Again, he'd apparently missed. Impossible. He knew he was a darn good shot, could shoot the eye out of a running squirrel at a hundred yards. Something was not quite right...but just then Homer appeared, urging him to signal the retreat.

"Let's get out of here," said Homer. "The boys don't like the way the Injuns all scattered. Likely the rascals are somewhere and figurin' on comin' back and catchin' us unawares."

Nathanael's back was up however. All he wanted to do right then was to stomp up to the old man and put a bullet in him.

"What are we waitin' fer?" asked someone else. "We don't want to be caught in some ambush so far from the rest of the army."

Clearly, the boys were spooked at the sudden encounter with the Indians and Nathanael felt the pressure to turn back.

"All right, let's go," he said at last.

A few minutes later, he found himself hanging back as the rest of the party headed back the way they'd come. A sense of unfinished business teasing at his mind, Natty couldn't go on until he settled affairs with the old Indian.

As the last man passed him, he turned and faded into the mist. A few minutes later, he'd returned to the village which by that time was only a collection of smoking ruins. The inhabitants still hadn't come back. Likely they were as shaken as his men had been and were miles away by now.

Slowly, he crept from tree to tree until coming in sight of the old man's lodge. The only one unharmed by the recent action despite being near the center of the village. The coincidence only added to Nathanael's curiosity as he watched the old Indian, still sitting by his fire.

Suddenly, he stood and entered his dwelling.

On impulse, Nathanael stole from cover and dashed to the lodge. Entering, he cornered the old man before he had a chance to do anything.

"Welcome young warrior," said the Indian, startling Nathanael.

"You speak English?"

"Yes. I learned it many years ago when the first wooden villages came to fish off of these shores. In those days, none of my people had ever seen a white man and we were very curious about them. I was young then myself and being bolder than most, I clambered aboard one of the ships when invited and was taken to England. There, I learned your language."

Nervous, Nathanael looked around quickly before replying.

"You're talking a hundred, two hundred years ago, old man."

"Longer."

"What...?" Nathanael managed, confused.

"It does not matter. I know why you have come." The old man fingered a small metal locket that hung around his neck. "You cannot put it into words, but you wondered why I was not harmed when you shot at me before. It is because of this." He lifted the locket away from his chest. "I obtained it in England long ago. It contains a gift from Wahn-di-ko that has given me favor for many years, but now I am tired of it. I have lived for too many years. That is why I am prepared to make a trade with you."

"A trade?"

"I give you the gift and in return, you kill me with your musket. In the heart. Do not miss."

"You want me to kill you?"

"Is that so hard? You are a warrior. You have killed before. Even now you go with many of your fellows north to kill again. What is one old Indian?"

At that, the old man lifted the locket from around his neck and presented it to Nathanael.

"Keep it with you always. With it, you will never come to harm. With Wahn-di-ko's favor, you will prosper."

Nathanael took the locket and clutched it tightly in his fist.

The old man stood back and pulled his thin shirt open, exposing his chest.

"Now, kill me!"

Almost without volition, Nathanael found himself tucking the locket into a pocket and raising his musket. He hesitated a moment and wondered if it was his imagination or if the old man's skin was really wrinkling before his eyes, spotting up, turning a pale waxy yellow...

Boom!

Nathanael pulled the trigger and the blast of his gun sounded like a cannon inside the walls of the lodge. Wondering if what he'd seen had been his imagination, he waited for the powder smoke to clear to make sure of his kill.

The old Indian lay there, his chest a bloody mess, but a smile nevertheless teased the corners of his mouth, an ironic smile it seemed to Nathanael who retreated from the lodge. Not waiting to reload his rifle, he quickly stole back into the surrounding forest, suddenly eager to catch up with the rest of his comrades.

Chapter One

Best Laid Plans

"A chicken farm?"

Glenn Springer still recalled the incredulity with which his revelation had been received by Paul Roundhouse, the chief accountant at Silver and Sax where he also worked as office manager.

He smiled at the recollection, especially juxtaposed against the high rises of downtown Boston that formed the backdrop to the thirty sixth floor office space rented by the firm in the John Hancock Tower.

It wasn't the kind of thing that often came up for conversation in such an environment, but it was one ventured by Springer when he sought some unofficial counsel from Roundhouse.

"A chicken farm?" Roundhouse asked again after nearly spurting out the mouthful of coffee he'd sipped just after Glenn mentioned his plans. "You mean, like roosters and clucking hens and heads being chopped off?"

Glenn laughed. "Well not the head chopping part, anyway. It's not that kind of farm."

"What then?"

"Eggs. It raises eggs for market in supermarkets and stuff like that."

"Eggs, heads, what's the difference? A farm is a farm in a nowhere backwater. Why are you even thinking of burying yourself out in Hicksville anyway?"

"It's not Hicksville," said Glenn defensively. "It's Bingham, Maine."

"Whatever. You mean you're serious about this? You want to buy a chicken farm?"

"I've been thinking about it for a long time. Well, about buying a farm anyway. But a chicken farm raising eggs is even better. Less labor intensive."

"But still, isn't that a little drastic just to get some fresh air? Why not just plant a garden in your backyard?"

"Hard to do that when I live in a condo in Lowell."

It would be even harder when he spent hours every day making the commute from Boston to his condo located in a restored mill building.

Renovating nineteenth century mill buildings was all the rage at the moment, especially in Lowell where such buildings stood empty and crumbling for decades before the federal government began pouring in urban renewal and national park funding into them. Now they were mostly high-end condominiums that had proven attractive to up and coming professionals who found the rents and real estate values in Boston not worth the quality of life involved.

Lowell offered the sophistication of an urban environment without the close quarters or crime levels of the big city. It was an easy commute from Boston. Well, it was supposed to be. Only forty-five minutes on a good day, more often work days meant an hour and a half at best.

Just now, Glenn was being reminded of why he'd finally decided to take the plunge into something he always thought of doing. Namely, moving away from the city completely for the wide-open spaces and slower pace of rural life. It was something that buoyed his spirits as he sat at a dead stop in the center of I-93, a four-lane interstate highway that ran straight as an arrow northwest from Boston to New Hampshire and points beyond.

Glenn eased the brake a little and inched up a few feet before being forced to stop by the endless line of cars that stretched farther than his eye could see. Likely there was an accident ahead that everyone had to slow down to look at, thus backing up traffic for miles.

It merely served to remind him of why he hated this commute. Forcing himself to be patient, he selected the classical music station on the radio and relaxed a little, telling himself things would soon be better. In his mind, he saw again the rambling forests of upstate Maine punctuated now and then by fields of produce arranged in geometric perfection. Potato fields mostly, he guessed, but plenty of corn too. By now the ears must be fat and ready for picking. A thousand roadside vegetable stands would be bursting with baskets of the stuff and streams of seasonal sightseers from Massachusetts buying it up for pots back home.

He wouldn't be one of them.

He pictured the farmhouse on the property that soon would be his. The several outbuildings and large coops filled with squawking hens and raucous roosters. Nothing to do but get up early in the morning and collect the night's eggs. Supervise the packing and meeting the truckers coming in to haul the eggs to warehouse distribution centers in Massachusetts. In the evening, relaxing by the fire and doing a little reading and bookkeeping until bedtime.

Glenn was imagining how good a night's sleep would be after days like that, out in the fresh air...

A horn blasted almost right alongside him, but traffic was still not going anywhere. *Jerk.*

Shifting mental gears, Glenn again recalled his conversation with Paul earlier that day. He'd had a bookkeeping question he wanted to run past him and couldn't do it without telling him about his plans.

"Seriously? A chicken farm?" Paul asked.

"Seriously. I always like the outdoors, doing work outdoors like raking leaves in the fall or mowing the lawn in the summer, going in the woods to look for saplings I could transplant to my yard. Stuff like that. I still think plenty of fresh air is the key to health. Spending all day in an office like this, breathing in that recirculated, climate-controlled air can't be good for you."

"Yeah, I've read those articles too. But why an egg farm?"

"Why not? I wanted to get a place where I could make a living, at least a modest one. Like I said, straight vegetable farming is labor intensive. Something I don't think I want to tackle at my age. But a chicken farm, especially one that was already established and had steady customers for its eggs, I could handle that. So, I looked around, checked the internet, visited a couple places, until I found a place outside Bingham."

"You already went up to look at it?"

Glenn nodded. "Yup. It's about a fifteen-hour drive from Lowell. Pretty rural. Farm country for sure, but really attractive countryside. So, I put down a security deposit and expect to close in a couple months."

"That soon?"

"You're welcome to come up and check it out after the sale."

"I just might take you up on that, Glenn. I don't know any farmers."

"Anyway, just wanted to ask you about balance sheets, liability, accounts payable and receivable, and payroll."

"Anybody but yourself on that payroll?"

"Well, I'll have a few people working to pack the eggs and, for now, there's going to be a local farmer I'm going to let work some of my fields. We're going to split the profits from whatever he grows on them."

"That'll complicate your record keeping a little but no biggie."

"Taxes?" asked Glenn with some trepidation.

"Right."

By that point, break time was about over and he and Paul made arrangements to get together soon at the local Starbucks to go over the accounting issues in detail. In the meantime, Glenn asked Paul to keep the chicken farm deal under his hat.

Be that as it may, news about his impending plans leaked out to the rest of the office and for the last few weeks, he'd been the target of some good-natured ribbing, even from Robbie Sax himself. Glenn just hoped Paul was better at keeping professional secrets than he was about chicken farms.

Suddenly, there was a break ahead and traffic began moving more steadily.

If he was lucky, he might make it home before dark.

Other books by the Author
at
Rogue Phenix Press

Extra Galaxia
Science Agents #1

Science Agent Jules Santros has two problems: he has to save the universe and avoid falling for beautiful 'Manda Mooney, sometime secretary for the Terran Consortium's Exterior Ministry but actually a secret operative with orders to keep him under surveillance. On assignment from Military Intelligence, Science Division, Jules is on the trail of a group of renegade scientists that plan on using dangerous black hole technology to tip the balance in Earth's war against the Outer Arm Coalition. Only thing is, use of such banned tech will set off an interstellar chain reaction that could consume the entire galaxy! Now, follow Jules and 'Manda as they team up and travel beyond known space to catch the conspirators and prevent Terran defeat in its war with the Coalition!

Novus Intelligens
Science Agents #2

They're back! And this time, they're a team in more ways than one! As Mr. and Mrs. Santros, Jules and 'Manda Mooney are now both science agents for the Terran Consortium's Military Intelligence. Join them on their toughest mission yet as they first become targets for murder then split up to find out who or what is behind a series of missing space freighters, the destruction of a Navy battleship, and a self-repairing spacecraft housing what may be a new form of life. When their paths finally reunite, Jules and 'Manda discover that the dangers they've faced individually, pale in comparison to the one they both must now face together: one that threatens two star faring civilizations and aims to make mankind, in particular, extinct!

About the Author

Pierre V. Comtois is a former newspaper reporter writing from Lowell, MA who has been editing and publishing *Fungi, the Magazine of Fantasy and Weird Fiction* intermittently since 1984. Comtois' book *Goat Mother and Others* was released in 2015 by Chaosium Fiction. *Marvel Comics in the 1980s: An Issue by Issue Field Guide to a Pop Culture Phenomenon* was published in 2015 by Twomorrows Pubs. Earlier volumes include *Marvel Comics in the 1960s* and *1970s*. The author has also written a number of books including novels such as *Strange Company* and *Sometimes a Warm Rain Falls*; non-fiction such as *Our Lives, Our Fortunes, Our Sacred Honor*; and short story collections such as *The Way the Future Was, The Portable Pierre V. Comtois, Different Futures,* and *Autumnal Tales*. Novels include *Scheduled for Extinction*, Desert Breeze Press (2018), and from Rogue Phoenix Press *Talismanic* (2018), *Extra Galaxia* (2019), and *Novus Intelligens* (2019).Comtois has also found the time to contribute non-fiction articles to such magazines as *World War II, America's Civil War, Wild West,* and *Military History* which have been collected in *Hazardous History*.